Sherdan's Prophecy

Jess Mountifield

Published by Red Feather Writing

Sherdan's Prophecy

Text © 2012, 2014 Jess Mountifield

2nd edition 2014

Cover art © 2014 Elizabeth Mackey

ISBN:1506173713
ISBN-13:978-1506173719

DEDICATION

To Bear. Your constant encouragement with what I write and my ideas helps to keep me going. Thank you for being my biggest fan and a great friend.

ACKNOWLEDGMENTS

Thank you to my husband, Phil, who has been the biggest support a person could ask for. To my mum for her continued encouragement. To my editor, Alex, for all his help making this story, and, to Adam and Anne for the final read through and all the help correcting my mistakes. To Keith and Elizabeth for the wonderful covers. I've been blown away by all the ways people have helped make this book something special.

Also a massive thank you to God, for the inspiration and seeing me through the tough times.

CHAPTER 1

Sherdan sat down and picked up the report from the desk in front of him. He lounged, half reading and half focused on the surveillance cameras. There wasn't really a need to be watching them; his security guards would be doing the same thing just down the hallway from him.

The report soon drew his attention away from the little stack of monitor screens. His good friend, Dr John Hitchin, had given him the document he now scanned through. Most of it was a medical report on the latest batch of recruits to their program.

The last few pages were more interesting to Sherdan. They listed the biological and chemical effects noted, as well as the different changes that could be made to the drug to reduce the complications and side effects it caused.

When Sherdan had finished reading all this he got up and went to the nearby bookcase. From the neatly organised shelves he pulled a leather-bound journal. He flicked through the pages, glancing at the neat handwriting which filled the first ten or so pages.

The rest of the book had a long list of names. He scanned through them, moving his finger down the list as he did. When he got to the person he was looking for he reached into the pocket of his suit jacket and pulled out a pen. With a sigh, he crossed the name out.

He did this for two more names on the thousands-strong list before going to the end and writing in seven more. By the last person he wrote the date and the number '5173' followed by '+7-3'.

With his task done Sherdan placed the book back. It blended in with the rest of the shelves and appeared no more important than the hundreds or possibly thousands of other books, lining the entire wall of the room.

Sherdan did not return to his seat at the desk, but sat down on the other side of the office in an armchair, by the blaze he had created less than an hour before. The brandy glass he had left beside his favourite chair provided a welcome distraction to his over-worked brain. He downed the rest of the alcohol and gazed into the flames.

The crackle and fizzle of the fire soon soothed him and half an hour ticked by on the grandfather clock in the corner. He ran his hands through his thick black hair a few times as he thought through some stressful things. He had a lot to plan.

The people in his program depended on him to make sure they had the new start in life they deserved. He intended to make the best life for all of them that he could; free from prejudice and judgement, free from unhelpful fear and stereotyping.

Sherdan was mulling over the next stage of his plan when a knock on the door disturbed him.

"Come in," he called out in his deep, English, upper-class accent. He looked towards the door on the left wall. It opened, and one of his security team walked in. He appeared the typical hired security guard. Black t-shirt and trousers, ear piece and upper body built like a tank. Sherdan knew there was a lot more to this man than first impressions gave.

"Sir, something set the compound alarm off less than twenty minutes ago but we are having difficulty finding out what."

"Twenty minutes?"

"Yes, sir. We don't think it's an animal," the guard said, anticipating Sherdan's next question.

"I had best go over there. I will take the lower route. Have the patrols doubled and keep me informed, Nathan."

"We already doubled the patrols, sir." The guard's lips did not move with this last message, even though Sherdan heard him as if he had talked normally.

Sherdan got to his feet as he was left alone. He fetched his revolver from the desk drawer. While he did this, he watched the monitors intently. The extra men on the compound cameras could already be seen, but there was no sign of anyone trespassing. He frowned. The alarm system was high-tech enough that they shouldn't get false alarms, but any intruder should have shown up on the cameras by now.

With his gun holstered under his jacket, he exited his study through another door on the opposite wall. He took a left turn down the hallway it led to and continued walking down it, past all the doors off, to what seemed to be a dead end.

When he couldn't walk any farther he stopped. The mirror which adorned the wall in front of him reflected only himself and the empty corridor.

He reached out and ran his finger over the left hand edge of the mirror frame. When he had found the right place, a faint buzzing noise started. He stood still as a beam came out from the top of the mirror and scanned his face, focussing on his eyes. When it had finished, the wall clicked and the humming stopped. A crack had appeared on the right hand side.

Sherdan pushed the wall and waited as it swung backwards. He stepped through the opening and shut the panel behind him. The mirror was clear from this side, allowing him to check that no one had seen him.

Once he was satisfied, he went down a flight of steps and into a plain concrete tunnel, lit overhead by many little lights. He walked for approximately half a mile in a straight line before turning a corner right and ascending an equally long flight of stairs. When he reached the top, there was an identical pane of glass and a circular handle set just below it.

Checking there were no observers on the other side, Sherdan pushed the centre of the handle and, after hearing the same dull clink, pulled the door towards him. He found himself in a very different room.

It was a much more military style. There was a fairly

standard metal-framed bed in one corner, as well as another container of brandy on a small glass table. There were no cosy furnishings and nothing as comfortable as the room he had been reclining in less than fifteen minutes earlier.

Sherdan didn't linger but stepped through the nearest of the three doors in the room. He was greeted by the gaze of the seven other males allowed in his command room. The monitors that filled one wall were all focused on the compound he was now in. Every camera on the west side had been fed through to the screens before them.

No one talked, instead waiting for Sherdan to command them. He looked at the nearest person, Jordan.

"Report!"

"Yes, sir. We've still not found the cause of the alarm, sir," the young man offered.

"Which one was set off first?"

"The farthest on the west, on Royal Fort Road... Three more alarms have gone off since, coming in this direction."

"Where are the patrols?"

"They've all concentrated on that area of the compound but no luck yet, sir," his commander offered before Jordan could.

"Thank you. Give me the microphone, let me talk to the men on the ground." Sherdan moved towards the main desk in the room, where all the important controls were. From this console he could communicate with every building that was part of the program, as well as control every door and window in the compound.

He soon contacted the chief patrol guard and had all the extra teams move to intercept all routes between the last tripped alarm and the room Sherdan was in. The intruder had made an almost direct path from the edge of the compound to the central hub, as if they knew where they were going. This worried Sherdan.

"Do any of the non-essential members of the program know that the alarms have been set off?" Sherdan asked the room. Two people shrugged, the rest looked at someone else.

"See to it that as few as possible find out."

Several of the men scurried to separate work stations and

pressed buttons. Thankfully it was late evening in December and most of the residents would be in the warmth of their homes. Very few would be out to notice the extra patrols near the compound, and many would be asleep already. Sherdan's impatience grew as the minutes ticked by and no one was found. By the time some unknown person had been eluding his staff for over an hour, he was pacing the floor. Everyone stayed out of his way. They did their best to coordinate the patrols, getting them to follow through to the zones as each one had an alarm set off. As the time ticked by, the intruder came closer and closer.

Jordan cried out as he spotted movement on one of the cameras. A young female, dressed from head to foot in black, snuck along the passageway on display, making her way painstakingly slowly.

"Where is that?" Sherdan demanded.

"Sector C, corridor 3." The young man grabbed the nearby microphone, "Patrols, target has been sighted. All please converge on sector C, corridor 3. Target is a white female, approximately five and a half feet, small build, appears unarmed, potentially dangerous..."

"Do not harm if possible," Sherdan interrupted. He didn't see the looks of shock which passed over every face in the room. He'd never said that before.

"Understood," came the voice over the radio.

Everyone stood and watched, tracking their quarry on the cameras and feeding the info to the patrols as necessary. It would not be long before she was hemmed in on all sides. Sherdan smiled.

CHAPTER 2

Anya stepped off the train onto the Bristol Temple Meads platform. She followed the few other people who had been in the carriage with her, down the steps, and along the tunnel underneath the other platforms. She tried to stay near the back of the group and not look too out of place.

For mid-December she wasn't wearing very much: black trainers, trousers and a black long-sleeved top that clung to her small frame. She had a scarf on, but the train had been warm, and until now she had needed nothing else. The first shiver ran through her as she put her ticket into the barrier and made her way through to the exit of the train station.

Anya hesitated in the last warmth of the building before stepping out into the evening air. She had a twenty minute walk from here to her destination. Determined, she set out at a brisk pace.

She had memorised her route by studying the map for several days, and even though she had never been to Bristol before now, she didn't make a single wrong turn.

The whole time she prayed in tongues under her breath. She had read a book many years earlier about a Christian woman who had lived in the slums of Hong Kong and had done the same everyday as she had worked and lived there. The gangs had never done anything to harm her.

When Anya reached the last bin on her path, she stopped, checked there was no one watching, and removed her scarf, placing it in the bin. She then continued as if nothing had happened. She shivered so much she could not tell if it was the cold, nervousness at her task, or, most likely, a combination of the two.

She arrived at her destination five minutes early, so stood and got her breath back on the corner of St Michael's Hill and Royal Fort Road. She knew she was already within his territory and briefly wondered if he knew of her existence already.

As soon as her watch said half past eleven she took a deep breath and walked down Royal Fort Road. She didn't have a plan for the next part. She wasn't even sure where she was going, only of why.

Continuing to pray, she walked towards the largest building she could see. For a moment her nerves got the better of her and she hesitated.

She looked for the nearest door while controlling her breathing in a vain attempt to calm her heart rate back down again. She walked against the wall to the only entrance she could see and tried to push it open.

It didn't move. It appeared to be a safety door that could only be opened from the inside by pushing a bar or handle of some kind.

Anya went to find another door, knowing she shouldn't waste time, but something made her stop. Instead, she put her fingers against the crack in the door and tried to pull outwards.

The door clicked and swung open. It was a fire door, but it couldn't have been latched properly as it had swung out with no resistance.

She sneaked inside and pulled the door shut behind her. She then crouched, listening and never ceasing to pray. Every moment her lips moved in almost silent words she couldn't understand.

Taking another deep breath, she moved from her spot. Picking her directions purely on what felt right at the time, she made her way through Sherdan's compound.

While she explored, she wondered what the man was like.

She was almost certain she wouldn't like him. How could she like anyone who ran a cult for their own benefit? He wasn't the reason she was here, however, at least not directly.

Several minutes of slow creeping passed before Anya found herself taking her first wrong turn. She had wandered into a storage room despite having been led there by her feelings.

She frowned and was about to return through the door when she heard the sound of approaching people. Being as quiet as she could, she shut the door and listened for any signs that she had been seen.

Whoever walked along the corridor did so cautiously. They took many minutes to pass out of earshot again, and at several points, when they had been right by the door, she had thought she would be discovered. She had felt so sure of it that it took her a few more minutes to calm her nervous shaking.

Anya continued sneaking, pressing her whole body up against the wall and walking sideways. Each slow step took her several seconds and already twenty minutes had passed when she moved through the third door.

The décor changed dramatically. What had been normally furnished rooms and corridors became concrete hallways and black walls, save for the lights at regular intervals. It was the first sure sign that she had travelled in the right direction. She sighed and continued praying.

Anya heard sounds from behind and moved across the corridor to a door on the right. She didn't wait to listen for people on the other side as she had at every other door but pulled it open and quickly ran inside. The light in the room came on automatically, showing her someone's bedroom, which was, thankfully, unoccupied.

She could hear the sound of people moving closer as she ran towards the bed and crawled underneath. Her heart pounded in her chest as the smell of accumulated dust and dirt filled her nostrils. She strained to listen for any noise from outside the room.

It suddenly occurred to her that the light would give her away if anyone looked into the room. There was no other door and the light had been triggered by movement. As if responding to her thoughts the light went out, plunging her into the relief of blackness.

Less than five seconds later the door was yanked open and the light blinked on again. She heard two people shuffle through the doorway. She had scrambled under the bed the wrong way to be able to see anything but the wall in front of her.

"Nothing so far," she heard a man say.

Anya closed her eyes in relief as they both walked out and closed the door behind them. For the moment she felt too shaken to continue.

She rested and waited until the light went out again. Before she could move, the door opened for a second time. More feet could be heard walking in. They stayed a lot longer than the previous set, but neither looked under the bed.

Almost as soon as they had left she slithered out from her hiding place. There had now been three sets of guards in a short space of time, and she needed to get a move on. They were obviously aware she was here and already searching for her.

She checked her watch. She had been in the building forty-five minutes. It would be a long night.

Biting her lip, she continued her escapade and made it to the end of the hallway. She found herself faced with a T-junction and hesitated for some minutes, unsure which way to go. The corridor continued in both directions before both ended in doorways.

Logically the right would take her in a similar direction to the way she had come, so she opted for the left. However, after several minutes' sneaking along the edge of the wall, she felt increasingly unsettled. For now she ignored her feelings and continued, but her unease grew.

Unable to disobey her doubts any longer, Anya turned around and headed back, more swiftly than before. She had barely reached the T-junction again when the sound of approaching footsteps came from behind her.

These sounded different to the previous type. They were moving quicker and not trying to hide the sound at all. She had nowhere to hide but the junction itself so she pressed herself up against the wall, hoping they would walk right past and not notice her.

She didn't dare breathe and hardly dared to look. The next few seconds felt like minutes until the two people walked straight past her.

Both of them were engrossed in conversation and neither noticed her. They wore lab coats and one carried a clipboard in his hands, explaining the contents.

Anya watched them go through the door at the end of the passageway and followed as silently as she could. She had now been in the compound for over an hour and the toll of being buzzed with adrenaline for that long was beginning to show.

The doorway opened to another corridor and Anya slowed again, having no idea where the two scientists or doctors had gone. She did not want to draw their attention.

She felt tired and had to try even harder to stay quiet as she moved. She was concentrating so hard it took her a moment to realise she could hear noises again. They were up ahead but she couldn't tell if they were getting closer.

Anya considered going back, but the door behind her started opening. She had no choice but to rush through the only other door off the room she was in.

She hastily turned and shut the door, only to notice that she wasn't alone in the room. The two men she had followed were staring at her.

"Hi," she said, not knowing what else to do.

She then waved. Neither of the guys said anything.

"I don't suppose either of you know where the bathroom is, do you? I get so lost here."

"Go left and it's the third door on the left in the next hallway." One guy pointed back the way she had come.

Anya hesitated. The last thing she wanted to do was go back out of the room. She had already noticed that there wasn't another exit, however.

"Where's your identity badge? Sherdan requires everyone who works here to have one," the guy said.

"Ahh, crap." She noticed that both of them had ID tags pinned to their lab coats. "I've gone and forgotten mine. I'm really ditsy like that. I mean, I am blonde." She pointed to her hair.

The guys just grinned. There was an awkward silence as Anya listened to the guards outside coming closer.

"So... I don't think we've met, I'm..." Anya didn't get to finish before the door behind her burst open.

"Don't move or we'll shoot," the guard said. Four men stood in the doorway with four very large guns aimed straight at her. "Hi," she said. Her game was up and she knew it. All of them came closer to her as she waited, unmoving. When the front one reached her, he pulled her hands behind her back and tied them.

He yanked the plastic ties so tight they dug into her wrists and made her wince. She was then patted down for weapons, but the only thing she had on her was her watch, and that was soon removed. She'd deliberately left everything else at home.

No one said anything to her but one of the guards leaned into the radio pinned to his chest.

"We've got her safe and secure."

"Bag her and bring her here," a voice came back moments later. Anya gulped. Before she had time to react a black bag was pulled over her head. Her world descended into darkness. She blinked a few times, hoping her eyes would adjust to the blackness but the bag was so thick they couldn't.

Both of her arms were grabbed. She flinched both from the aggressiveness of the guard and from the pain of her bonds digging in even further. She was steered towards the door.

As soon as she had been brought out into the corridor, she was spun on the spot until dizziness spilled her into the arms of one of her captors.

"Walk," someone yelled. Both of her arms were grabbed again as she was marched off, now so disorientated she could have been going back into the same dead end room.

The only thing she knew for sure was that her bindings were too tight. They rubbed as she walked and dug so deep that she could feel the first few trickles of blood running down her hands.

CHAPTER 3

Sherdan paced as he listened to the radio chatter. His men were closing in on the woman, but so far she had still not been captured. He had watched her dive out of shot when she had obviously heard the approaching guards, but there wasn't a camera in the room she had sought refuge in.

He sighed with relief when he heard the patrol's report of her capture and demanded her brought to him.

"I want to know how she might have got in and have it prevented from ever happening again," Sherdan yelled at the room. He went to his retreat and poured himself a brandy.

Glaring at the opposite wall, he waited for her to be brought before him. He was furious, both that the woman had eluded capture for so long and that she had somehow gained access to his facility in the first place. He wasn't going to let her see his anger, however, as the last thing he wanted to let an enemy know was how well they had managed to pursue their goal.

For someone who appeared very under-prepared to overcome his defences she had got a long way into his compound. He knew his men were well-trained.

While thinking this over, Sherdan picked up a report he had left on the coffee table earlier and flicked to half-way through. He retrieved his favourite pen from its usual place and pretended to be making notes on the document as if it were of great importance.

This was how he looked a few minutes later, when the patrol knocked on the far door. Sherdan bid them enter and watched, pen and paper still in hand, as the woman who had interrupted his evening's relaxation was marched into the room.

She shivered and waited with the black bag over her head. He briefly admired her figure. The skin-tight stretchy fabric of her top made full use of her athletic shape. The tips of her blond hair poked out of the bottom of the black bag, which Sherdan finally let the men remove.

Anya blinked several times and squinted at him. Her shivering had stopped but she didn't say a word and appeared to be calm in every other respect.

"Who are you?" Sherdan asked, breaking the silence. The four guards all stood waiting for their next commands.

"Who I am isn't important," she replied. He was impressed by her well-spoken accent. There was a hint of the Somerset lilt in her voice, but it was mostly as upper-class as his own accent.

"I do think it's important and I need you to tell me."

"Why I am here is more important." She stepped towards him. "Are you Sherdan Harper?" He nodded but didn't speak.

"Then I would like to see the prophecy you have."

Sherdan blinked, but it was the only outward sign of shock he gave. No one but Dr Hitchin and himself knew about the prophecy.

"My church have sent me to read it if you'll allow it. We don't think it's wise of you to make plans for the end of the world and not include Christians, I mean, it's partly a Christian concept."

Sherdan didn't respond to this at first. The guards were all listening intently and he didn't want them to know about the prophecy at all.

This girl, who refused to tell him her name, knew something she couldn't possibly know. Yet all he knew about her was that she definitely wasn't part of his program.

"I'm afraid you are very much mistaken about any kind of prophecy. I am not Christian and do not believe in any end-of-the-world stories. Now if you don't tell me your name and why you are really here I will have to resort to some less pleasant methods to find out the answers I want."

"I can't tell you my name and I have already said why I am here," she replied without hesitating. It was like his threat had not been taken in at all. He didn't really think she was lying, but she obviously did not realise the level of danger she was in.

Sherdan couldn't do anything to protect her without raising more suspicions from the already curious guards. He had no choice but to hand her over to his interrogation team. If she was as smart as she appeared to be by sneaking so far into his facility she would make up something much more plausible and give him something to work with.

"Take her away and interrogate her," he said to the nearest man. Sherdan didn't look at her, but went straight back to his document and fake notes. They put the bag back over her face and removed her from both the room and his presence.

As soon as she was gone he shivered and decided to see if Hitchin was awake. They needed to talk. Sherdan needed a rational explanation for how she knew about the prophecy.

He left his refuge and made his way to Hitchin's laboratory. If he was still up and about, he would be working.

On his way Sherdan passed the exact spot where the girl had been captured but he didn't note anything of importance. It astonished him how close to him she had come. She had to know something other than what she was saying.

Hitchin wasn't asleep yet and was checking something in his microscope in the lab. He greeted Sherdan enthusiastically.

"Hello, Hitchin, how are you today?"

"Not bad, thank you. How are you, though? You look like a bear with a sore head." Hitchin looked at Sherdan over the top of his glasses and waved him towards a stool. Sherdan didn't sit down.

"Not great. We just had a break-in. I don't think anyone but the security teams noticed, but nonetheless, we've had someone get past your defences."

"I assume they didn't get far?" Hitchin seemed totally unfazed by this news.

"They got farther than I'd have liked, but most worryingly,

they knew about the prophecy. They asked to see it. I denied its existence, of course."

"Of course, a wise move. Let's face it; most cults have something prophetic they follow. He could have been any old crackpot who heard of us."

"You didn't tell anyone about the prophecy, then?" Sherdan looked piercingly at Hitchin.

"Of course not. There is only one time I've mentioned it to anyone and it was only when I wrote it down and gave it to you. You have the only copy." Hitchin didn't look away or even blink.

Sherdan sat down and sighed. Hitchin didn't hesitate in pouring them both a drink. Sherdan didn't refuse the gesture then or when he was poured another, straight after downing the first.

They continued to drink for several hours while Hitchin steered the conversation away from the intruder and everything else to do with it. Sherdan didn't even correct his assumption that it was a male who'd entered the compound, despite it being a female.

When Sherdan finally left to go to his house and get some sleep, they were laughing over the day they had first started their program. Sherdan himself had been the first subject, followed by Hitchin. Those had been good days.

It wasn't until the walk back through the underground route to his house that the intruder invaded Sherdan's thoughts again. Normally he could forget about anyone not in his program with ease, but something about her unsettled him.

When he arrived back in his study he went to pour a final brandy before sleeping. The fire had almost died down in the three hours since he had left it. He didn't bother rebuilding it.

Instead, Sherdan took his nightcap to his desk. As he did, he noticed that one of the monitors was showing the footage from the intruder's cell. He moved the channel to his larger central screen and sat down. The guards had wasted no time in starting the interrogation process.

While he sat watching, the guard yanked her up from her chair by nothing but her hair. He yelled in her face as she remained impassive and non-responsive. Sherdan was impressed that she could remain so calm in the face of such abuse.

When the guard still did not get the information he wanted, he gave her a right hook into the face. She went flying back over the chair she had been sitting on and landed on her shoulders. The table mostly hid her body from Sherdan's view, but he winced regardless. That must have hurt.

As the burly man lashed out and kicked the girl in the side, Sherdan reached out and switched the TV screen off. He couldn't watch that right before sleeping. It usually wouldn't have bothered him at all, but either the alcohol or something else had made him more sensitive to this female's suffering.

Sherdan finished his drink and went to his bedroom. He sank into the warmth of the duvet and looked around his comfortable, yet large, room. He had insisted it be constructed in the image of the upper-class bedrooms of the early nineteenth century, with an oak panelled effect just over half way up the walls, and it contained a four poster bed in a matching wood. The rest of the room was a deep burgundy colour.

The fire his maid had lit was still reasonably well-fed. Sherdan turned the last of the electric lights out to fall asleep in the cosy glow cast by the blaze from one side of the bed.

It was Sherdan's alarm that woke him the following morning. The room was still dark and cold. His head hurt from the alcohol he'd consumed the night before and he didn't want to get up. He knew he had to.

He had three meetings in the morning so he needed to write some notes for a press conference the following day. He would need to be very careful with what he said. Thankfully, he had been given a list of probable questions his interviewer would ask. That was something he could plan for.

As usual, his breakfast was laid out in his dining room. He helped himself to a small amount of scrambled eggs and bacon before turning to the selection of fruit. He didn't like to eat a lot before a big day. It made it harder to think.

While eating, he briefly flicked through the paper, but nothing of interest caught his attention. He didn't need advice on what to do with his last week before Christmas, and he really didn't need to know that yet another celebrity's husband had been caught sleeping with some easy blonde. If they were stupid enough to get caught they should pay the price.

When he had finished, he got up and went through to his study. He immediately noticed the central monitor and couldn't help but turn it on again. The table and chairs were gone and in their place a bucket of water sat.

The girl was drenched and kneeling in front of the water. Her hands and feet were manacled behind her to a metal hoop in the floor. Her tattered clothes, as well as the floor around her, were splattered with her blood.

Thankfully the guards were nowhere to be seen but she didn't get up. Her lips were moving even though there was no one to listen to anything she said. Both her eyes were closed, but he suspected that her right was swollen shut anyway.

For a moment he desired to rush into the room, undo her bonds and carry her to safety. He soon reminded himself that she had brought this upon herself. He would be kinder to her when she finally talked, if she hadn't already.

While Sherdan watched, her captors came back. She didn't even stop talking or acknowledge their presence in the room. She continued her kneeling, ceaselessly murmuring with her eyes closed. Sherdan wished he had installed a sound feed to satisfy his curiosity over what he assumed to be praying.

It was possibly just rambling as a result of what she was going through, but she had already informed him of her faith. He wished to know which it was, as it appeared to be helping her.

She didn't stop speaking until one guard grabbed her, shoved her head into the bucket of water and held her there while she struggled against him. As soon as she was let up, she coughed and spluttered and went straight back to her ritual.

Sherdan watched this happen another three times before he was interrupted. The security guard who had spoken to him the night before was back.

This time it wasn't bad news, but his agenda and several different reports, including the weekly report on base security.

Without the girl's addition to the report it was otherwise a very healthy break-down. Any other security issues had been dealt with so effectively that he was impressed with the guards.

"Is there no update on information the girl has divulged yet?" Sherdan asked when he noticed the missing report.

"No, sir. They've not got her to speak yet."

"I guess they took a break to sleep."

"No, sir, they've been trying all night. She's one tough chick. She just keeps talking in this language no one understands and ignores almost everything they try and do."

"Ignores it?" Sherdan looked pale but he tried not to let his guard see how moved he was.

"Yes, she feels the pain for sure. She flinches and cries out occasionally, but she carries on talking right after. Me and Matthew have never seen anything like it."

"Thank you, Nathan. Have me informed as soon as she does say something. And get them to feed her. We'll need to keep her alive until she talks."

"Yes, sir." The guard saluted Sherdan and left. Sherdan looked back at the screen. They had given up on the water and each held an electric baton. He felt sick just knowing what would come next. Reaching out, he switched the monitor off again. He hoped she'd talk soon.

CHAPTER 4

Sherdan had finished two of his morning meetings before he thought of his prisoner again. His third meeting was with Hitchin.

"Has he talked yet?" Hitchin said as soon as he saw Sherdan. Sherdan grinned at the notion that he still thought it must have been a male who'd caused all the trouble the night before.

"We've not got her to talk yet, no, but the men are working on her and it won't be long now."

"Her? You mean it's a female?" Hitchin's eyes went wide.

"Yes, this cute little blonde thing. Looks really are deceiving in this case."

Hitchin laughed and Sherdan soon joined in, even though he wasn't sure he felt like doing so. The same overwhelming urge to protect her had come over him again. He dismissed it and decided to find a woman to share a night with at the next available opportunity, in case that was the cause.

When they had stopped laughing, the two of them discussed the report he had read the night before.

"As you can see, the developments shown by each test subject are still varied. No two subjects have yet developed the same enhancement."

Hitchin pointed at various things on the page as he explained.

"I've done my best to log each one, and what seems to have changed. None that are particularly useful have come up in the last batch, but they may well be in the future."

"What about the next batch?"

"I've got another five ready to administer the drug to. I know it's a small group."

"After tomorrow there should be plenty of volunteers. Your next batch will be much larger."

"Shall I begin the treatment?" Hitchin asked.

"Yes, but make sure to monitor them very closely and keep them here for an additional twelve hours."

"Really? Do you think it wise to take up so much time with each group?" Hitchin raised an eyebrow.

"Our mortality rate is too high still. Only about eighty percent of people are surviving the treatment, and we should be aiming for closer to ninety-nine percent. Otherwise we are wasting a lot of our time. I want you to focus on that."

Hitchin nodded and Sherdan got up to go. He was about to leave the room when Hitchin stopped him.

"Sherdan, I think I might be able to help with your intruder. If someone can get me a DNA sample I can get it run through the ID base for all known covert organisations to see if she's a spy or an assassin. There's a particular patient I have in mind who should be able to help with that."

"I'll have a sample of her blood sent over for you. I'd like to know her name and who really sent her. I don't buy her church story even with the constant praying. Well, at least it seems to be prayer. No one understands it." With that Sherdan left. He passed on Hitchin's request and went back to his study for some peace.

It was mid-afternoon, and Sherdan had finished preparing his answers for the interview before he allowed his focus to drift back to this girl again. He tried to resist the temptation to turn on the monitor and continue watching, but his hand moved and flicked the switch by its own will.

His prisoner lay sideways on the floor. Her trainers were gone, showing two little feet that would have been pretty had her toenails not been a bloody mess. Her clothes were torn even more and barely kept her modest.

She looked exhausted but still she whispered. He was struck by the peacefulness in her face. Peace in the midst of great pain and chaos.

For the next half an hour he watched. She lay there, talking, until she finally fell asleep. Sherdan sighed with relief. Sleep would give her strength, and for some reason this comforted him. The respite was short-lived.

The guards had been instructed to wake any interrogation subjects if they tried to sleep, and in their minds this one was no different to the others. They soon kicked her awake. She continued to whisper, almost oblivious to the abuse, as Sherdan reached out and stroked her on his screen.

He frowned and got up. He needed to be busy, not feel sorry for this stupid prisoner. He went to his personal gym and tried to block her out of his thoughts as he ran on his treadmill.

An hour later he had succeeded in pushing the girl from his mind, as well as running eight miles. Tired, he reclined in his favourite chair, with his back to the haunting cameras. He looked over the provisions report he had been given in his first meeting of the day.

By the time he had finished he was much happier. The program was now almost entirely self-sufficient. The gardens were producing enough fruit and vegetables that food wasn't a problem. The fish breeding program would be at a stable cycle in less than two weeks. Their only worry was a good supply of fresh water.

The underground stream they had found would only support another few hundred people if their mains pipes were cut off. Sherdan made a note to get his workers on exploring an alternative supply. The facility needed to be entirely self-supplied by the end of the year.

Later that evening, Sherdan was sitting by the fire with a brandy in one hand and his Kindle in the other. He had been reading some of the old classics, and the Count of Monte-Cristo was his latest. It was moderately fitting for his mood at the moment.

He had an original version from the first print run on his

shelves, but didn't want to damage the pages or spine, as it was over a hundred and fifty years old.

Sherdan was disturbed from reading by the daytime guard at the end of his watch.

"Sir, I've got an update on the female prisoner."

"Ah, brilliant. What has she said?" Sherdan enquired of the older man, but as he looked past him he saw the TV screen. As he spoke, the guards were plunging her head into the water bucket again.

"She's not said a word, sir. She's a stubborn one, make no mistake."

"Then what is the update for?" he almost yelled.

"She's refusing to eat, sir. They've tried to feed her three times today after your order came through but she just leaves it untouched. She'll drink plenty of water, though she gets a lot of that in many ways," the guard said as he glanced at the monitor.

"Thank you. Get them to keep trying. Don't bother updating me unless she says anything in future," Sherdan replied and motioned for the guard to leave. The man didn't hesitate, sensing Sherdan's anger.

As soon as he was alone he got up and poured another brandy. Why didn't the girl just talk? She had to be suffering. He wasn't going to let her die without speaking. However, there was no way he could allow it to get that bad.

Sherdan tried to put her from his mind. He needed to sleep to be well rested for his interview the following morning. Despite his efforts, he went to sleep with the image of her bruised and bloody body fixed in his mind. He awoke with the same picture.

When he had finished preparing to travel to London he checked the monitor. The girl lay still, her mouth moving slowly in faint whispers. There were fresh bruises and cuts on top of the old and her breathing looked more laboured than it had before.

On his way out he checked with the security guards that no messages had come through for him in the night and he asked them to inform the interrogation team that he wanted their prisoner kept alive. He also suggested that it would be wise for a doctor to see her and check she would survive further questioning.

With a lighter heart Sherdan got into his chauffeur-driven car and relaxed as he was driven the two-hour journey to London. While he was travelling he went over his notes and what he wished to say.

He couldn't be too careful with the words he used to describe their gifted community. It was too soon to let the world know the whole truth, but it was definitely time they knew he existed and had plans for the future.

Once Sherdan felt suitably prepared, he reached for his laptop. He wanted to search for examples of Christians praying. He still couldn't decide if his prisoner was talking incoherently or actually praying. Despite what he had told Hitchin, he mostly believed her church story.

It took him a few minutes of searching relevant keywords before he stumbled on a page mentioning praying in tongues. The page informed him that Christians believed the Holy Spirit gave each person their own unique language to pray in.

He listened to several samples of people praying and sometimes singing in what they called tongues. The languages were all widely different, and Sherdan found it hard to believe all of them were real, but it did seem to be what his prisoner was doing.

Traffic was awful in London and, despite allowing almost an hour extra to do his journey, he was late for his designated arrival time. As a result, he was rushed through make-up and plonked down on the sofa opposite his interviewer, Emma Dobs. The program wouldn't have too many viewers, as it was a lunch time show, but Sherdan knew it was a big start.

Emma was a brown-haired mousey sort of woman with a big smile. She made idle conversation with Sherdan while they were waiting for the cameras to go live. Thankfully, they didn't have to wait long.

Their off stage director was soon counting them in and Sherdan was being welcomed onto the show. He exuded a cool charm and grace as he thanked his host.

"You run a commune of people in Bristol that's grown rapidly over the last few years. Why don't you tell us about it?"

she launched straight in.

"Well I'm not sure that commune is quite the right word for it. It's more of an organisation. There are about five thousand people living in the area, and they are all very gifted individuals. A lot of them have come to Bristol University and have stayed to help with the projects."

"And you work at the University, correct?"

"Yes, I have been working there in one of their research departments for roughly ten years. The University itself is the centre of our organisation."

"What exactly does your organisation intend to do?"

"To start with, we are looking for anyone who wishes to have a new start in life, who thinks they have a gift or talent that is currently being wasted. We will take applicants from any walk of life into our program."

"What will people gain from joining you?" Emma asked, probing further. Sherdan smiled before responding.

"We hope to give each and every person a new sense of purpose as well as all the training and support they need to forge a successful and fulfilling life."

"This all sounds too good to be true. Where's the catch?" The hostess looked very shocked when Sherdan laughed.

"Well, the University is an education institute, so in part it is as good as it sounds, but to recoup some of the costs of training, etc., we do ask each participant to work for a few hours a week at jobs which support the community."

Sherdan paused thoughtfully until he noticed Emma was about to speak. He didn't give her the opportunity, but continued instead.

"However, these hours always allow for any necessary program requirements and don't start until each member has settled onto their course and is fully committed to staying out the course to its completeness." Sherdan finished his little speech with another smile.

The interview had gone exactly as he wished. He relaxed as Emma thanked him and informed the viewers of how they could apply. His work was done here. Dr Hitchin would have many more test subjects for his subsequent batches.

The world was also finally aware his organisation existed, even if they knew nothing else yet. It would not be long before he could show the world everything he'd been working on.

As he was getting back into his car, he had a phone call from Hitchin.

"We've found the girl. She's a normal civilian. Her name's Anya Price."

"Thanks, Hitchin." He hung up on his friend as he mulled over this new information. He liked it.

Sherdan smiled the whole drive back to his home. He even stopped off at his favourite sea food restaurant in Bath on the way.

While he was there he observed an attractive young female alone on a nearby table. She spent the length of his meal writing in her notepad, and hardly even glanced up when the waiter took her empty plate away.

When he had finished eating he got up and went over to her. Before she could say anything he had offered to buy her a drink. She said no at first but, when he promised to let her continue writing if she wished, she said yes and let him join her.

Four hours later he left her house, satisfied. She had been very impressed by the car and chauffeur, and Sherdan had dictated the rest of the night without objection.

He closed her front door as quietly as he could. He had left her sleeping and didn't expect her to notice he was gone until the morning. He hadn't left any contact details.

When Sherdan got back he made the mistake of going to his study first. The first thing he saw was Anya; still praying and still being interrogated.

He flicked the monitor off, but the last image was burned into his vision and he continued to see it long after the real thing had disappeared. Until she talked he couldn't do anything to stop it.

Sherdan fell asleep as quickly as he usually did, but his sleep was far from peaceful. Everywhere he turned he saw a small-framed blonde girl on her knees praying, her big brown eyes imploring him for help. He turned away, only to see blood dripping from his fingers and hands. Not his own blood, he wasn't the one hurt.

He tried to flee from it all but the path didn't lead away. Instead it doubled back to the same place. Always Anya, kneeling, begging for mercy from a hooded man.

The hooded man taunted her while Sherdan watched. He then reached into his cloak and pulled out a huge axe. She tried to get away as it was aimed at her, but she was still manacled to the floor. As the axe came down Sherdan yelled out.

With a jump he sat up in bed. His torso shook and sweat poured from every pore in his body.

He turned to check the time. It was only half four in the morning. Sherdan threw back the covers, pulled on the nearest clothes and grabbed his security radio from the bedside cabinet. He rushed down the stairs while calling for the attention of his guards.

"Is everything all right, sir?" the radio squawked.

"Er... Yes. Please have my car ready to take me to the compound as soon as you can."

"Yes, sir. Are you sure you are all right?"

"I am..." Sherdan trailed off as he walked into his study. The monitor was right there in front of him. He flicked it on and watched, struck dumb, as Anya crawled backwards, a look of intense fear on her face.

Her eyes were fixed on the guard who stood nearby, jeering at her as he undid his belt buckle and stepped out of his shoes. Anya pulled herself away from him as Sherdan noticed her lack of trousers. They were in a heap against the wall. Her torturer soon added his belt and shoes to the pile.

"Sir?" the radio broke the silence and stirred Sherdan into action.

"Nathan, please contact the interrogation team and request they stop immediately. I am going to take over the situation myself."

"Yes, sir. Right away, sir."

With that Sherdan rushed out of his study and through the front of his house. He didn't pause as he moved past his personal guards except to grab his long black coat and hastily pull it on. He still clutched his radio as he rushed out to the car.

"Done, sir... Thank you, sir. I think a new approach might be..."

"I understand, Nathan," Sherdan interrupted. He then got into his car and urged his chauffeur to drive fast.

CHAPTER 5

Fear shook Anya as she was escorted away from Sherdan. No part of her had expected him to deny the existence of the prophecy. It briefly flashed through her head that there wasn't a prophecy at all, but she dismissed the thought as soon as it occurred to her.

Several members of her church had confirmed her dream. God wanted her here and she would trust to that, whatever happened next.

Sherdan had been calmer and more calculated than she had expected. He was clever and in control of his emotions. She knew he would be a difficult man to persuade otherwise once he had decided on a course of action. Thankfully she had God. She had seen Him defeat more powerful men, though she knew He didn't act in every case.

Either way, Anya knew she was in danger and the testing of her obedience to God had only just begun. She already prayed that her faith wouldn't fail her, no matter what she was put through.

The second blindfolded walk lasted much longer than the first. She started to swell around her bonds until she could no longer move her hands without an excruciating stabbing pain lancing outwards from her wrists.

Despite all this she continued to pray. While her lips moved continuously in tongues her head was free to pray in English. She prayed that Sherdan would be blessed and his heart would be opened; that he would know love and all the wonders that came with it.

Then she prayed for her escorts; that they would be forgiven and shown mercy even if they showed neither themselves. She didn't really do it out of any sense of love for them, more because it was what she had been told to do. Finally she prayed for herself, for God to grant her enough strength, faith and love, that whatever happened she would know Him for the rest of her days.

Her prayer was interrupted by arriving at her cell. The bag was swiftly removed from her head and she found herself forced into a sitting position at a small table.

The room only had a single light bulb, the table and two chairs, one of which she had been sat on. It looked a lot like the scary rooms in movies where organisations took suspected spies. She knew it was meant to frighten her. Knowing everything was God's will kept her calm.

"We'll start this the easy way, miss. Cooperate and it will stay nice and civilised. My name's Jack and I'm one of the senior guards here. Who do you work for?" the guard said as he sat down in front of her. Anya suspected that this was going to be a long night.

"I work for myself. I'm an artist," she replied.

"Who sent you then?"

"God."

The guy got up and came around to her side of the table. Anya looked at him, trying not to let her fear show. He waited for a moment as if expecting her to change her answer. She didn't.

"I don't want to do this the hard way, I really don't."

"Neither do I," she replied.

"Then I need to know more. Why don't you tell me everything about why you're here, in one long story, seeing as my questions aren't working."

Anya nodded and spent the next forty-five minutes explaining all about her dream, what she had told her church pastors and that many others in her church had said the same thing. She had volunteered to come see the prophecy and find out for sure.

She could tell the guard didn't believe a word she said but it was the truth, and not lying was all that mattered to her. The only thing she didn't say was her name. Something stopped her, and she wasn't going to disobey any directional feelings.

For the next two hours they repeatedly covered the same ground. Eventually he lost his temper; he didn't believe her story and wanted her name, but she wasn't lying even though she refused to divulge her identity. There was only one direction things could go from there.

Anya hadn't exactly seen it coming, but she wasn't surprised when he began to threaten her with violence. In response, she resumed praying in tongues.

He called her a whore and yanked her up out of her seat by her hair. She winced, not by being hauled to her feet, but because her hands had caught on the back of the chair. The numbness that had resided in them gave way to a sharp pain, which shot through both her hands before turning into a dull ache.

When she refused to answer his next question he punched her. Her left eye felt like it had exploded as she went flying.

For the next hour Anya's world was nothing but yelling and abuse. She prayed in tongues and kept her eyes closed so the sight of her own blood wouldn't frighten her any more than she already was.

The entire time she did her best to focus on relevant bible stories, though few came to mind. Her favourite book, Esther, was the clearest. Esther had fasted before going before the king and risking her life, and Anya had copied her example, fasting for three days as well. By the end of the hour she simply prayed for God to end her time and take her to be with him.

Mercifully, as soon as she thought this, her tormentor stopped his violent lashings and dragged her to the centre of the room. He cut the plastic bindings, relieving the pain in her wrists, before transferring them to the manacle-style metal cuffs already there. He bound her ankles as well so each hand was connected behind her back to the opposite foot via a short chain which passed through a large metal hoop affixed to the floor.

The clanking chains felt like needles stabbing into her throbbing head so she kneeled still and prayed. As Anya focused on God she started to sing to him softly, still in tongues. In response to her worship all the pain melted from her body. Despite everything she had endured, for now, she felt none of it.

She had no idea how long they left her like that before her guard was back. The next few hours rolled into a haze of repetition. He would talk nicely until he lost his temper and got violent; finally, he would give her a break when he thought she'd had enough. The entire time she would attempt to pray.

While she was alone she catnapped, but if she appeared asleep someone came and woke her up, and never gently. One such time a second much younger guard didn't leave when she resumed her prayer vigil but had the table and chairs removed. Anya knew it was time for the next stage, whatever it was.

When the latest guard returned with a large bucket of water Anya actually smiled. She knew what would happen next. This test wasn't about pain, but panic. Her immediate response was to pray for the presence of the Holy Spirit.

She turned her mind to her first ever encounter with God. It had happened when trying a new church at the age of twenty-one. She had suddenly felt overwhelmingly peaceful for the first time in her life. Anya hadn't been to another church since.

Time and time again her head was dunked into the bucket and she was held under until her lungs ached for breath. Just when she thought she might drown she would be allowed to breathe.

Calmness lay on her like a cloak. Rather than feeling worse, as the guards had hoped, Anya soon felt refreshed. She'd never thought it possible to feel calm in the face of such hate, but her confidence in God grew all the more as a result.

Eventually the bucket was taken away and her captors returned with small sticks. Anya looked puzzled until she was hit with one. The electricity caused her body to spasm.

When even the electric shocks didn't get her talking they gave her another break and brought her a plate of food. Her hands were freed and she was encouraged to eat.

Anya picked up the plate and had a fork full ready to shovel into her mouth before she thought. God had asked her to fast and in one unguarded moment she had almost ruined it all. She put the plate down again and turned her back.

The rest of the day passed in a blur. She left all three meals completely untouched. The guards continued to try new methods to get Anya to talk, but she had nothing else to say and she knew Sherdan realised that. She only had to fix on God and at some point she would be delivered, one way or another.

Anya had been puzzled by only one thing that day, sometime between her second and third meal. A nurse had come in, taken some of her blood, and left again. They had not spoken and the guard had held her still while it happened.

She was left alone all night – at least she thought it was night; it was the only explanation that made sense. She prayed and rested. Her whole body was racked with pain but she knew God was close.

Every time she felt weak or defeated, a fresh wave of the Holy Spirit would flow over her and bring the peace and warmth of her maker. Jesus understood. What he had suffered had been far worse and God had honoured His own son for the trials he was put through.

The following day was a haze so alike to the first that Anya wondered if she had finally fallen asleep and it was just the haunting remembrance of her ordeal so far. It made the torture easier to bear if she pretended it was just a dream. A horrible dream, but a dream nonetheless.

As the day progressed she spent less and less time conscious. Jack was back, and he was nastier than the second guard had been. Anya sighed with relief when his shift was over and the second guard came back.

"Don't be too soft on her," Jack said as he was relieved.

As if placating his superior, the younger guard resumed the interrogation with more force than Anya expected. He was soon interrupted by another young male in a lab coat. Her guard left, leaving her alone with the new arrival. They stared at each other while she prayed. He seemed to be analysing her. She eventually raised an eyebrow in question. He smiled.

"I'm a doctor. You can call me James. What's your name?" he said.

"I'm pleased to meet you, James. Why have you come to visit me?"

"I've been asked to check you over. No one wants you to get too sick." At this he moved towards her. He gently checked every cut and bruise and listened to her breathing before whispering goodbye. He shut the door behind him with a gentle click in contrast to the slams of the guards when they entered or exited.

No one came back. Anya drifted where she lay. Suddenly she felt herself prodded. She opened her eyes but no one was there. She closed her eyes again and let herself drift. Moments later she felt another prod. Again, when she opened her eyes no one was there.

Anya looked around the room, confused. The story of Samson popped into her head. Every time he had fallen asleep, his wife had taken whatever he had said was the source of his strength. If he had stayed awake and not said anything he would never have been betrayed. Anya lifted herself up onto her knees and continued praying. She did everything she could to stay awake.

Several hours of her vigil passed before she could no longer stay kneeling and she collapsed onto her side. Still, she fought off sleep. Slowly her eyes closed, although her mouth still moved in silent prayer.

When her lips had finally stopped moving and her senses had dulled to the outside world, she felt herself floating off into the distance. As if from a strange distant land she heard a soft click. She ignored it, wanting to continue into the oblivion of deep sleep.

What seemed like minutes later she heard a faint shuffling sound that came closer the longer it went on. It couldn't be placed by Anya's brain at first, but it eventually made its way through the fog.

Her eyes snapped open. The first thing she saw was the older security guard. He stopped his creeping and looked at her. Pure anger burned in his expression.

"The doctor informs me that I have to stop what I've been doing to you to get you to talk. He seems to think I'm not doing a very good job. I don't like disappointing the boss. So I've come up with the perfect way to get you spilling the truth."

Anya gulped. She didn't like the glint in his eyes as he looked at her. She shifted backwards from him as far as her chains would let her. All the while he walked towards her, menacing step after menacing step. He grinned. She shivered.

Suddenly he lunged at her. She struggled against him as he grabbed hold of her trousers. He ripped them off and flung them against the wall.

Her bonds prevented her from defending herself with anything but her mouth. She bit into his shoulder. He yelled out and back-handed her. Miraculously, the strain of her struggle broke the ring in the centre of the room and, although she was still bound, she no longer found herself fixed to a single point.

Anya thanked God and dragged herself away from the vile man, despite the pain that flared in her limbs. The guard made his intentions clear as she watched him remove his belt and shoes, and fling them to the same place as her trousers. He never took his eyes off her.

"I'm going to enjoy this. I've never had a good little Christian girl," he said as he advanced towards her again. She tried to back up even further, completely overcome with fear, praying out of habit rather than desire.

He was less than a foot away from her when the door was flung open, crashing against the wall.

"What?" the guard snapped furiously at their disturber.

"Sherdan is on his way. We've been ordered to stop."

"I'm in the middle of something. It's half four in the morning. He'll be asleep." The guard turned straight back to Anya, who had used the time to slide around him and put more distance between them. He grabbed her leg and pulled her back. She screamed.

"Jack! You have to stop. He's really on his way." The younger guard and two others all came into the room as she was let go. Jack spat at her.

"I'll be back to finish this later. The boss won't do the dirty work for long. You're not his cup of tea." Anya wept as she was left alone.

CHAPTER 6

Sherdan bit his lip as he sat in his car. Despite the driver breaking the speed limit, it didn't seem fast enough. Horrible images of what might be happening to Anya flashed through his head. He had to stop her being tortured. No matter why she was there, he just couldn't let it go on any longer. He had never felt so sure of anything.

As soon as the car had stopped, Sherdan rushed into the main compound. He didn't stop to speak to security but ran straight by them and through the door. Anya's cell had been deliberately placed near the heart of the building, almost as secure as the command room.

Less than five minutes later he arrived at the right room. Four of his security team were outside. They stopped their heated argument when they saw Sherdan approach. He instantly recognised the guard who had been about to rape her and relief washed over him.

"Let me in to see her," he snapped before he had even reached them. Only one guard responded and rushed to unlock the door for him. Anya cowered in the far corner. She was reasonably calm, but tear tracks could plainly be seen on her grimy face.

"Get me a chair and turn off the camera feed into the room," Sherdan commanded. He was obeyed without question. Anya gulped, obviously expecting more of the same.

The second they were alone together he sat down. He couldn't look at her. She was so close to him and so helpless. He felt like a monster but his pride wouldn't let her see his remorse.

"Hello, Anya Price," he said, when he had managed to get his emotions under control.

She raised her eyebrows at the mention of her name but didn't speak or move from her position in the corner. He couldn't blame her.

"How do you know about my prophecy?" he asked, admitting it existed for the first time. She didn't respond at first. After a few minutes she stopped hugging herself quite so tightly. She cleared her throat and winced. Sherdan waited, not wanting to frighten her further.

"I dreamt of you in a big mahogany panelled room. One wall was filled with books. The opposite had a large fireplace built of Bath stone. You got up and went to the bookshelf third from the right. You took what I think was the sixth book from the left, on the fourth shelf from the bottom." She closed her eyes as she said it as if she were picturing the location.

Sherdan looked amazed. She had described his study and the location of the right book in perfect detail.

"In the book was a prophecy you were given and after that was a list. Your name is first on that list."

Sherdan nodded but remained silent. She didn't offer him any more information and, to his surprise, she no longer prayed.

"You won't speak of the prophecy or anything related to it to anyone else in my program. Is that clear?" He looked at her properly for the first time since being in the room. She nodded. He got up and went over to her, keeping his eyes fixed on her face.

Anya drew back at his approach so he slowed his movements and held out his hands to show her he meant no harm. Despite being reasonably close, it still took him some minutes to move closer.

When he reached her he undid all the manacles and helped her put on his coat. She tried to stand, but her feet wouldn't support her.

Without hesitation, he lifted her, cradling her body against him. She arranged his coat to keep herself covered and he walked with her to the door.

Neither of them spoke or even looked at each other as Sherdan knocked on the door to the cell. They were both let out to the open mouths of all four guards. Shock soon turned to anger on Jack's face. Sherdan felt Anya cling tighter to him as he walked past the men who had tortured her for almost three days.

He retraced his entire journey right back to his waiting car, where he placed her gently on the back seat and strapped her in. Still, neither of them said anything.

Anya's eyes were closed before he had walked around to the other side of the car. He knew she would sleep for a while, now her ordeal was over. He watched her sleep until they reached his house, and then carried her inside. She didn't stir as he took her to the bedroom beside his, and she remained asleep the entire time the doctor examined her. Sherdan then locked her into her room.

Feeling peaceful for the first time since news of Anya had reached him, he went to his study to await breakfast. The monitor that had displayed her cell had been changed to show her new room, where he watched her sleep in comfort.

The doctor had hopes that she would recover over time, with no serious scarring or permanent injury. There would always be marks around her toes, ankles and wrists, but it would be minimal and fade over time. It would hardly be noticeable after a year or so.

Psychologically, there was no way to say for sure how long it would take her to recover, if she would ever completely do so. The doctor hadn't said the last part but Sherdan didn't need him to. The only relief to the overwhelming guilt he felt was what he had managed to prevent.

Sherdan still couldn't decide if she had told him the truth, but no one else knew the exact location of the prophecy. Some higher power had to be at work.

Until Hitchin had given him the prophecy he had never believed in anything spiritual. People existed because the planet supported life. Slowly, he had seen parts of the prophecy come true, but there was no mention of this girl in it. He had no idea where she featured, but he would keep her locked where he wanted her until he could find out.

When Sherdan's breakfast arrived, he informed his maid that the spare room was occupied and locked, to only be accessed by him. He also informed her that there would be two for each meal and he would take his guest's meals to them. If the maid was puzzled by any of this, she didn't show it.

As soon as he had eaten, he went to see his security guards. Nathan and Matthew had already knocked off, leaving him with the guards on the morning shift, Ed and Julie. They nodded acknowledgement of him.

"I'm going to be spending the rest of the day in the room with Miss Price. I want to continue questioning her when she wakes," he lied. He really wanted to make sure she didn't wake alone in a strange place. "Please have any messages passed to me there, but don't let anyone disturb me unless it's urgent."

"Yes, sir. Very good."

"I shall have my laptop with me, so emails will be the best way to contact me," Sherdan added as he walked away.

Wasting no more time, he fetched his laptop from his study, along with its power supply, and walked up the two flights of stairs to the top floor. There were only two bedrooms on this floor, his and the one now occupied by Anya. Both had en-suite bathrooms, and were separated by the hallway.

He quietly turned the key in the lock and went into her room. She was still fast asleep and he watched her peaceful breathing, mesmerised. Only her matted, bloody hair and the purple bruise on one eye gave any indication that her life wasn't perfect.

Sherdan sat down on the armchair facing her bed and propped his computer on his knees. Until now he had been distracted from his duties, but he needed to return to them. There would be applications to go through and more plans to be made, as well as an update on Hitchin's next test batch. With any luck he would already be seeing some good results.

When Sherdan had finished replying to the important emails, he checked the central database of all the applicants so far. For each person applying Sherdan had people running a family, criminal and government employment check. The information was then uploaded along with their CV and application form for him to look over.

There were already over a hundred people in the database. He smiled. This was much higher than he expected and could potentially mean there were many more people who had sent CVs. They wouldn't be uploaded for him to see until the other checks were done. With only one person working on it, they must have put every waking hour into the task since his interview.

Sherdan started with the applications from older people with less family. They would be easier to convince to take the drug and would be missed less if things didn't go according to plan.

Several hours later Sherdan had approved twenty-two of the applicants and authorized them to be invited for a two-week trial period at the University. There were another sixty-five possibles that Sherdan stuck on a waiting list in a rough priority order.

The remaining fifteen were rejected, although none of them would be informed of that. They would be told the same as the sixty-five on the waiting list. They would all be asked to wait until a place was available.

Of the fifteen rejected, two were above sixty and probably wouldn't survive the drug treatment. Three were foreign and hardly spoke English. One had been a political activist for communism during their university years; someone who believed in equality wasn't what Sherdan wanted.

Five had worked for the government in some capacity and could never be trusted in the next few stages of the organisation's development. The final four had too much past criminal activity and would look bad if reporters snooped at his accepted lists. Bad press now wouldn't be useful. If things changed, they would be bumped up to the waiting list.

Before Sherdan could start anything else, his maid knocked at the door. She had brought lunch up. He thanked her but didn't let her see inside the room. Anya stirred at the noise but didn't wake up. She continued to sleep all afternoon, missing both lunch and dinner. The only time Sherdan left her side was to visit the bathroom.

Hitchin had no news to report yet so Sherdan continued processing applications while he waited. Not long before the doctor was due to check up on her, Anya finally opened her eyes. She immediately focused on Sherdan and tried to sit up.

The movement attracted his attention and he rushed over as she winced in pain. She didn't try to move again.

"Thank you," she said slowly. It looked like it hurt to talk. He sat on the edge of the bed but got up when she pulled away, creasing her face up with pain once more.

"Don't keep moving. You need to lie still," Sherdan implored,."I'm not going to hurt you." He put his hands up to show his actions would match up with his words as he sat down again. Her eyes never left him, and they were tinted with fear.

For a moment there was only silence. He could hardly look at her. The look of pain in her eyes bothered him.

"Can I see the prophecy now, please?" she asked. Sherdan started. Of all the questions he had expected that hadn't been it.

"No, you cannot, and never will be allowed to. You need to rest."

"I am here for only one reason: to read that prophecy." Her eyes blazed. She was angry at him. "As soon as I am well enough to move I shall continue searching for it."

"No, you will not. You may have been upgraded to more comfortable accommodation but you are still my prisoner, and, until I have the answers I wish for from you, you will remain that way," he hissed. Inwardly he protested; this wasn't how he had wanted their conversation to progress. He'd wanted gratitude and polite conversation. He'd wanted some idea of where she fit into his future, not hostility and threats.

Most importantly he hadn't expected to be surprised. No one was unpredictable to him. That's how he had managed to get so far in life and meticulously plan for everything he wanted.

Thankfully, the doctor arrived. Either because she remembered her promise, or because she was too tired to argue, Anya didn't mention the prophecy. Sherdan sat back down in his chair and allowed the doctor access to her.

James was pleased she was awake and discussed all her differing ailments with her at length. He made her wiggle all her fingers and checked her wrists for permanent damage since she could now tell him what hurt and what felt numb. He then did the same with her feet.

Anya expressed concern about her nails growing back but it was too early to tell for sure. She then waved off his attention to her face. Very little damage had been done in that regard.

When the doctor tried to pull back the covers to examine the rest of her body, Anya stopped him. Her gaze was on Sherdan, who had sat and watched the entire process so far.

"Sir, I think Miss Price would like some privacy. Would you mind stepping outside?" Before James had finished speaking, Sherdan had got up and walked over to the window, putting his back to them both. James shrugged at Anya, who reluctantly let him pull the covers back.

"She's going to need a change of clothes," the doctor called out as he checked over the bruises on Anya's torso and thighs. Sherdan didn't respond.

"I think there might be a fractured rib; it's hard to tell. You're covered in bruises from the last three days. I should know for sure in a day or two."

He helped her roll over so he could see her back. It wasn't as bad as her front. Her bonds had prevented many blows reaching her central back. It was a blessing. Her spine was mostly untouched, as were her kidneys. Both would have been badly damaged by the blows that had landed elsewhere.

The doctor rolled her back and covered her back up again. She smiled and thanked him as Sherdan retook his seat at the end of the bed.

"One last thing. I've brought some pain killers with me. They should help you rest." He stretched his hand towards the briefcase he had left by the door. It opened on its own, and a small packet of pills flew out of it and into his hand. She gasped in shock. He smiled but continued as if nothing had happened.

"Take one of these every four hours, or just before you sleep if you can cope without them the rest of the time."

"Doctor..." Sherdan growled.

Anya didn't get a chance to say anything else as both men suddenly left the room. Sherdan was furious at James.

"She didn't know about the drug and its abilities," he snapped at the doctor. James' face went white. "Leave us and come back tomorrow evening." Sherdan didn't wait for a response but went back into Anya's room and slammed the door behind him. She looked frightened. He stared at her and paused, losing himself in the depths of emotion in her big brown eyes.

"You weren't meant to see that," he tried to say casually. She visibly relaxed.

"I suppose there's no point me asking what exactly that was?"

"Would you like to know?"

"I'd like to see the prophecy more, but I would like to know what that was too, if it's something you will share."

Sherdan nodded and sat back down again.

"Nine years ago Dr John Hitchin and I stumbled upon an enzyme which had a marvellous effect on the human brain. It encourages the brain to map new neurological pathways, resulting in a new and completely unique ability in each person who takes it."

"Why has there not been any news of this?"

"It is the best kept secret of this facility. No one who has taken it is allowed to leave the area, and until I disclose it, the world will never know about it."

Anya frowned. And he could guess what she was thinking.

"That now includes you. You will not be allowed to leave here."

"Not ever?"

"No, not ever. Now, I have work to do and you need rest. I shall see you in the morning. All the windows and doors will be locked, and even if you did manage to break out in your state, there are patrols and guards enough to bring you back. Goodnight, Miss Price."

CHAPTER 7

Sherdan slept very well that night. Things had not gone amazingly with Anya but he had all the time he wanted with her. She would remain his prisoner as long as he wished.

He beamed when he thought of all the new applicants. The lady processing them, Janet, had asked for some more help. He had assigned her another worker who had a very special ability of being able to work out what was and wasn't true in written words. It wouldn't make their job too much quicker, but it would help.

Sherdan himself would take weeks to go through every application and Dr Hitchin would be kept busy for months with all the new test subjects. It was time Sherdan focused on growth and taking their organisation to the next level, but it would get increasingly difficult to keep all the abilities hidden from the public and keep everyone with an ability from leaving if they wished.

His first task of the new day was planning his next move. He already had an idea of what it would be, as he did for many years to come. There were always new situations and scenarios to be taken into account, however. Planning for the future was a constant mix of preparation and adjustment.

By the time lunch rolled around he was fairly sure of the plan going forward. He would need to talk to the chief of police for Bristol but the man had been in Sherdan's pocket for years now and he had no doubt that his wishes would be honoured.

He went to see Anya again while he ate lunch, but she slept through all the time he could spare to wait. He grew concerned when he noticed that she still hadn't eaten anything. It was now her fourth day in his compound without food.

For the rest of the afternoon Sherdan visited Hitchin. Hitchin had wonderful news. One of the people in the new test batch could separate compounds by filtering them through his hands.

He thought there might be something in the man's sweat that separated things. If so, they would have their water problem solved. They would be able to recycle all of their waste water. Of course, they would only need to do as much as they required to supplement the supply they already had, and at the moment there was more than enough.

They then planned where all the new recruits were going to live, as well as the size and frequency of the test batches. Finally Sherdan ran his plan for controlled expansion past Hitchin.

His friend helped him with the fine tuning, and by dinner time Sherdan was almost skipping back to his house, though no one who saw him would be able to tell he was so happy. It was only his voice that gave it away as he greeted everyone and stopped to chat with as many of the residents as gave him the time of day.

With a smile on his face, he took his charge some more food. She wasn't awake when he arrived but she stirred a few moments later when he sat down in his usual chair.

"Hello," she said when she saw him. She looked better than she had the day before. Her eye wasn't so puffy and swollen and she had washed her hair. He smiled at her and came over.

"How are you feeling?"

"Better, thank you."

"Good. I brought some dinner up for you. It's shepherd's pie. I hope..."

"Thank you, but can you take it away, please," she interrupted. He raised an eyebrow. "I'm fasting."

"Fasting? Whatever for?"

"I won't eat again until I've seen that prophecy." Sherdan sat down again. She didn't stop looking at him. Nothing this girl said ever seemed to be normal to him. He wasn't used to being surprised by anyone.

"I'm not showing you the prophecy."

"Then I'm not eating."

"Fine," Sherdan snapped. There was an awkward silence.

"Where am I?" she asked a moment later, oblivious to his anger.

"You're in my house. My bedroom is across the hall."

"It must be causing quite a stir in your family to have a girl locked up in the adjacent bedroom." Sherdan laughed as she smiled.

"I'm alone here. None of my immediate family is alive anymore."

"I'm sorry."

"Don't be. It means I can lock young women in bedrooms without the complication of explaining myself to a relative. Only four people know you are here, and one of those is your doctor."

She nodded, taking in the implied meaning. He was surprised how calm she remained. Other than her insistence to see the prophecy, she hadn't shown any sign of objection. He'd half expected her to attempt to break the door down.

Their conversation didn't progress any further as the doctor arrived to do another check-up. He changed Anya's bandages and checked over her bruises. He was pleased with her progress, although he reiterated to Sherdan that she needed clothes.

Sherdan and James both left when Anya yawned; she still needed plenty of rest.

The following morning when Sherdan took her breakfast she again refused to eat and asked to see the prophecy. He said no. Lunch was the same, and dinner. When Sherdan reminded her she hadn't eaten in five days she looked thoughtful.

"It's eight, actually." Sherdan was surprised for the third time by her. "I fasted before I came... I was nervous, so I fasted and prayed to succeed in what I was being asked to do."

"You need to eat."

"No. I need to see the prophecy."

Sherdan sighed. He didn't want to keep going over the same thing.

First thing the following morning Sherdan went to talk to Hitchin about Anya. He wanted advice on how to persuade her to eat, on top of checking over the abilities of the new group of subjects.

They had found that the people living within the program were generally happier if they could get involved with the future of the organisation. A sense of belonging in their new family and life was important. Hitchin and Sherdan spent a long time discussing where abilities could be useful to make sure people could be involved.

Spending time with Hitchin helped Sherdan refocus and, by the time he had to leave for his meeting with the chief of police, Sherdan was confident again.

"Jeremy, so good to see you. How is your daughter? Did she get her degree result reviewed?" Sherdan asked politely. Jeremy, the chief of police shook his hand.

"She did. She got her first after all and has that top-notch job I was telling you about."

"Fantastic. I did hope it would all get resolved." Sherdan smiled. He had arranged it. The lecturer had managed to find the young woman some extra marks and the employer had gone to school with Sherdan.

"What can I do for you?"

"Well, I need some information regarding policing private land and reclaiming public roads for my compound."

"That's a big operation."

"There's bound to be complaints, especially when we close the roads off."

"I understand. I'll make sure any complaints are dealt with quietly but effectively."

"Thank you, Jeremy. I'll make sure this one is remembered."

Sherdan had everything he wanted. He fetched the plans he'd made and took them back to his house for the guards to execute, before continuing with his duties.

As usual, he went to see Anya with her dinner. Her first

question was a request to see the prophecy. He answered as he usually did.

"What does it matter if I see? I'm locked in this room and you've told me that I'll never leave. What would be the harm in showing me?" Sherdan didn't reply but walked over to the window.

"We always talk about this one thing. Can we not talk about something else?"

"What do you have in mind?" she asked.

"Why do you willingly put your life on the line for your God?"

"Because he gave me my life. He can take it away. I was created to do His will."

"But isn't death by starvation suicide?"

"No, He won't let me die. He'll either keep me alive or tell me I can stop fasting."

Sherdan looked at her again. She was so calm, but evidently very tired. He didn't understand her faith. After a pause she looked away.

"Can I have some clothes, please?" Anya asked, her voice trembling a little.

"Anything in particular?"

"Well, I'd like the clothes I've got at home if you could fetch them, but at the very least a change of underwear and some jeans and t-shirts. It would mean I could get out of this bed when someone else was here."

"Me, you mean?" She nodded. "I'll get something fetched for you."

"Thank you."

As soon as Sherdan had left Anya, he went to his security team. Nathan was at the desk. Sherdan passed on Anya's request for something to wear and asked him to find out her address and fetch some of the clothes in her house. He wasn't going to tell her that he'd done as she asked, just show up with them one day.

During breakfast the following morning, his maid, Anne, lagged after bringing the food through to him. He raised an eyebrow at her.

"Are you going to need me tomorrow, sir? What with it

being Christmas, I was hoping to spend the day with my husband and daughter."

"Of course, Anne. Take the following day off as well."

"Thank you, sir."

Sherdan hadn't noticed the date and had forgotten all about Christmas. He would have to remind Hitchin that they had agreed to spend the day together. He also promptly informed the guards that they could have the day off as well.

By the end of the afternoon Sherdan had approved a total of two hundred more people for the program and added almost another thousand to the waiting list. All the preparations for the next stage of his plan were ready and would go into action before the twenty-seventh. Hitchin had been reminded to come for Christmas dinner, and Anya's clothes had been fetched.

It was Christmas Eve and he knew of nowhere he wanted to spend it more than in Anya's company. He took her dinner and her clothes. She thanked him for the clothes and he begged her to eat with him. She refused. Sherdan lost his temper.

"You stubborn fool, you're killing yourself. You had better eat tomorrow!"

"What's so special about tomorrow?"

"It's Christmas!"

"I will eat when I see the prophecy and not before, regardless of the occasion."

Sherdan glared at her but she sat at the top of the four poster bed, calmly waiting. He picked up her dinner tray and left the room with it, slamming the door as he did. He turned the key with a lot more fervour than was needed.

Anne had already left so he had to take Anya's tray to the kitchen and clear it away himself. He banged and clattered everything around the kitchen.

Anya was so stubborn and difficult to talk to. He wanted to get to know her and she didn't want to talk about anything but the stupid prophecy. Sherdan caught himself in the middle of his thought. He had never been so sure he wanted to get closer to somebody and this surprised him. He had no idea what was different about this girl. He didn't love her. He hardly knew her.

When he had finished tidying up the kitchen he went through

to his study to have a nightcap before sleeping. He noticed Anya crying on the TV monitor as soon as he was in the room. He sat and watched her cry herself to sleep while he drank almost every drop of brandy in the nearby decanter.

Christmas day dawned bright and sunny. There wasn't any snow, although they had already had some earlier in the winter. Sherdan had been up less than half an hour when Hitchin arrived, giving him no time to see Anya.

He was soon talking to Hitchin about some of his issues, although he was guarded in what he said. Without being able to explain why, he didn't want his friend to think Anya meant more than she should. He didn't tell Hitchin that much about her, but he did talk about her dream.

"It is possible she has some purpose in our plans somewhere but I wouldn't worry yourself about her. She is locked up right here with no chance of escape. She really won't be leaving. Don't fret if she's uncooperative now. She'll come around in time," Hitchin reassured him.

"You really think so?"

"Of course. You have her right where you want her, and since when have you had any trouble getting women to do what you want them to?"

Sherdan and Hitchin both smiled and chuckled at this and then reminisced of old times together, when they were both courting at university themselves.

They spent the rest of the day together amiably chatting and hardly noticed the time go by. Hitchin was the only person he spent large quantities of time with. They talked for so long that it was almost midnight by the time Sherdan was left alone. Anya had been forgotten about and unvisited all day.

He rushed up the stairs to see if she was still awake, forgetting to check the security camera first. He turned the key quietly and opened the door with as little noise as he could manage so he wouldn't disturb her if she had already fallen asleep. He was pleased to find her wide awake and standing at the window, staring at the night outside.

"I was watching for snow," she said as if that explained everything. Sherdan just nodded. "I haven't ever had a white

Christmas so I pray for one every year. There's not really anything left of today though."

Sherdan still didn't say anything. She hadn't moved from the window so he took the time to admire her. She was wearing some black jeans and a loose-fitting smock top. She looked a little hippy with her bare feet.

"Did you have a good Christmas?" she asked, giving him her full attention at last. He nodded and walked farther into the room. She sat down on the edge of the bed.

"If I'm going to be kept here a while I would appreciate having a Bible."

"I think that can be arranged." Sherdan smiled. She hadn't asked to see the prophecy and had actually said something conversational. Hitchin was right. Time would achieve everything he wanted and she would live here on his land for the rest of her life if he wanted her to.

"Do you mind if I join you for a bit? I'm not feeling like sleeping yet." Sherdan asked.

"By all means, I'm wide awake myself."

She moved over on the bed to make room for him. He smiled and sat down beside her. She soon struck up a conversation with him about past Christmas memories and hopes for the new year.

Over the next couple of hours they talked of everything from politics to money and careers. They were almost polar opposites in everything. He was a scientist, she an artist. She had a large family, he had hardly any.

The only thing they agreed on after many hours searching was that the best form of leadership for any country was a benevolent dictatorship, although she called it a righteous monarch.

By the time they had come to this conclusion they were both getting sleepy and, having made themselves comfortable, it wasn't long before their eyelids were drooping.

Anya dropped off first but Sherdan had hardly noticed before he too fell into a deep sleep right beside her on the bed.

CHAPTER 8

When Anya woke up she was surprised to find she had company. It took her a moment to remember what had happened the night before. Sherdan was fast asleep beside her and she didn't want to wake him. She grinned as she thought of what people might say if they saw the two of them in that moment. It looked like they had done more than sleep beside each other.

Her body still hurt in a lot of different places but she was also thankful. The worst two and a half days of her life so far were over. She was a little angry at Sherdan but God wanted her here until she had seen the prophecy.

The first few days she had been in Sherdan's house were a little blurry. She remembered the doctor and how nice he was, and seeing Sherdan at meal times, but the rest was a sleepy haze. There was no way of knowing how long she was going to be here but she felt calm and peaceful. She'd had a few nightmares in the last few days but they were soon stopped by praying. At the moment she felt strangely safe.

She didn't like being alone so much, however, and very quietly settled back down beside Sherdan. While she waited she studied his peaceful features. It had been a pleasant change to talk to him rather than argue.

Anya prayed for him. He had told her about the drug he'd

made and that he planned to follow his science experiment wherever it led. She knew he disapproved of her faith, but liked how tranquil being with her felt. At this particular moment in time, while he slept, he appeared the more peaceful of the two of them.

About half an hour after Anya had awoken, Sherdan finally stirred. He opened his eyes to see her lying beside him. She smiled.

"Good morning," she said. He didn't move back or get up but stared at her until she blushed and looked away.

"I'm sorry. I guess I fell asleep."

"It's okay. I did, too. I think it's the first time I've shared my bed with someone since I was five."

"I'm honoured to be the first." Sherdan grinned.

Anya blushed again.

"I've got to go. Do you want breakfast?"

She looked away. She was starving but couldn't give in at the last minute. Sherdan got up and went to the door.

"When are you going to visit me next?"

"I can come back at lunch, if you'd like?" Anya nodded. "Very well."

He left her and she sighed. All his barriers had come back up this morning. For a little while, he had let her beneath his cool calculated exterior and told her about himself. Sherdan was a very intelligent man and extremely logical. He connected two different things very quickly and had a great deal of intuition. It was a shame he had such loose morals.

Anya wandered slowly around the room. Her toes were the only part of her still bandaged, and every other wound was healing well. She thought it was pretty impressive, considering how little she had eaten, although she had rested plenty to try and make up for it.

For the rest of the morning she prayed. She missed her family and friends and was sure they'd have missed her over the Christmas period.

When it was time for lunch she curled up on the bed again. She didn't want Sherdan to see how much better she was just yet. He brought her a tray of food, as usual. She sighed and opened her mouth to tell him she wouldn't eat but as he put the tray on the bed beside her she noticed there were also two books. She gasped.

"I thought both of these would make you happy."

"What made you change your mind?" she asked.

"You are right. You're going to be here a while. As long as I want you here, in fact. I figured there wouldn't ever be anyone else you can tell."

"Thank you."

"You're welcome. Now I have a lot of preparations to make; this evening is a big evening. I will leave you to your reading."

Anya grabbed both books as she beamed. She tucked the Bible under her pillow and flicked open the second. There, in Sherdan's handwriting, was the prophecy. She glanced over it, checking it was authentic, and then tucked into the plate of food.

He had brought her leftovers from the Christmas dinner the day before. Turkey had never tasted so good.

She then sat back and let her food digest for a bit. It had been so long since her last meal that her stomach hurt. She sighed; her mission for God was almost complete.

CHAPTER 9

Sherdan had a little bounce to his walk as he made his way down the steps. It had made sense to let her see the prophecy and start eating. He wanted her to stick around for a long time and she really wouldn't be telling anyone else. In less than twelve hours any chance of her ever escaping would be drastically reduced.

He went straight to his security guards. They confirmed that all the preparations for the evening were complete, so Sherdan went over to his command bunker. The changes would need to be coordinated from one place, and all the residents informed.

Today was the first step for his organisation to act as a separate entity, and it was a day Sherdan had been looking forward to for many years. Hitchin had predicted it and now it was coming to pass. Their plans would pick up pace from this moment and there would be no stopping them.

Everyone waited for Sherdan in the command bunker and greeted him when he joined them. There was a tense silence before he gave his first few orders. The visible changes would need to be deployed in a quick and orderly manner. As progress was made, a buzz of excitement grew and continued to grow until Sherdan picked up the microphone and addressed everyone within the organisation.

"Hello everyone. May I have your attention for a moment? I

have promised all of you a better future, where you are all valued. This evening we take the next step in that future. Tonight we will be putting up barriers on every road and path into our land. No one will be allowed in unless invited by us. For the next while we would ask that all residents also stay within those barriers, to minimise the workload of the guards and security. Congratulations, everyone!"

As soon as Sherdan had finished this speech he nodded at the person standing next to him.

"All teams move into position. In a few minutes we'll be going into action," the commander, Graham, said into his radio. The security teams were all heading up the changes and policing the barriers. To start with, there would just be simple road blocks and signs but they had all the resources needed for much more secure measures, if necessary.

Sherdan smiled and sat listening as everything he had planned was executed. The teams placed their barriers and signs with quick efficiency. The only hiccup was a car that had driven onto their land as a cut-through before anything had been placed and needed to be let out at the other end. Thankfully, it was late on Boxing Day, and not many people were out on the roads.

The following day would be a different story. It was a working day and he had closed off a lot of roads. This day had been in planning a long time, however, and Sherdan had made sure no major roads were closed off. He wanted to make a point, not start a disagreement.

Sherdan stayed in his command room for the next hour, in case any problems arose. There was the odd issue but as usual the smoothness of change was a testament to the planning and organisation he inspired in his people.

Of course, the many extra abilities helped. Each one was unique and fitted in well. There was one woman who could turn plants, fruits and vegetables that were decaying back into perfectly healthy food again. One initiate could control the weather within a small range, although he still needed a little more practice. Sometimes it hailed when he tried to make it rain.

When Sherdan had satisfied himself that everything was

going according to plan, he decided to take a walk back to his home with a few detours around the land. No sooner had he left the compound than he was approached by a resident. The man shook Sherdan's hand and had a large grin on his face.

"Congratulations. This is a marvellous step," the man enthused.

"Thank you. This couldn't have come about without the help of everyone here, and it is just the first step in a full plan for independence and rights."

"I'm very glad to hear it. If there's anything else I can do just let me know."

"What's your new ability?"

"I can create heat in anything just by making the atoms vibrate."

"That's a wonderful ability. I'm sure it will be very useful over the next few weeks and months. Only three days ago, I think, in an email I was given, I was informed that there were concerns over keeping the winter greenhouse hot enough. I will reply and inform them of your ability."

Sherdan found his hand being shaken again with even more enthusiasm than the first time. He then said goodbye and allowed Sherdan to continue his walk.

Everywhere he went he was stopped by people wanting to congratulate him or offer their support. The general air of excitement buzzed around the entire area. To add to the fun, just as he began to head back to his own house, the first few flakes of snow fell. He smiled and radioed for his car so he could return to Anya and a late supper together.

Despite the car arriving swiftly and bearing him home, it was gone eleven by the time he informed Anne he was back, and not far off midnight when he took a tray with food for two to Anya.

CHAPTER 10

Anya had read through the prophecy once already but found it made little sense to her. After giving herself a moments' rest, she looked over it again.

When the lion, beaked by an owl, rises from the dead remains of an old nest, a leader will come to the faithful. His wisdom will see through all veils and be the final judge. People will perish without his guidance. With him, enlightenment will be gained and gifts of devotion bestowed. He will lead his people to a better world as they prepare for the end times.

The end will be known when many signs have been seen and plans made. It will come like a great flying eagle, reaching great speed as its destination approaches.

The first sign of the coming end will be the rising up of the gifted people. They will flock to the leader as bees to nectar. He will teach them and lead them in the ways of the Ox. Every member will become like the great roots of a tree. Spreading upwards and outwards they will sap everything they need to feed the tree growing beneath the surface.

When the three spoons of prosperity are gathered

together with the plough, a badgers' set will be made. It will grow and form until it can no longer be contained within its shell. It shall keep its desires secret but parade its existence to all, growing fat from the ignorance of the weak.

Then comes the great shedding. The badger will detach itself from the world around and shed its skin to reveal the gyroscope underneath. Only the worthy will be able to cross the void between the untouched and the enlightened.

The world will react with fear at first, until the men with the silver sceptre extend their pledges of allegiance. One by one each oppressor will fall and be judged until all of the evil is separated and made known. Utopia shall blossom, fed by the submission of the unworthy, until all of the righteous and unburdened can rejoice together.

Even after a second run through, it confused her, but what she could make of it she knew to be wrong. It implied the world's end would be replaced with some kind of utopia built on slaves of the unsaved. She knew this could not be true, as the Bible said otherwise.

Anya picked up her Bible and flicked to Revelation, skim-reading through it. It definitely didn't agree with the prophecy. She then read through the prophecy several more times. She needed to tell her pastors what it said, and she knew Sherdan would never let her take it from him. There was no other choice but to memorise it. When she was happy that she would remember it, she would leave and tell her pastors.

It hadn't escaped her notice that Sherdan had told her she would never leave, but God had got her in here and He could get her out again, even if she had no idea how yet.

She then prayed. She wished for God's guidance on her next move. Sherdan had changed since she first met him and she knew her actions were partly responsible. God would have the last say in what she did, but she wanted to leave on good terms with Sherdan if she could, and sneaking out of his facility would not be conducive to a lasting friendship.

Anya was still praying when Sherdan came back. He apologised when he noticed her kneeling on the floor. She went to get up but found her legs had gone stiff. He helped her move to sit on the edge of the bed.

"Do you often pray on your knees?" he asked. She shook her head.

"Only when I particularly feel that way inclined. Often when I am showing that I submit to God's will over mine."

"It is snowing," Sherdan told her. She suspected he had deliberately changed the subject but she didn't mind. Snow was one of her favourite things. She hobbled over to the window.

"Your feet still hurt?"

"Yes, they are taking a while to heal. They still look horrible"

"The doctor assured me that the scarring would hardly show in a year or so."

"To be completely honest, I don't mind if it does. If any of it does," she motioned to her wrists as she watched the snow fall and settle outside.

"Really? I'd have thought you'd want it to fade quickly."

"No. God looks at my wounds the same way I would look at the wounds Jesus suffered – with love. Jesus had many wounds because he was obedient and took our place. Now I have wounds and scars because I was obedient."

"I think God, if he existed, wouldn't allow people to be hurt."

"I know he exists and uses all my hurts for my good." She shrugged and continued to watch the snowflakes fall in swirling patterns.

"So you're obedient to a God that asks you to endure torture?"

"My God gave everything, including his life. He can ask everything, including my life."

"I don't understand."

"I'm happy to bear the scars of my obedience because I'm not alone in doing so."

Anya looked at Sherdan but it was evident he still didn't understand. She might as well be talking a completely different language. She sighed and went back to watching the snow. Sherdan stood with her for a bit longer before going and getting the book that held the prophecy.

"I assume you've read it."

She nodded.

"And?" He looked hopefully at her.

"It's wrong."

"I disagree."

"I thought you probably did." Anya rolled her eyes.

"It has been coming true."

"Of course it seems right; it's vague. But it disagrees with the Bible."

"So you'll ignore it as being false regardless? How noble of you."

"It doesn't really matter what I think. I shall inform my pastors and let them decide. I would like to leave now, please." She stepped away from the windows and towards Sherdan. He scowled.

"I'm not letting you leave."

"You won't be able to stop me if God thinks it's time I did so."

Sherdan came back around from the other side of the bed, shaking his head as he did.

"You don't seem to understand, Anya. I want you here until I have figured out how you fit into this." He waved the book under her nose. "No deity of any kind will be removing you until I am done with you. Is that clear?"

"I don't belong to you, and don't think you can keep me trapped in a normal house for long." Sherdan laughed but Anya didn't find it entirely unexpected.

"Things have changed since you arrived. This is no longer just a house in the centre of a normal estate. You're in the centre of a half-mile radius of land, all sectioned off. If you escaped this house you would still be stuck on land where every person would bring you right back here. You do belong to me, and you had better get used to the idea."

Sherdan stormed out of her room before she could reply. She soon heard the familiar click of the lock. Tears slid down her cheeks at his outburst.

She wasn't really upset that he was trying to keep her prisoner. She knew that wouldn't stop God. She was upset because she had wanted to leave as Sherdan's friend. He had made it perfectly clear how angry he would be at her if she escaped against his will. She had to try, however. God's last command to her had been clear: get the prophecy and bring it home.

Anya had enough sense to sit, calm herself and pray for God's blessing before attempting any kind of escape plan. She knew her door was locked and Sherdan would hear her attempting to break it down, so she considered picking the lock.

There wasn't anything particularly useful to use as a pick, except possibly cutlery from the dinner Sherdan had brought her. It had been forgotten thanks to the argument.

She added lock-picking to the potential list and went to the window. All the windows were locked so no exit through them would be quiet. She also noted that she was two floors up from street level and there wasn't any way down but to jump. She'd be lucky not to break something without God's protection.

Her only sensible option was to try lock-picking unless God explicitly told her otherwise. She picked up the knife from the food tray and went to the door. She soon found that it was far too large for the keyhole and swapped it for the fork. The fork wasn't much better, and Anya was soon kneeling in the middle of the floor, begging God for his assistance.

Half an hour later Anya sank into a heap of frustrated tears. She knew God had heard her, but if He'd answered she couldn't hear it. She didn't want to be here any longer. Her heart ached to be home in Bath, with people who cared for her, where she felt safe and loved.

Anya soon got up off the floor and got into bed. She was tired and knew she always felt more emotional when tired. She would sleep and try again in the morning.

CHAPTER 11

Fury raged through Sherdan as he stomped down the stairs. He returned his book to its place and paced his study for the next hour. Anya was so ridiculously stubborn. Couldn't she see that he was significantly more powerful than her God?

When Sherdan had finally calmed himself down he went to bed. He wanted to be rested for the morning, just in case he was needed. He suspected there would be a request for interviews from news teams as well. After all, it was not normal to reclaim public roads and completely seclude an entire set of buildings from the surrounding city.

Anya was calm at breakfast and didn't make any demands. He didn't stay long. Things had soured between them and for now she wasn't his main focus.

Sherdan headed over to his command bunker as soon as he could. It was so early that he was one of the first people there. Rush hour was still a few minutes away and so far so good.

Over the next half hour his entire team assembled and waited in case they were needed. Sherdan sat down to await the events of the next few hours.

He listened to the radio chatter as the occasional person got aggressive or confused by the road signs. For the most part the guards handled all the people wanting to drive through without needing any assistance. There was only one occasion when the commander, Graham, had to remind the security guard to remain calm.

Sherdan was about to leave the command room when a phone call came through for him from the chief of police. He was quickly handed the phone.

"Jeremy, how are you?"

"Dr Harper, I'm very well, thank you. I just thought I ought to phone to let you know that the mayor has decided he's not very happy."

"I thought all complaints were going to be handled?"

"I'm sorry. The mayor isn't someone I can easily deal with."

"Arrange a meeting with him for me. Invite him to come and visit so we can discuss any issues he has."

"Do you think that's wise?" Jeremy asked.

"Just arrange it. Preferably for next year. As soon as you can."

"Of course."

Sherdan slammed the phone down and swore. No one said anything.

"I want a background check on the mayor of Bristol. Find out everything you can about him and have it all forwarded to me." Several of the people in the room leapt into action while Sherdan sat down, thoughtfully. After a few minutes he got up again and went to see Hitchin. As usual, Hitchin was in his laboratory.

"To what do I owe the pleasure of this visit?"

"I need to know when all our new residents are joining us."

"First thing in the new year. The fourth of January for most of them."

"We may need to get them here sooner. I've got problems with the mayor."

"Hmm... I'll see what I can do. How's everything going with Miss Price?"

"She's as stubborn as usual. I let her read the prophecy. I wanted her to eat, and she's not going anywhere."

Hitchin raised an eyebrow.

"What did she make of it?"

"She told me it had to be wrong."

"Well, I'm sure she'll realise she's wrong when more of it comes true, and if she doesn't, then it doesn't matter. She's inconsequential."

"Oh, of course. I... I am sure that she'll see the truth in time. How could she not?" Sherdan replied, trying to convince himself as much as Hitchin. Hitchin could tell his friend wasn't completely confident.

"Everything has gone exactly as it should so far. Miss Price is evidently part of this whole thing somehow, but I'm sure all will become clear with her. I've been having some snaps of something lately. There might be some more involving her."

"Really?"

"Yes. It's only coming in snapshots, but something is coming through. I'll let you know what it is as soon as I do."

"Thank you," Sherdan said and sighed.

They then talked over the new batch's powers. So far, all of them were alive and showing good signs. Hitchin was already preparing for the next, larger batch. Sherdan left him to his work. There was a lot for both of them to do.

The next two days passed in a blur of organisation and work. Sherdan had all the information on the mayor fed to him. There wasn't much to work with but he'd make the most of it. The meeting had been scheduled for the fourth, the same day all the new residents were set to arrive. The mayor had wanted to come straight away but Sherdan had refused; he wanted more time.

Anya was still being awkward. He had caught her twice trying to pick the lock to get out. He warned her not to keep on trying but he did not know what he would do if she continued to ignore him. Hitchin still hadn't told him where she fitted into things.

He still visited her every meal, but they barely talked. This time, on entering, he noticed she was puffy-eyed and stood at the window. The bandages were gone and her face only had a few small fading cuts. Everything else she kept covered up with her clothes.

Realising she was upset, Sherdan lingered. He just stared at her while she looked outside.

"All the snow has melted," she said.

"You like the snow?"

"Love it; it makes winter and cold worthwhile." Sherdan didn't know what to say, "Are you going to keep me here forever?"

"I will keep you here as long as I want."

"And how long will that be?"

"As long as I want it to be."

Anya sighed. "I just want to go home."

"You know too much."

"I'm..."

"This is not a debate," Sherdan interrupted and stepped towards her. He was angry again. Tears welled up in her eyes. "I guess your God hasn't rescued you. Do you still think He will?"

Anya turned away from him. She shook and wouldn't look at him. There was a long and awkward silence until he left. She continued to cry.

Sherdan ran his hand through his hair on the other side of the doorway. The girl was a complete pain but he didn't want her to cry. He'd been doing everything he could to keep her happy. He'd given her her own clothes, a Bible, even the prophecy. He tried to talk to her and make her feel welcome, but she always focused on leaving.

The schedule for the rest of the day was so tight Sherdan didn't even get to see Anya at dinner. He had arranged a large New Year's Eve party in the University's main function room and he was technically the guest of honour. He instructed Anne to take an evening meal up to their guest and gave her the key just before leaving.

Sherdan didn't really want to be part of such a social event, but he did wish to create a buzz of excitement in the residents before his meeting with the mayor, just in case. Hitchin had promised to come to give him some light relief at points along the night.

The social side of the event passed slowly. Sherdan was preoccupied, and although able to make small talk, he took no satisfaction in it. Anya had upset him.

Hitchin soon noticed that his friend wasn't quite up to his

normal standard of working a crowd and asked if there was anything he could do to help. Sherdan shook his head.

"No, I will work everything out with Anya... Miss Price. Just keep up all the good work you are doing."

"As you wish. Do try not to worry over her. She is here for a reason and I'm sure she will begin to see this project our way over time." Sherdan just nodded as their conversation was cut short by another guest joining them. Very few of the residents knew Anya existed.

For the rest of the evening Sherdan moved around the room, making polite conversation and surprising many residents when he remembered their names. He was greeted with smiles and enthusiasm wherever he went. At least something was going right.

When it struck midnight everyone clapped and cheered. Sherdan swiftly moved to the front of the room to address everyone.

"Thank you all for coming... A new year has begun." He had to pause for the clapping to subside, "This new year isn't the same as any year before. We are on the verge of greatness. A greatness only made possible by everyone here."

There were more cheers. Sherdan smiled and waited.

"Every person will play a crucial role going forward, and I'm positive we will all do our part and make two thousand and eighteen a year to remember. Happy New Year, everyone!"

Everyone cheered again. Sherdan had kept it short and sweet, as well as being complimentary of the people in general. It had worked. He kept a smile fixed on his face as he went back to his drink and people began talking amongst themselves again. He wasn't allowed to enjoy the excitement for long, however, as he soon got a call over the radio from Nathan.

"Sorry to disturb you, sir. I think Anya has escaped."

"What! When?"

"Only just now, sir. I saw it on the security footage. She's sneaked out somehow."

Sherdan swore and walked out of the function room and through the rest of the building.

"Graham, the female prisoner who recently attempted a

break in on our compound has escaped her cell and is loose in the vicinity of my house. She must be stopped from leaving the grounds. Mobilise all security right now."

"Yes, sir."

"Let me know the second she's sighted."

Sherdan ran out into the streets and towards his home. He swore every few steps when he realised how much she could affect his future plans. She could also get him in a lot of trouble if she told the authorities about everything that had happened to her.

When Sherdan reached his home Nathan was outside, talking on the radio. Nathan shook his head when Sherdan ran in his direction.

"We've not found her yet. There's no sign of her."

"Has she got past the perimeter?"

"Not that we know of, but she's not been sighted. She only needs to jump the right fence."

"Crap. We have to find her. Have a security team drive over to Bath and her house to check if she manages to get all the way back there."

"Yes..." Nathan trailed off and looked past Sherdan. Walking towards them, completely calm, was Anya.

"There's no need," she said. Sherdan ran over to her, livid. She stopped in the middle of the road, apprehensive at the look on his face. He grabbed her wrist, making her wince, and then dragged her back into his house.

Although she didn't resist, he still bundled her inside as fast as he could, acting like he had to force her. She hissed in pain as he accidentally banged her against the doorway through to his study and she tripped on the first step in his over-eagerness to get her upstairs. Finally, he shoved her onto her bed. She pulled away, fear in her eyes.

"Nathan, find Anne and get her to bring me the key to the guest room," he yelled into the radio. Anya curled herself up on the bed while he stood at the foot of it glaring at her.

"It's not Anne's fault I escaped," she told him.

"Then how did you escape?"

"God didn't like you mocking Him. He gave me what I

needed to get out."

"No, He didn't. You're still here."

"I'm only here because God wants me to be."

"No!" Sherdan flicked her dinner tray off the sideboard in his anger. "You are here because I want you here."

"I came back. I had made it all the way off your land. God told me to come back."

"Well, forgive me for not believing you... Ah, Anne, there you are. Are you sure you locked Miss Price in after you were last here?"

"Positive, sir. I double-checked."

"She escaped afterwards at some point."

"The door was locked, I already told you. Anne locked me in just as she was meant to." Anya got up off the bed and stood boldly between him and Anne. Of the two of them, in that moment, it was Anne who looked the most frightened.

"I'm really sure I locked her in, sir. I knew it was important."

"Very well, Anne. The key, if you please, and then you can go."

Anne handed him the key, which he instantly pocketed before she scurried off. Sherdan then turned to Anya, who gulped and took a step back. He walked towards her and she put her hands up.

"Look, I came back and you have me here again. There is no harm done."

"There is harm done. Do you want me to turn you back over to my interrogation team?"

"No, and neither do you."

"I've half a mind to continue what they were doing," Sherdan growled. He took another step towards her and she backed up into the wall.

"Sir, you need to come see this," Nathan's voice said over the radio.

"I'm very busy right now, Nathan."

"It relates, sir."

"We'll continue this later," Sherdan hissed at Anya before leaving and locking her in. He went straight through to the security desk.

"This had better be good."

"Sir, you need to watch this. It's the feed from Anya's room." Nathan offered Sherdan the seat as he hit play on the camera feed. Sherdan noted that it said five to midnight. Anya was pacing the room, praying. Each time she walked past the door she tried the handle, getting more forceful each time. Then, on the fifth try, the door just clicked open. Sherdan gasped.

There was no possibility that the door hadn't been locked the first four times but the fifth it was somehow not. Sherdan made Nathan replay the feed several times.

"That's not all. Look at this feed." Nathan switched to an outside camera that showed Anya walking right past the security guards at one of the road blocks as if they couldn't see her. When she had regained her freedom she stopped and turned her face upwards.

He watched her mouth move in a thank you that could only have been to her God. A single snow flake then drifted down and landed on her upturned face. She smiled and paused before going back the same way she had come, still invisible to the guards less than ten metres from her.

Sherdan sat back in his seat, completely speechless. Nathan waited while he thought.

"Don't let anyone see these or know about them until I've decided what to do with her, is that clear?"

"Perfectly, sir."

"Thank you, Nathan."

With that he walked back to his study. He would need to go see Anya shortly but he wanted to get his thoughts straight first. One thing was for sure, someone or something wanted him to know that Anya was there for a reason, not just because Sherdan wanted her here. He hoped it was something Hitchin could explain to him.

The man had told him he'd been getting snapshots of something new. Hitchin wouldn't hear of this incident, however. Sherdan wanted the security of knowing Hitchin saw Anya as important without being told so.

Sherdan went back to Anya's room, much calmer than when he'd left. She sat on the bed with her chin on her knees. She had her arms wrapped around herself and she pulled her legs up even closer as he came towards the bed. She looked so frightened that it stopped him in his tracks.

"You're safe... I'm calm now. I've seen the footage from the camera outside the room. I don't think the door was locked properly," he lied. Anya's eyes went wide but she kept her thoughts to herself.

"For now things will continue on as if this incident didn't happen, but if I ever catch you trying to escape again I will not be as nice as I have been, do you understand?" she nodded but still didn't speak. When he did not move but continued to stand in her room, she fidgeted. He sighed. This whole event had set things back dramatically.

"I'm here for now, anyway," she broke the silence.

"Because your God wants you to be?" Sherdan mocked. She looked away, her pain evident. It only made him angrier.

"I don't want to argue. Can we talk about something else?" she asked. Sherdan looked shocked. He sat down on the edge of the bed as she wiped her eyes.

"I don't want to argue with you either. You do need to stop trying to escape though."

"Okay. For the next little while I won't try to leave."

"Promise?"

"You have my word."

"Good, now we can move onto other things."

Anya smiled, although she still looked like she might cry at any moment. He didn't think wishing her a happy new year was wise, especially as it had begun snowing again. They talked of trivial things for half an hour, before she yawned. Sherdan left her to sleep. It was almost two in the morning.

CHAPTER 12

Everything ran smoothly in Sherdan's world for the next couple of days. Anya didn't try to escape and all the plans for his organisation progressed. He put several measures in place, just in case the mayor didn't react favourably to their discussion in a few days. Sherdan also did a few more news interviews, mostly local, but each time they gained even more applicants to their program.

On the third day of the new year, Hitchin came to find Sherdan late in the evening. This was very unusual for Hitchin, especially without warning. Sherdan's first thought was something must have gone horribly wrong.

"I've just had a new vision," Hitchin said as Sherdan poured them both drinks. "Anya was in it." Sherdan smiled. Just what he wanted to hear.

"Go on, friend, tell me all about it." He fetched a paper and pen to make notes.

"Well, you were standing at the top of a great flight of stone steps outside a very grand building. Anya stood beside you, though ever so slightly behind. She wore a white dress and was with child." Sherdan raised his eyebrows but didn't interrupt Hitchin.

"Then the vision moved on. You sat on a throne and were placing a small silver crown that was a small, delicate version of your own on the head of someone blonde. I assume it was Anya, but she was bowed at your feet so I couldn't see for sure."

"Anything else?"

"Yes. The child grew up. It was a boy. He was being taught by his mother, about all the child's abilities. She had one, and the child had several. He was the first child between two parents with abilities."

"And you're sure of this?"

"Positive. It was just like the previous visions. Anya is to be the mother of our great nation. You will crown her to be your queen and she will submit to you. It even explains why you stopped the guards when you did. She is to remain pure for you and you alone."

"Very well. Thank you, Hitchin. I appreciate you telling me this. It makes things much clearer."

"What do you plan to do with Anya now?"

"I will need to think about that very carefully."

"Understandable. Rash decisions are not wise. Let me know if you have any questions at any point regarding the vision. I will do everything to help it come to pass, assuming it's what you wish?"

"Of course. I wouldn't try to defy one of your visions. Anya will give me a child and heir."

Hitchin left and Sherdan sat for some time, thinking this over. He had hoped Hitchin would see something concerning Anya. Now he had to get her to see that he was following the same force that had brought her here. The same force that had helped her escape only to send her back to him, to be his wife, and queen.

She did belong to him; he had been right all along. He smiled as he thought of all the implications of Hitchin's vision. Saying he was pleased would have been an understatement. He couldn't deny that he found her attractive.

He had a few nagging doubts. It did seem a little too convenient, but he knew Hitchin had never lied to him, and he truly must have had this vision. It would just be a matter of time before it came to pass.

Getting up, he hurried to the security cameras to check on

Anya, but she was already asleep. He frowned. He had hoped she would be awake and he could talk to her. Nothing else was in his thoughts except his desire for her. At that moment very little would have stopped him showing her their future in a very practical way.

After a few minutes of gazing at her on the camera his brain kicked back in and he went to take a shower of much cooler temperature than normal. Sherdan didn't want to frighten her. He wanted her to develop feelings for him as strong as the ones now blossoming in him. He could court her with the assurance of knowing his success was guaranteed.

He vowed to let her know of his intentions as soon as there was a sensible opportunity. She would be his wife and wouldn't resist him or anything he wanted.

Sherdan's sleep that night was filled with images of Anya. The smile as she looked up to him at the altar and they kissed. The ability she might gain from the drug and, of course, the enjoyment of making their son. His focus was kept by this last part for so long that he awoke finding he would need fresh bed sheets. It only made him grin as he realised that hadn't happened since he was a teenager.

When he noticed what the date was, he groaned. He was snapped from his indulgent thoughts back into cruel reality. He hardly had time to say hello to Anya when he took her breakfast. He needed to help Hitchin with the new residents until the mayor arrived for their afternoon meeting.

Greeting the residents, however, kept him busy enough that he didn't notice the time passing. There were many new eager faces ready to take the drug and start their new lives. All of them had signed the non-disclosure agreement before coming. It was just the first step in making sure the enzyme stayed a secret.

Sherdan stood at the front of a packed lecture hall and told all the new residents about the treatment. He had members who had previously taken the drug show off their new abilities.

There were gasps similar to Anya's when James took the slide-show buttons from Sherdan's hand from across the lecture hall. Nathan then popped in to say hello and introduced himself while not even opening his mouth. This talent achieved a round of applause.

By the time Sherdan had finished his warm-up speech, everyone was enthusiastic about having the drug. They'd been chosen by Sherdan because they would get excited. He left them all in the care of Hitchin and went back to his home. The mayor was on his way over.

Sherdan had barely finished lunch when the mayor was shown into his study. He offered his visitor a drink and seat before sitting down himself.

"Jeremy reassured me that you're a very reasonable man, Dr Harper."

"I try to be."

"Then you'll understand that I wasn't happy to find a large area of my city closed off to the public without me being informed."

"I'm sorry to hear that you were uninformed. I hope someone has since corrected their mistakes and shown you all the relevant paperwork I filled in to reclaim the roads between the buildings on the land, collectively owned by me and all the residents here."

"They did, yes."

"Then what can I discuss with you, Mayor?" Sherdan asked, gaining the upper hand in the conversation. He wanted to be the one steering the meeting, not the mayor. For the moment there was an awkward pause.

"You do realise that although the roads are now privately owned, something I'd never have approved had I been aware, you cannot change them without attaining planning permission?"

"I am aware. The residents here and I simply wish to control who passes through the estates we own."

"That is something I am meant to control."

"As you controlled that incident with your secretary?"

"Is that a threat?"

"I just want to have my say on how the land I own is protected from the outside world. The people here want privacy. I'm merely giving it to them."

"I do not think it's healthy and will be doing everything I can to have your rights to do so revoked. You will be opening these roads again shortly, Dr Harper."

"I don't think so. I have plans for this land, plans the residents approve of. I will only warn you this once. Don't get in my way."

"You do not have the power you think you do, Dr Harper. Good bye." With that the mayor got up and Sherdan had him shown out by the security guard.

He sat in thought for some time before he radioed the same security guard.

"Have the next layer of our defences put into place around the entire perimeter, as detailed in section three of the defence report I put together."

"Yes, sir."

"Also, schedule in a full program-wide announcement for tomorrow evening."

Sherdan spent the rest of the evening in the command bunker, ensuring that the plans for the next line of defence were put into place properly and swiftly. He was using technology that hadn't been tested in any real situations yet and wanted to make sure it was deployed correctly.

He also wasn't sure how quickly the mayor would have his claim to the roads overturned. Legally, he knew that he was on dodgy ground, but there was no going back on their journey now. The residents wanted this as much as he did.

Over the last three years several abilities had been combined to make an emitter that blocked anyone without the drug in their brain from being able to pass through. To anyone else the emitters would act as a barrier, sending the person dizzy, as well as making it impossible to walk forwards.

Each little device only worked on a very short range, because they weren't electrically powered. The last thing Sherdan wanted was an electromagnetic pulse killing their best line of defence.

A large number of these devices would be needed, however, and they would need to be deployed so that there were no gaps in the perimeter. They would also need to be out of sight.

He had drawn up a map with suggested locations, but it would need to be tested before full confidence in it was achieved.

Anya was fast asleep by the time Sherdan finished his duties for the day. He watched her sleeping on the camera feed for the second night in a row, before heading to sleep himself. He would have to tell Anya of their future the following day. One day's delay wouldn't hurt.

When the following day dawned he rushed to Anya's room with breakfast. He'd had a small table placed in one corner so they could eat together. She joined him at it and smiled at his chirpy greeting, but they only talked of inconsequential things while they ate.

He waited until she had finished her scrambled eggs on toast and put her knife and fork down. He stared into her eyes as she sat opposite him, making her fidget uncomfortably.

He would normally be tidying up their breakfast things and hurrying to go now, but he sat still. Now that it came to telling her, he hesitated. Even with the assurance of success, he felt a little nervous.

"I've had Hitchin approach me recently about you," Sherdan began. Anya raised her eyebrows. "He's had another vision of the future. One involving you."

"He's the person who came up with your prophecy as well, isn't he?"

"Yes, and I know you don't believe it, but I do." Anya sighed, but Sherdan pretended he hadn't heard her and continued, "He saw us marrying and you carrying our child. Not only that, but you had an ability, and as a result our child had more than one ability himself. I knew you were part of the future here but I didn't know how."

Sherdan beamed at her while she sat with her mouth open.

"You're not happy?" he asked her.

"I don't know what to say. I didn't expect you to say all of that when you said there was a vision of me."

"Say yes."

"Uhhh... I'm not sure I can." Anya couldn't look at him.

"I'm not giving you a choice."

"You're used to getting your own way, aren't you?"

"Yes I am."

"Well, you can't force someone to love you."

"I'm not asking you to love me." He meant that, but the concept of no love did disappoint him more than he'd expected.

"I'm not sure I can do what you ask without loving you."

"Well I guess you should start thinking about that, because we will get married and we will have a child." Sherdan finally got up to leave. His excitement had quickly turned into anger.

"Wait, please." She got up and went over to him. "Please don't plan anything yet. I will want to think about what you've told me and process it. I'd appreciate it if you didn't rush this."

"You'll consider doing this willingly, then?" His anger dissipated in an instant.

"I will consider anything at this point. I've not been given any other reason by God for being here. But I really don't want to feel pressured. It won't help me decide."

"I will let you think then." Sherdan bent down and kissed her on the cheek before going.

CHAPTER 13

Anya sank into the dining chair. She shook with her shock and emotion. Her mind could barely grasp what she had been told. God had asked her to stay but not told her why. She couldn't quite get her head around being asked to marry a man she didn't love and give him children. Was there any point resisting, however, if he was going to insist?

For this thought, Anya almost hit herself. Of course there would be wisdom in resisting Sherdan if God told her to. He would make sure she was vindicated in trying to do only what God wanted. She did the only thing she could at this point: she got down on her knees and prayed.

Did God bring her back for this reason? What were His plans for her and how would she explain to Sherdan if they didn't match up with his idea of their future?

She got very little answer from God. He didn't tell her that it was why she was here, but equally she didn't get told not to marry Sherdan. She knew she wanted to start with the marriage part of Hitchin's second vision, if she agreed to any of it.

Anya got up and punched her pillows a few times. She hated the idea of being forced to do anything. The only reason she was in this predicament was because she had walked back at God's command. She paced as she ranted at God.

It was His fault she was in this position. She had never

expected to be locked in Sherdan Harper's guest bedroom and be told she was going to be the next Mrs Harper, when she had left home in December.

It occurred to Anya that she'd also never expected to like Sherdan either but she actually found him attractive. However, it wasn't her idea of wedded bliss to marry a guy so evidently controlling.

She sat down on the edge of the bed and cried. She didn't love him, but she didn't hate him either, and she felt totally lost in terms of guidance. This wasn't the kind of decision-making she'd ever expected to have to do.

Anya went around in circles, alternately getting angry and upset. She only talked to God to rant at him. Sherdan found her like this when he came back for lunch.

She immediately tried to appear calm. She didn't want to make him angry at her. His temper was volatile and scared her. If he thought she would say no she had a pretty good idea of how he would respond.

Sherdan smiled at her and she tried to smile back, but it came out as more of a pained grin.

"You don't look so good," he told her.

"I'm fine. I just have a small headache. All this thinking."

"You are thinking about our future, then? Good. I was a little concerned you were buying time before refusing me."

"No I'm genuinely thinking about it, but that doesn't mean I'll necessarily agree to what you ask."

"I've already said, we're having a child. It has been foretold."

Anya looked away and sighed.

"This is hard for me. Please, can you not try and be nicer about it?"

"I am being as nice as you deserve. It is you being stubborn. I'm offering you everything and asking very little in return."

"Forgive me if I don't see it that way."

"So you've decided to try and resist this?" Sherdan hissed.

"No, I've not decided anything."

"You will be my wife, Anya. It is our future, and why you came here." She didn't reply. She could see the look in his eyes. He believed what he was saying. Arguing further would only cause him to grow more angry and possibly violent.

It worried her that even if she agreed to marry him, giving a child to a man she didn't love had the potential to be a very painful experience. The mere thought of it made her stomach churn. It put her off her lunch in an instant. She stopped eating and Sherdan looked at her with concern on his face.

"I don't feel like I can eat any more," she said in answer to his questioning gaze.

"Get some rest." Sherdan got up and left her, but she knew resting was impossible. She had a thousand questions and fears running through her head. What if she said no? What would Sherdan do in response? She didn't think he could force the marriage. He couldn't make her say yes at an altar.

There were plenty of other things he could force on her, but she had seen his anger at the guard that had tried to rape her. She didn't think it was a coincidence that he had rescued her at that moment, but there was no knowing what he might do when angry now.

Anya turned to God again. She really needed his guidance. She didn't even trust herself to make a sound decision. This time when she prayed, she felt God's Spirit fall down on her.

It calmed her and helped her to remember that God would be with her no matter what happened. Just as he had been with her in the prison cell, He'd be with her in her situation with Sherdan. He would also help her stay of sound mind. She didn't want to develop Stockholm syndrome, though she wasn't even sure what it was exactly.

She had made her decision finally. She didn't think that God had asked her to stay for this reason. It made no sense that He would ask her to stay and then not confirm why.

It didn't mean that marrying Sherdan wasn't something that was part of her future, but God appeared to be leaving the decision for that part of the plan to her. She was sure she wouldn't give in to fear.

Anya continued praying on and off for the rest of the afternoon, often pacing and enjoying feeling God's closeness.

As she passed by the mirror, on one of the many paths back and forth, she stopped. She stared at the mirror. Only her clothes were reflected back at herself.

She put her hands over her mouth to stop herself from screaming out loud, but she couldn't see them as they passed where her face was meant to be. As they moved against her skin she felt the cold of her fingers, but still only her clothes could be seen.

Anya stared at the reflection of the room until she faded into view again. As soon as she could see her whole body properly, she went up closer and prodded her skin as if she wasn't sure it was real anymore. She calmed her breathing and paced again. Every few minutes she checked the reflection in the mirror, but nothing happened.

She was still trying to somehow disappear again when Sherdan came back. She stopped moving the second he entered the room, and stood like a deer in headlights before glancing at the mirror. She was still completely visible.

"I thought I suggested you should rest." He wasn't very happy.

"I wanted to pray."

"You pray a lot."

"There isn't much else to do," she explained, while trying to sound like she wasn't complaining.

"You could think about us."

"That's what I was praying about." Sherdan looked at her, hope in his eyes. She hurriedly looked away. "I'd like some time to get to know you better."

"How much time?"

"I don't know." Anya shrugged.

"I'm not giving you any more time to get to know me. We're getting married."

"You can't make me say yes to you if I don't want to. We won't be legally married."

"You'll say yes if you're carrying my child."

"I won't have sex with you either."

"I never said you would need to consent to that part," he said with a slight growl. Anya frowned but stood her ground.

"I know you won't force me. You've already rescued me from that once," she replied. Her stomach was moving around like a boat in a storm but her face remained stern.

"You and I are destined to be together."

"If that's really true, what is the harm in waiting and letting me get to know you better?"

Sherdan didn't respond.

"Wouldn't you rather I willingly walked down the aisle and willingly carried your child?"

"Of course."

"Then give me some time to get to know you, especially if you think it's inevitable. That means you don't have to force it. It will happen when it will happen."

"What if it doesn't?"

"Then the vision was wrong and both of us have been spared from making a huge mistake."

"I'll think about it."

"Thank you," she replied. She wasn't sure she meant it, but the hardest part was over. She had told him what she thought, and he'd not grown too angry. He wasn't happy but he wasn't about to force her into anything either.

They ate dinner together, having finally reached a sort of truce. Anya relaxed in his company and Sherdan soon cheered up again.

When he left, taking their empty plates with him, she went to watch the snow falling. The snow from New Year's Day hadn't yet melted and now a fresh veil was forming over the footprints, snowmen and various other sculptures that had been made.

This was where Sherdan found her when he came back. She jumped when he entered. He had never come back after eating with her before. He joined her by the window to watch the snow.

"Are you not busy this evening?" she asked.

"No. I have some spare time."

"Can we do something? I'm bored of being by myself."

"Yes... If you'd like, we can go out in the snow." She looked at him, her eyes wide. He laughed.

"Can we make a snowman?"

"If you'd like. You'll need to wrap up warm." Anya didn't waste any time grabbing a jumper, coat and scarf from the old oak wardrobe where she had hung them. He helped her put everything on and then took her hand and led her downstairs. She went where he pulled her, doing her best not to appear to be awkward at all. This was a huge step in trust and showed he was softening to her.

When they reached the security desk he made her sit down, surrounded by the guards, while he put his own coat and scarf on. Again, she made a deliberate act of cooperating and putting his mind at ease. She twirled on the swivel chair, making everyone else smile.

Excitement was evident on Anya's face as Sherdan took her hand again. His grip tightened as he opened the front door. She lingered just outside, letting the first few flakes fall on her face before following him out onto the lawn. His own front garden had a perfect covering of snow.

She didn't hesitate in falling over backwards into the crisp white sheet, yanking her hand out of Sherdan's in the process. He was about to complain when he saw her laying on her back moving her legs and arms up and down, shifting the snow out of the way as she did. She then held out both hands for him to help her up.

"Snow Angel," she explained as she pointed to the pattern she had made in the snow. He laughed.

"It's beautiful."

"You make one." Anya's eyes gleamed in delight. Sherdan looked at her as if she'd suggested he did something really stupid, before looking back at the snow and laying down beside the first snow angel. He mimicked her actions and then let her help him back up as she laughed.

Before Sherdan could take her hand again she had slotted her chilly fingers into the deep pocket of his coat.

"I should have got some gloves," she said as if it explained her actions.

"You really do keep your word, don't you?"

"Of course. Don't you?"

"Sometimes. It depends."

"How do you get people to trust you if you don't?"

"There aren't many people I want to trust me."

"I want everyone to trust me... Come on, let's make a snowman as tall as you." Anya took her hands out of his pocket and ran off before he could grab hold of her. She heard him suck in his breath as he prepared to yell at her.

She scooped the mountain of snow off the low wall at the front of the garden and patted it together to form a giant snowball. She added to it until it grew too large for her to hold then Sherdan helped her roll it around the garden, careful to avoid the snow angels.

CHAPTER 14

Their hands touched as Sherdan handed Anya her hot chocolate. She was curled up in his favourite chair, with him sat on the floor beside her, near the roaring fire in the study. Her cheeks glowed and her hands were pink as she warmed them up on her drink. Her smile, like a child's on Christmas morning, spread more warmth through him than the fire ever could.

She soon finished her hot chocolate and yawned. Normally, he would have let her rest at this point, but he didn't want to this evening. He liked having such amicable company in his study, even if she had sat in his chair. He watched as her eyes closed and imagined her sitting there some months from now with a very large bump. The thought made him smile.

He allowed his mind to wander as Anya fell into a deeper sleep. He had been happier since Hitchin had told him why Anya was here. It comforted him that she had a purpose, that his reaction to her torture had been more than him going soft.

Sherdan knew they would not be able to wait long to have children, however, if theirs really was to be the first with multiple abilities. There already couples within the program, and who knew when a woman would fall pregnant.

It had also occurred to him that Anya would need to take the drug before she got pregnant. Giving it to her wasn't something he had thought much about, considering that she might die.

Knowing she would live changed things. He decided to suggest it to her in the near future. He would give her the choice for now. If he needed to force her, he could do so at a later date. She seemed to like feeling as though she had a choice, even if he knew that she didn't. Offering her more time had made her significantly more amiable. He just hoped she would not want too much more.

It didn't bother him that she had been let out of her room and then encouraged back by some miraculous force. As far as he was concerned, the very force that had given Hitchin the vision had also brought her back. It was comforting that she wouldn't really ever be able to refuse.

Everything else aside, however, he didn't want to hurt her and really hoped that when the time came she would be ready and willing. He gazed at her lovingly; she was fast asleep in the chair and had been for a while.

Sherdan felt reluctant to disturb her but he would need to sleep soon himself, and despite the progress, he wasn't leaving her outside of a locked room. He didn't trust her that much yet.

As carefully as he could, Sherdan slid his arms underneath Anya. She soon stirred and looked at him through sleep-hazed eyes.

"Bed time," he whispered. She struggled against him as he lifted her.

"It's okay, I can walk." Sherdan didn't let her go, but moved with her towards the stairs. He noticed that she was lighter than she had been the first time he carried her, making it easier for him to carry her smoothly.

He placed her in bed and pulled the covers over her. She dozed again before he'd even finished, but he wasn't so fortunate, and lay wide awake in his own bed for several hours. His thoughts were full of their evening together. He had never enjoyed snow so much.

It had been a long time since Sherdan had taken time off, let alone been silly with someone for an entire evening. The snowman they'd built had been huge. He couldn't remember ever making one so large as a child, but the best creation by far had been the snow angels. He had taken several photos of those.

When Sherdan woke up the following morning he sighed and didn't want to get up except to see Anya. They had breakfast together, as had become normal, before he had to continue with his work.

The morning post brought a letter from the mayor concerning the roads. He had found a legal loophole that meant he could claim the roads back for public use. Sherdan had been expecting it.

He wrote a letter back, politely declining and offering to negotiate an alternative. He knew that the mayor would say no but he wanted to appear reasonable wherever possible. There was also the fact that it would buy a few more days before they would need to progress to the next stage.

Sherdan soon went over to the command bunker, although he lingered briefly to straighten the carrot-nose on their snowman. After a morning of arranging and coordinating, he spent the afternoon with Hitchin.

The first batch of the applicants had taken the drug, boosting their numbers by twenty. There wouldn't be any new talents yet, but with a few days or so in Hitchin's care some interesting things would start to happen.

Sherdan looked over their test results and reports so far, and then went to introduce himself to everyone in the medical rooms.

All the test subjects greeted him enthusiastically. A few were a little nervous, but he soon boosted their confidence. When he went back to Hitchin he had a query to make.

"The young girl in the batch, Ellie, how old is she?"

"She's nineteen according to her application," Hitchin said, once he had pulled out her file.

"Can we get that checked? I'm not sure she's that old."

"They will have checked when she applied."

"I know. I would just like it double-checked."

"Of course, I'll have that done. Can you tell what any of their powers are yet?"

"No, not yet, but I'm sure it won't be long."

"Do you want to add Miss Price to the next batch?" Hitchin asked in as relaxed a manner as he could manage. Sherdan looked thoughtful for a moment.

"Not yet. I've only just told her about your vision."

"Did she respond well?"

"Not at first. She's requested time to get to know me."

"Be careful how much time you give her. She needs to take the drug and have an ability before the child's DNA is mapped." Hitchin frowned at him briefly. He knew his friend thought he was being too soft on Anya.

"I'm aware. I won't leave it long."

"Let me know when you want her added to a batch then."

Sherdan nodded and left the scientist to continue his work. He was a little concerned that he hadn't been able to see any of the new abilities yet in the latest group of residents, but for the moment it was only a passing thought. He wanted to focus on Anya again for the coming evening. He would need to suggest she take the drug. Hitchin was right, he couldn't wait much longer.

He found Anya pacing and praying again when he joined her later. She seemed a little preoccupied while they ate and she only gave him one, or two, word answers to his questions.

"Is everything all right?" he asked when he could ignore it no longer. She nodded. "Have you thought any more about our situation?"

"A little. I enjoyed yesterday evening."

"Good. I did, too. I have been hoping to present something else for you to think about." Anya frowned but didn't say anything. "I'd like you to take the drug."

"I'm really not sure I want to."

"I need you to."

"Biblically, it goes against everything I believe in. The body I have already is the way God created me to be, with all my limitations. I'm sorry Sherdan. The rest I can consider, but I will never willingly take that drug."

"You won't go away and think about it? It would be difficult living in a community of people who had taken it if you were the only one who hadn't."

"I really won't change my mind on this one. I won't take it." Sherdan looked off into the distance while he tried not to snap at her. She would have to take it at some point, but he didn't want to spoil their evening together by arguing.

Anya didn't need to know that he wouldn't take no for an answer until he injected her with it. There was even the possibility of doing it while she slept so she would not know until afterwards, but he would only do that as a last resort.

They spent the rest of the evening playing cards and talking about their childhoods. She had owned many pets, and Sherdan hadn't ever been allowed a single one. He'd also had no brothers or sisters whilst Anya had one of each.

She'd not had a poor upbringing but it hadn't been anyway near as rich as Sherdan's. He had inherited a large amount of property, which was the basis for his current situation. He himself had proved clever enough to have a natural science degree from Cambridge.

Sherdan saw Anya look down at this. He reached out his hand and tilted her chin back up. She looked sad but held his gaze this time.

"I don't think less of you because you are an artist with a more... simple life."

"But if I marry you that shall no longer be the case."

"Do you not want the money and power I offer?"

"It is not the money or the power that bothers me; it's the temptation and corruption that comes with it."

"You think me corrupt?"

"I think you're too used to getting your own way." Sherdan frowned. He felt his anger rising up inside him and did everything he could to suppress it.

"You may be right," he said, shocking himself. Anya's eyes went wide. "I usually get what I want."

They parted from each other as happily as they had done the night before. Sherdan decided to talk to Hitchin about giving Anya the drug without warning. She would have to forgive him for going against her will. He knew it would upset her, but she was right, he wanted his own way and was not very good at taking no for an answer.

The following day, as Sherdan expected, the police had turned up at several of the road blocks and requested they be removed. He personally went to each one and explained that it was private land and he didn't have to. The police left all but one after speaking to him, giving him time to have the last few emitters put in place.

He wanted to go talk to Hitchin but knew he needed to keep abreast of the situation with the police. It wouldn't be too long before they had all the paperwork sorted and would insist on moving the barriers. He doubted they would try and take the barriers away themselves, but even if they did try, they would soon realise it was impossible.

Sherdan estimated that it would only be a day or so before they would have their third and final line of defence set up. Thankfully, the additional technology was easily attached to each emitter, and over half the area was already protected.

The work he had to do kept him from focusing on Anya. As a consequence she had gained time before he would force her to take the drug.

Just after lunch Sherdan received a phone call from the mayor. It wasn't something he had expected.

"Dr Harper, my police chief has informed me that you are still refusing to open the roads."

"Yes, I did warn you that I wouldn't."

"I'm giving you one last chance to cooperate."

"I really don't think you understand. Nothing you have the power to do will open the roads."

"I beg to differ."

"Do you have anything else to tell me?" At this the mayor slammed the phone down. It wouldn't be much longer before his arrest was ordered.

As Sherdan expected, the police were soon trying to gain access to detain him. He told the security guards to stand back and let the police try.

He sat down and watched on the camera as both policemen walked towards the barrier and suddenly stopped. They quickly stepped back and looked at each other. Confusion reigned on their faces. Sherdan laughed as they tried again. They would be doing that for a little while.

"Keep me updated with events, please," Sherdan radioed the

two security guards. He then focused on getting their next line of defence in place. There was no knowing when they would need it at this point in time, but it was best to be prepared. Late in the afternoon he finally got to go see Hitchin. As usual, he greeted him happily.

"I spoke to Anya about taking the treatment."

"And?" Hitchin put down the lab goggles he had been wearing.

"She was adamant that she didn't want to take it."

"She needs to take it."

"I know. Can you prepare a treatment for her for two days' time?"

"Of course. We'll want to monitor her health, just in case."

"Yes, why don't you bring the drug over in two evenings' time and we'll bring her back here once you've injected her and calmed her down."

The police spent the rest of the day trying to get into the area to arrest Sherdan. None of them succeeded, and reports came in of the police getting very frustrated. Most of them gave up. The few that remained sat in their cars and waited, not really knowing what to do.

This put Sherdan in high spirits for another evening with Anya. The last two evenings had gone very well. They had managed to avoid arguing and he found she was letting him into her mind a little. He still hoped she would completely open up to him before long. He wasn't going to allow anything less.

CHAPTER 15

Every afternoon for the last four days Anya had managed to turn invisible. The first time it had shocked her, and since then she had practised every moment she knew she'd be undisturbed. She did not want to be interrupted by him again.

Thinking of the night before, she stopped pacing and went to the window. She could see their snowman sitting on the edge of the front lawn. The rest of the snow was melting, but the snowman still stood tall and proud.

For most of the day Anya had been preoccupied with going invisible, but she knew she needed to be careful when she tried it. She didn't want Sherdan to know that something was different about her, and he sometimes came up to see her when she least expected it.

At first, she had wondered if it had been her mind playing tricks on her because of trauma. It wasn't until she managed to disappear again that she realised it was really happening. Her first thought was that Sherdan must have given her the drug against her will, but it had only worked while she had been praying.

Once she had achieved the same thing for a third time, she stopped pacing and praying, and just stood in front of the mirror. She focused on the way she had felt right before her reflection had disappeared the first time.

For several minutes nothing happened. She sighed and closed her eyes. When she opened them again she couldn't see her reflection.

Unlike all the previous times, she stayed invisible. Anya had expected it to fade as it had done every time before, but after fifteen minutes, nothing. She gnawed on her bottom lip, worried she would be stuck like that. Thankfully, after concentrating hard on wanting to be visible again, she saw herself slowly appear in the reflection before her.

She didn't dare try again after that, and waited for Sherdan as normally as possible.

When he did finally come to see her, he was later than usual and looked a little flustered.

"Is everything all right?" she asked.

"Yes, everything is going well. I am busy preparing things for the next stage. This area of land shall be a fortress within the next week."

"With me locked at its centre."

"It's the safest place for you."

"Perhaps."

"Are you still completely against taking the drug and gaining an ability?" Sherdan asked. Anya did her best not to let her confusion show. She'd assumed he'd already put it into her system.

"I don't want it, but I suspect it's the kind of thing you'd do to me while I slept if you really wanted it to happen."

"No, I have more respect for you than that. I might still force it upon you, but not in secret."

"You'd still make sure you had your way then?"

"Of course."

Anya smiled at Sherdan when he said this. She didn't seem able to be annoyed at him for anything. She'd also noticed that, since their evening in the snow, he had been much more open and honest with her.

If he hadn't already given her the drug, however, it meant her invisibility must have come from somewhere else. In that moment she almost told him about it.

"Sir? I think you had better come take a phone call that's just come through for you," the radio squawked, disturbing their evening together.

"Who is it, Nathan?" Sherdan replied.

"The chief of police."

"I'll be right there." He rolled his eyes at Anya. She laughed.

"Seems you're in trouble with the law."

"Well, they have been trying to arrest me for most of the day."

"So my future husband, and the possible father of my first child, is a hardened criminal." They both chuckled.

"As I said before, you're safest here."

With that, Sherdan left her for the rest of the evening. She sat and pondered everything he had told her. Not everyone got personal phone calls from the chief of police when they were being pursued for arrest, especially when the very act of phoning showed that the police knew where he was and, therefore, could apprehend them.

She was also sure he'd been truthful about not giving her the drug. The only other way she could conceive being given the gift of invisibility was God, but this kind of ability was a new trick, even for Him.

Anya was still thinking this over when she fell asleep. It even continued to puzzle her the following day. She had no intention of looking a gift horse in the mouth, however, and stood herself in front of the mirror as soon as she knew she would have privacy for more than half an hour.

She focused on the same feeling as the day before, and her reflection disappeared in front of her eyes. Anya grinned. It was an awesome feeling, even if her clothes were still visible.

For the next few hours she practised moving between her normal state and invisibility. Each time the transition got quicker and took less concentration.

Anya gasped several hours later when, in transitioning from visible to invisible, all her clothes fell to the floor. She tried to pick them up and her hands went straight through them.

She hesitated, not knowing what to do next. As she stood thinking she faded back into view until she could see herself naked in the mirror, her clothes still in a pile under her feet.

Suddenly it dawned on her that, if her hand had moved through the clothes, in the same state she might be able to move through other things. She picked up her T-shirt and held it in her hands.

Anya took a deep breath and focused on the needed feeling. As usual, she turned invisible. She paused and concentrated again. A few seconds later the top fell to the floor and, no matter how hard she tried, she couldn't pick it up again.

As soon as she was sure she couldn't lift her clothes, she reached out to the bed. Her hand passed right through and she felt an odd sensation as it did. Feeling very brave, she stepped right into the bed. Her lower half tingled all over until she stepped back out again.

She grinned as she allowed herself to fade into view again. There was no way Sherdan could force her to do anything she didn't want to anymore.

She danced around the room and thanked God. She was as free as she wished to be. The weight and stress of the last few days fell from her and she laughed with happiness at her newfound liberty.

Picking up her clothes, she pulled her underwear back on but she was disturbed by the sound of footsteps outside the door. She froze with only her lower half clothed.

The key turned in the lock. Anya did the first thing that came into her head, and her jeans and thong fell to the ground again. In her invisible state she glanced at the clock. It was only half four. Sherdan was early.

She watched Sherdan come into the room, followed by someone else in a lab coat. He was one of the two guys in the laboratory she had walked in on. In his right hand was a syringe. She knew what was in it. Sherdan had at least warned her.

Anya smiled to herself as he scanned the room. He looked straight over to where she stood, but he was completely oblivious to her. He put his finger to his mouth and looked at Hitchin and then walked silently towards her bathroom to knock on the shut door.

"Anya, are you in there?" he called. She didn't respond and

had to resist the temptation to laugh. He knocked again before trying the handle. The door opened without resistance. Sherdan marched in and checked behind the shower curtain.

"She's gone!"

"The door was locked." Hitchin motioned towards the now open door behind him. Sherdan shrugged and ran from the room. Hitchin fixed a cap onto the syringe and followed.

With a very large grin on her face, Anya allowed herself to go visible and put her clothes on. As soon as she was decently attired, she left her unlocked room and followed the two men to Sherdan's study.

CHAPTER 16

Sherdan had been preoccupied all morning by Anya's remark the night before. She had said her future husband was a hardened criminal. It had been the first time she had referred to a relationship with him in a positive way, if you could call being a criminal a positive thing. Either way, it had made it very difficult to focus on his work.

The chief of police had phoned when he had finally heard of the arrest claim out on Sherdan. He'd also been informed of the interesting barrier they had. Sherdan had laughed and refused to explain. He'd warned the mayor. Admittedly, he had wanted a little more time before needing the lines of defence he was already using but he'd made his point.

The news had featured him and his compound all the morning. It showed clips from his interview as well as a few home videos of the police trying to walk past the barriers. None of the reporters could explain what had happened and, although they also interviewed the police officers, none of them could comment on what was wrong. There had been fresh requests for interviews as well as a huge boost in applications.

Sherdan had spent most of the morning talking to the security guards as the police kept trying to come in and arrest him. It was important that the guards didn't do anything threatening that would give the police a reason to use violence in gaining an entrance, especially shooting at anything or anyone.

Around mid-afternoon, Hitchin sent Sherdan an email informing him that the injection for Anya was ready. Sherdan finished up what he was doing and left the security commander in charge of the command bunker. Now that he could give her an ability, he wasn't going to waste any time.

Hitchin was eager to inject her himself and Sherdan couldn't see any reason to object. He would then be on hand if any immediate health problems arose.

Sherdan hoped that, even if it made her angry at first, she would finally decide to be his bride and embrace her new life with him. Their conversation the night before had shown him that their relationship was progressing nicely.

Despite the recent encouragement, Sherdan was still nervous in the car on the way to see her. Hitchin seemed entirely unaffected, but Sherdan couldn't talk to him. He didn't want to let Hitchin know how much he wanted Anya to be willing. Allowing someone to say no to him wasn't normal ,and not something he wanted people to be aware of.

He led Hitchin upstairs to her room. The last thing he expected was for her to not even be there. He noticed the pile of her clothes in the middle of the floor and assumed she was having a bath or shower. How wrong he was. He ran from the room as he reached for his radio.

"The prisoner is free again. Please mobilise all security teams. Don't let her reach any of the perimeters. Be advised the police are still lingering at several of the major barriers."

"Yes, sir," Graham said. Sherdan then sat himself down at his desk to pull up the camera feed for her room. Hitchin came in several seconds after.

They watched for ten minutes before they saw Anya stood in front of her mirror in the clothes that he'd seen on the pile, staring at it intensely.

A noise from behind the two men made them both jump and turn around.

"Hello," she said as she walked into the room, pulling down her t-shirt as if she'd only just put it on. Sherdan's mouth fell open before he stood up. He walked towards her and raised his arm to backhand her. She shrank back, her eyes wide.

"Sherdan!" Hitchin yelled. He was pointing at the screen.

"What?" Sherdan was furious and didn't appreciate the interruption. Anya grabbed his arm bringing his attention back to her.

"This," she said as she disappeared. Both men gasped. Her clothes came towards Sherdan before they fell to the floor in a heap.

"I seem to have an ability," she explained from somewhere in front of him. He reached out his arm and waved it in front of him. He couldn't feel anything. "That was right through me."

"Oh my God."

"I'm still working out exactly how to do everything, so excuse me a moment."

Sherdan watched Anya's pile of clothes lift up and leave the room. He then turned to Hitchin. The surveillance footage played behind him, completely forgotten by everyone. Sherdan suddenly regained cognitive thought.

"Stand down security. She's been found."

"As you wish, sir," the radio answered.

"Hitchin, I don't think we'll be needing that injection."

"No you won't be," Anya answered as she rejoined them.

"I would like to run some tests," Hitchin said as he got up out of his seat. Sherdan nodded as he smiled at her.

She stood there, before him, with an ability; an ability that would enable her to leave, and yet she was still here, looking relaxed and calm. Not only that, she had a light in her eyes and a grin on her face which said even more to him.

"I'd like to start with a blood test," Hitchin interrupted the unspoken conversation.

"Of course, Hitchin. I'll bring Anya into the lab tomorrow. For now, I think the two of us need some time alone."

"I'll see you both tomorrow then."

Hitchin didn't get a reply. Sherdan held Anya's gaze and everything else was forgotten. Neither of them noticed the scientist leave. Sherdan went towards her and took both of her hands in his.

"I'm sorry for getting angry just now."

"You're forgiven."

"Will you show me your ability again?" She nodded, and within seconds all he could see was her clothes. He could still feel her hands in his. His eyes went wide as he gave her fingers a squeeze.

"There seems to be two stages. This is where I'm invisible but still solid, and this one..." she said as her clothes became a pile on the floor for the seventh time that day. Sherdan grinned.

"I think I like this part."

"I can pass through anything in this state."

"Go back to being solid but invisible," he requested. He soon felt her hand touch his. He reached out and took it firmly, pulling her closer and closer to him.

"Sherdan," she warned. He reached out and grabbed her left arm. Despite not being able to see her, his lips met hers several seconds later.

Just as he'd suspected, she didn't protest or stop him. He wrapped his arms around her invisible body. She finally thought he had gone too far and melted out of solid form and out of his arms. He sighed.

"I was enjoying that."

"A little too much. I've still not made my mind up about your friend's vision."

"Yet you are still here."

"God wants me to be."

"You want to be with me, you mean?"

"I will go wherever God calls me without reference to anyone else."

"So why do you think you're here?" he asked as he sat down.

"I don't know yet, but for now I'm here."

"I want us to marry."

"I know. You're going to have to be patient."

"Don't keep me waiting for too long." Sherdan watched as her clothes got up and walked from the room again. A perfectly visible and attired Anya came back. She sat in the seat opposite him.

"For now I will stay here and, for the most part, do as I'm

told."

Sherdan felt like swearing. All the control he had was gone, and she knew it. Anya could do as she wished, and nothing could stop her. His only hope was her belief in her God. He knew she had no respect for Hitchin's prophecy or vision.

He sat for some time so deep in thought he didn't remember that he wasn't alone. He stayed that way until she got up, came over and knelt in front of him.

"I know that you're not happy that I won't do what you want and you can't make me, but I'm here now and not going anywhere. I believe in living in the present." She kissed him on the cheek. "I don't know about you, but I'm famished."

She smiled at him and he couldn't help but respond in the same manner.

For the first time since she had been in his house they ate together in the dining room. He'd never had a woman eat with him in that room, and he enjoyed the change. She looked completely at home in the dining chair, sat back, her meal finished and a half-full glass of wine in her hand. He'd had the dining room lit by candlelight, and she looked beautiful in the flickering glow.

They spent a very pleasant evening together, making it the third out of the last four, and talked of nothings all evening. She loved to watch sci-fi films, and they discussed their favourites for a long time. Oddly, they agreed on most of the good ones. Not long after, they were both sat side by side, watching a film with a bottle of wine and two glasses.

He had to carry her up to her bed again after their evening's entertainment. She smiled at him from her bed once he'd tucked her in.

"Thank you," she whispered.

"What for?"

"For making my life exciting."

"Was it dull before?"

"Not exactly dull but nowhere near as interesting as it has been the last two weeks."

"Well then, you're welcome."

Anya smiled before rolling over and closing her eyes.

Sherdan lay in bed thinking of the last few days for many hours. He felt happy despite his lack of control concerning Anya. She had stayed.

For the next few days he would have to focus on the development of the program. There were still many hurdles to overcome, and things were moving faster than even his original predictions. It was good that he had planned ahead.

Anya came with him willingly to the laboratory in the morning. She didn't want a huge number of tests but she wished to eliminate the possibility of her having been accidentally given the enzyme. He agreed at the logic.

Hitchin had already prepared to take blood samples and test them. Sherdan left her with his friend while he went to continue his work in the command bunker. He didn't really want to be with them while they investigated the source of her gift. He hadn't been able to tell she had one, let alone what it was. This unsettled him. His own ability should have alerted him to hers.

He hoped that there was a slight difference in her blood somewhere, but he didn't want to be there when they found out. For now he had other matters to sort out.

The check had come back on the young woman from the latest group of residents. She had lied about her age. She was only seventeen, not nineteen, and the worst part was that she hadn't got her father's permission to be there. They had essentially given a minor the drug and helped her run away from home.

Sherdan sighed. They couldn't let her leave, but legally they would have to let her father take her home. He'd have to think long and hard about what to do with Ellie. Now he had two girls to worry about, not just one.

He had the information passed on to Hitchin so he could confront the child. Sherdan would leave it up to him to decide what to do after that.

He turned his focus back to running the compound. Other than the hiccups with Anya, everything had been going according to plan. Their final line of defence was now fully in place.

Sherdan was also going on TV the following day. It was

time he did another news interview to announce some more of his plan. He wouldn't be anywhere near as prepared as he had for the first interview, and it would be live. He would have to think on his feet, but that did not bother him.

Hitchin soon emailed him to let him know that he had finished with Anya. She'd refused to allow any tests other than the blood test. Every time Hitchin tried anything else she used her power to move. Sherdan went to the laboratory as soon as he noticed the message.

Anya sat on a swivel chair at one of the desks, spinning cutely and making him think of their evening in the snow. Hitchin was ignoring her and was processing the blood samples he'd taken. She smiled when she saw Sherdan, but didn't stop her circles.

"How's everything going in here?"

"Well," Anya replied. Hitchin's face said otherwise. "I can't get Miss Price to allow any further testing."

"No more is necessary for the moment," she said.

"Anya, please?"

"No. You can determine whether it's your drug in my system or not and leave it at that."

"Don't make me angry." Sherdan stopped her from spinning in the chair. She stood up.

"No, Sherdan. I don't belong to you, and it's time you realised it. I won't just do what you tell me to do."

Without thinking, Sherdan slapped her. She stood in shock for a moment, before she vanished and her clothes fell to the ground in front of him. A few seconds later the laboratory door opened. Sherdan rushed after her.

"Anya, get back here now!" He looked both ways in the hallway but couldn't tell which way she'd gone, let alone if she'd heard him.

"Stupid girl," Hitchin said when Sherdan came back. "The power of her new-found ability has gone straight to her head."

"She thinks it's from her God." Sherdan picked up the pile of clothes.

"She needs to learn to submit to you and your wishes; that she's been brought here to be your wife and supporter, in all you do."

"How can I show her that when she can disappear when she wants?"

"That slap was probably an effective start. Show her you mean business and she'll come around. I've seen it. You'll have her in her place soon."

"I had best go find her. She'll want her clothes. Let me know the test results as soon as you do."

Sherdan walked out into the hall and headed towards the nearest building exit.

"Anya?" he called when he heard a noise nearby. The fire door in front of him opened by itself.

"Anya, come on, I know you're there. Stop hiding."

"I will not submit to you just because Hitchin thinks I should." He watched as her footprints ran off into the snow and towards his house. He hoped she didn't feel temperatures in her invisible state.

He went back to his work, leaving her to do as she wished. He could not lose focus on the bigger task because of a single woman. Hitchin could help him persuade her to submit to him, even if that meant trying out the inhibitor they were testing for their abilities, assuming she had exactly the same drug in her system.

For the rest of the day, Sherdan worked in the command bunker. The police had backed off with their attempted arrest after the mayor had been forced to admit Sherdan had filed all relevant paperwork. On TV, the news reporter had made a point of saying the only reason Sherdan had done anything wrong in the eyes of the law was because the mayor didn't like what had happened to the roads.

The same news reporter would be interviewing him the next day, and this made Sherdan even more confident it would go well.

He took Anya's clothes up to her room as soon as he got back to the house. A small part of him expected her to be gone and back in the safety of her own home. Instead, he found her sat on the bed, reading one of the books from his study.

She'd put on fresh clothes. He instantly noticed the bruise on the side of her face, where he had hit her, and his stomach churned. He regretted it but could not let her know.

Anya thanked him for returning her clothing and went straight back to the book.

"Do you want to eat here or in my dining room?"

"Neither. I've already eaten." She didn't even look up from her book.

"Fine." Sherdan left her before he got cross with her. The image of the bruise played in his head and he knew he would not forget it in a hurry. Hitting a woman had never had such an effect on him before, and he wasn't sure he liked the fact Hitchin had not only approved but encouraged it. He guessed that in her mind he'd already done a lot worse by letting her be interrogated.

He sat down on the bottom step and sighed. He had got used to eating his meals with someone and did not want to eat alone.

With his head in his hands, he sat and thought. He had no idea how he was going to get Anya to marry him. If it hadn't been for Hitchin's vision, he wouldn't have been sure he even wanted her to be his wife. His ideal partner probably wouldn't have had a religious faith or been so opinionated.

Anya refused to eat breakfast with Sherdan as well. She also seemed more happy than not when he told her he wouldn't be around for dinner, because he had a news interview and had to be in the studio when they would normally eat. He swore as he left her room. She was being completely unreasonable.

Hitchin emailed the test results to Sherdan when he arrived at the compound. The enzyme in her system did not match the enzyme they had been giving people. That was all the information included in the email, except for Hitchin asking him to come to the lab when he had a chance. Sherdan knew that more had been found out. He excused himself from his duties as soon as he could.

"Hitchin, what other information do you have for me?"

"Ah, Sherdan, you want to look at this." Hitchin pulled up a computer image of the blood sample on a microscopic scale. He used the mouse pointer to circle the enzyme particles in her blood. He then showed an enhanced image of the enzyme, and the different shape it was in comparison to their own.

"So it's different? Can you map the enzyme in her and see if it's better than our drug?"

"Unfortunately, not from the computer images I have of it."

"Well, you've still got the enzyme in the blood haven't you?"

"Come and see." Hitchin led Sherdan over to the microscope and fed a slide in marked 'Anya B1'. Sherdan looked at it for some time before pulling back and looking at Hitchin.

"I can't find any enzyme in her sample."

"No. There isn't any of it left in any of the blood samples I took. It has completely disappeared from her blood."

"Surely that should take longer?"

"Yes. It should leave traces, too, but there are none. It's like it wasn't ever there in the first place."

"That's not possible," Sherdan said, frowning.

"I'm going to need to do more testing."

CHAPTER 17

Sherdan thought about Anya's test results as he was being driven to London for his interview. If it wasn't the enzyme that had given her an ability, then there was a possibility someone else had done something similar. The only other explanation was the existence of some higher being or force, a force that wished Anya to be with him and to soon be his wife.

When Sherdan arrived at the news room he did as he had done at the previous interview and became lovely and gracious in an instant. His host, like last time, was female, and he charmed her while they were waiting for their slot. He watched from the edges while the rest of the news was broadcast. He would be last on the air, before the weather.

There wasn't much in the news except the continued chaos in the Gaza Strip. Sherdan smiled slightly. It wouldn't be long before they had something else to talk about, something much closer to home.

Sherdan was waved onto the set when it was finally his time to speak. He was introduced in a very formal way, and a clip of the police trying to get into his facility was shown to the viewers.

"Dr Harper, it appears that your facility has technology which the rest of the world doesn't know about. Could you explain how you've managed to keep such advances from the public and what you intend to do with it?"

"The technology is a recent development by the people within my program. As I've said before, I give people the chance to start again, to find a new talent and put themselves to use. There are many other great developments and projects, thanks to the people who have joined me."

"Why have you put all these barriers up if people are welcome to join you?"

"The residents who've already joined me feel that their privacy is important. They, like me, understand that other people can often feel like they are threatened when a group of people make huge leaps in technology. This feeling of threat can make people do things they regret. The barriers are there to protect my residents from the people that might react, whether they be a few individuals, a city, or a government."

"You don't think that you make the threat appear worse by segregating your community?"

"It potentially does, but it's not meant to. We mean no one any harm, and anyone is welcome to join us. I do want my residents to feel safe, however, and this is one of the precautions."

"Thank you, Dr Harper. Am I right to understand that there's been an arrest notice put out for you?"

"Yes, there was for a few days. The mayor of Bristol is one of these people who reacts with force when unsure of things. He didn't like me privatising the roads between my residents' houses."

"But that arrest request no longer stands?"

"Not that I'm aware of."

"Do you have any other surprises in store?"

"Yes. A few, at least." Sherdan smiled. "I've not finished with my plans in the slightest."

"Can you tell us some of your plans?"

"Not very easily. None of them have been fixed. I think the number of people who are part of the organisation will grow, and with that may well come changes. I do intend to continue as I've started, and I think people will be hearing more of us in the future."

Sherdan's interview ended there. He'd not really said much. He still didn't think the time was right to tell people of the residents' abilities, but it wouldn't be much longer. Eventually someone would leak the information, and he wanted to beat them to it.

Thankfully the news reporter did not seem to know about Anya or the minor they had living with them who hadn't obtained parental consent. No one had even reported her missing yet, despite it being almost an entire month since she had become his prisoner.

It had never occurred to him, until that moment, that someone might be missing Anya. She had family and friends who may not know where she had gone, let alone if she was even still alive.

By the time Sherdan got back it was late evening, and he'd narrowly missed another police attempt to arrest him at the studio. If he'd not left promptly they'd have caught him. There were police at every one of his own barriers. The driver kept going past them all so no suspicion was aroused.

His chauffeur automatically drove to a small building half a mile away and pulled up into the garage. Built into the floor was a lift that took the car down into a tunnel and allowed Sherdan to travel along into his compound and up into his own garage. He'd hoped not to have to use it yet but the fresh arrest attempt had been unexpected.

When Sherdan arrived back, Anya was in her room reading and, although she remained polite, she didn't do anything to keep the conversation going. He left her alone again, not wanting the hassle.

He suspected she resented him for hitting her but he didn't know for sure. He had no intention of apologising for his actions either way. She would have to accept him for who he was. He accepted her, despite disliking her belief system and several other things about her.

The following day, Anya finally asked about her test results. Sherdan hesitated before giving her an answer. Here was an opportunity for him to get her to submit to more tests.

"Unfortunately there was a problem with the blood test.

Hitchin would like to do another, and will possibly need to do other tests to figure out for sure if it was our drug or not."

"Oh, that's odd. Hitchin told me that the blood test should be enough to figure out if the enzyme was the same."

"Well, at the very least, he's going to need you to do another blood test."

"I'll come to the lab with you this morning then," she replied and put her book down.

Neither of them spoke the whole journey over to the main command facility. Sherdan didn't know how to repair the rift between them. It had always been Anya who had made the conversation progress, and without her effort he ran out of things to say.

She didn't need showing where to go, and said goodbye to go into the lab, not expecting him to come too. He couldn't think of a reason to accompany her and, after a moment's thought, had to pull out his mobile phone and email Hitchin.

Hitchin had asked for Anya to be sent for more tests but not for the reason Sherdan had told her. Hopefully Hitchin wouldn't let Anya realise that. The last thing he needed was another reason for her to be angry at him.

When Sherdan settled down to his work in the command bunker he had an email waiting for him from Ellie's father. He'd figured out where she had gone and wanted her back. Sherdan had to think very carefully about his response.

Hitchin had spoken to the girl and she didn't want to return to her home. She'd also developed her ability: when she touched people she could tell exactly what they were feeling; a very useful skill.

Sherdan knew to be as polite as possible to what would be a very worried father, and simply explained that Ellie hadn't informed them of her true age and, upon speaking to her, they had learnt that she still wished to stay. He didn't point out that forcing her back home when she wanted to be in the program wouldn't be helpful. He wanted to strike up a trustful correspondence with the father, if he could, and tried to sound like he only had Ellie's best interests in mind.

Sherdan moved on to finding out why he was under arrest

again. As far as he was aware, the mayor had dropped the original charge against him due to its lack of success. He soon had Jeremy on the phone.

"Hello friend, I hope you are well?"

"Very well, thank you, Dr Harper. How can I help you today?"

"I believe I'm the target of another arrest attempt, but I'm completely baffled as to why, this time."

"I hadn't heard of anything... Just let me check our database for why... Ah, yes, here it is. Apparently several of your residents who have left have complained about manipulation and coercion into the program."

"Can you tell me who? Because as far as I am aware no residents have left,"

"I can't find out from this database. I'd need to look into it and probe further to see if they're real complaints."

"Please do."

Sherdan put the phone down and immediately requested a full check of every person within the perimeter. If residents had left and gone to the police, then he wanted to know before Jeremy.

While he waited for the information concerning his residents and replies to his earlier emails, Sherdan continued to make preparations for the next stage of his plan. His next stint on TV would include a big announcement. It was possible that already-strained political relationships would get even worse as a result, and many things would change about life, in a very short space of time.

It soothed him that the entire facility was now self-sufficient in every way. They had enough food and water, and a continual source of energy from harnessing many of the different talents the residents had developed.

Sherdan ended his day by going to see Hitchin. Anya had returned to the house after letting him take more blood. She hadn't even let Sherdan know she had left; Hitchin had done that for her.

"The samples are the same as last time. There's the same similar enzyme in her blood work but, the second I tried to figure out what it was, it faded out of the sample. In all three samples, it didn't fade out until I tried to map the exact molecular structure of it."

"What are you saying?"

"Something doesn't want us to know how she got her power."

"Something?"

"Without doing further tests I can't say what, whether the enzyme is designed to fade out of the blood once out of the body, or if something is helping Anya's ability to stay a mystery to us. Quite simply, scientifically I can't explain it."

"I'll try to persuade Anya to do more tests."

"Oh, before you go. Could you check in on the few left in the latest test group? There are three who haven't figured out what they've gained yet, and we could do with knowing."

"Will they all have developed them yet?"

"Possibly not, but it's rare for three out of twenty not to have one yet." Sherdan nodded and went through to the ward.

There were two middle-aged women and a man in his fifties. He smiled and conversed with all three for a few minutes, checking they were happy and comfortable. Oddly, Sherdan couldn't see if any of them had a power, and definitely couldn't figure out what they might be. He went back through to Hitchin.

"Sorry, friend. I don't think any of them have abilities yet. Start the next group while you're waiting for these ones to develop."

"Of course. Come back soon, though."

"I will come as soon as I can find time."

Anya waited for Sherdan in his study that evening, and he walked in on her before he realised she occupied the room.

"What were my test results?" she asked before he'd had time to acknowledge her.

"It's not the same enzyme." Her face lit up. "It's behaving oddly, too. Hitchin would really like to do more tests."

"I don't think more are necessary. God's given me one of your abilities. I know everything I need to know."

Sherdan slammed his laptop down on his desk. She ignored his anger and left the room. He hesitated before following her all the way to the top of the house.

"I know we don't agree whether some kind of God has anything to do with this, but I would really appreciate it if you let Hitchin do further tests. We just want to know for sure that the change in you isn't caused by us."

"You said it yourself: it's a different enzyme."

"It is, but it could be a mutated version of our own. For your health..."

"My health!" she interrupted. "Don't lie to me, Sherdan. This is purely your curiosity and disbelief, and has nothing to do with concern for me."

"I do care about you, Anya."

"You were very good at showing your 'care' when you let me be tortured for over two days, and when you locked me up right after."

"That was before I knew you."

"So what was meant by hitting me? It's not the first time you've got so angry you've hurt me or gone to do so, either."

"Is that what's bugging you about me?"

"What doesn't annoy me about you?"

Sherdan glared at her and left the room before he made matters worse. He slammed his way across the hall to his own bedroom, leaving both doors rattling in their frames. She was impossible. He paced as he ran their argument through his head.

Her Christian beliefs made her stupid. If he even slightly questioned them she got offended and continued assuming everything unexplainable was her God. Sherdan himself wasn't perfect, but he was only trying to find out the truth and do what was best for her. As his future wife he, did care about her wellbeing.

When he finally emerged from his room, she had already eaten dinner without him and locked her door from the inside so he couldn't disturb her. He didn't know when she'd taken the key, but it infuriated him all over again, especially when he learnt she'd taken the only spare key as well.

Before Sherdan went to bed, he received a reply from Ellie's father. His email sounded very angry, and he demanded that Ellie be sent home, as well as expressing his disbelief that she wanted to be there.

Sherdan did not reply right then. He wanted to think carefully about his response, and the email had been sent late enough that he wouldn't be expected to still be awake. The longer he could delay the father going to the police the better, assuming he hadn't already.

Sherdan didn't want to have an active arrest warrant when he did his announcement, if at all possible. It would make some parts of the plan significantly harder if there was.

CHAPTER 18

The smile on Anya's face gave away her feelings as she lay on her back in Hitchin's lab. Sherdan ran his hand over her exposed stomach. The sound in her ears was the heart beat of their little baby. Hitchin held the other end of the stethoscope against her stomach.

When she'd given Hitchin back the instrument, Sherdan was left alone with her. He went to kiss Anya but she pulled away, a sadness in her eyes he'd not seen before.

"I have something to tell you," she whispered and looked away. Sherdan's stomach churned. It wouldn't be good news. "You're not the father. I'm sorry, Sherdan, Hitchin is."

Sherdan yelled into his pillow as he woke up. He groaned when realised it hadn't been real. It had felt so vivid. He shivered and his breathing slowed back to normal. He didn't dare close his eyes again, even though there were still several hours until he needed to be awake.

He got up and went out into the hallway, up to Anya's door. He stood outside, aware that she'd locked herself in. After a few seconds he heard her cry out. The door opened, allowing him in.

She lay on the bed in the dim, lamp-lit room. Her whole body poured with sweat. She'd kicked off the covers while she had been thrashing and exposed a great deal of her skin in the over long t-shirt she wore. He tore his eyes from her body and focused on her face. It was screwed up in fear and pain, but her eyes were still closed.

Sherdan went to her while her eyelids flickered in the familiar movements of a dream. The look on her face and the continued uncomfortable murmurings and movement pained him.

He reached out to stroke her cheek and called her name. She screamed and threw herself off the bed and, somehow, into his arms. She immediately burst into tears and fought against him, disorientated by both his presence and by not being in her bed. He held her and hugged her to him.

"It's okay, Anya, you're safe. It was a nightmare. It wasn't real," he whispered.

He repeated the same sentiments again and again until she calmed down, sobbing gently against his chest. After a few moments she stopped and pulled away from him. Her embarrassment was evident as she covered herself back up with the duvet. He stayed by her bed, concerned.

"Are you all right?"

"I am now, thank you."

"What was it?"

"Hitch... Nothing. Just a nightmare. I hardly remember it now." Sherdan frowned. She'd almost said Hitchin's name, he was sure of it. She leant back against the head board and closed her eyes. She was very weary.

"It's not the first nightmare, is it?"

She laughed and looked at him.

"I was tortured for two days; of course it's not the first." Her words were harsh but there was only softness in her eyes.

"I'm sorry."

"They will fade. Already I'm forgetting what happened."

"It won't ever happen again."

"Perhaps not. Not to me anyway. Would you put others through it?" Sherdan couldn't look at her.

"You expect a lot of people."

"No more than I expect of myself."

There was an awkward hush for a few moments. He reached out and stroked her arm.

"I had a nightmare too."

"What scares you, then?" she asked. Sherdan hesitated. He wasn't sure why he'd even mentioned it and didn't know if he wanted to tell her what it had been about.

"I was betrayed by someone I thought I could trust." He didn't look at her as he said this. He didn't want her to see how much it had affected him.

"I'm not tired now. Would you like to play cards until morning?" she suggested. He nodded and smiled.

For the next three hours they sat together at her small table and played many different card games. It helped him relax and he filled her in on the recent developments in the world, as well as his plan's progress. She'd seen his latest TV interview.

"You flirted with the news reporter," she told him. He laughed.

"Only a little."

"You won't be able to do that once you're married."

"Perhaps not, but I'm not even officially engaged yet, let alone married."

When their early morning was up, Sherdan hesitated before leaving. The yellowing bruise on her face had haunted him the whole time he had been with her.

"I'm sorry for losing my temper and hitting you. I shouldn't have done it."

"You don't agree with Hitchin that I should be beaten into submission, then?"

"How do you know he advised that?"

"I didn't leave the lab straight away that day."

"I don't agree with Hitchin, no. Violence is not always right, but I do think you'll be my wife, one way or another."

Sherdan felt only a little better as he went to try and sort out everything to do with Ellie. Her father's anger needed to be handled delicately. He fired up his laptop in his study and sat down to compose an email to her father.

To Edward Johnson,
I hope I haven't said anything which has led to the idea that I would keep Ellie from returning to you if that

is her wish. I am merely trying to resolve this issue in a manner which has the best result for everyone involved. Your daughter came here of her own free will and even lied about her age to get past the security checks that we have in place to stop this exact situation from happening.

Your daughter has informed my staff that she still wishes to stay, even though you don't want her to. I would also like to point out that if her desire to be here was made up, then she would not have left her home, so many miles from here, just to get here. However, I understand that as a parent you are concerned for the wellbeing of your child and, in your worry, our assurances may not be enough.

I propose that this coming weekend you travel here and, over the course of the two days, let our staff show you around our facility and what Ellie is doing here. It will also give you and your daughter time to talk over her decision. At the end of the weekend, if you still wish to take your daughter home, we'll refund all your travel expenses and allow you both to leave.

Seeing as Ellie will be eighteen in three months, we'll offer her a place on our course again when she is old enough, as long as both of you stick to our non-disclosure agreement. I've attached the document. You'll need to provide a signed copy to the guards on the way in, as well as photo ID. If you have any other queries my staff will deal with them for you.

Yours sincerely,
Dr Sherdan Harper.

With that issue sorted, Sherdan went into his office. He had a report waiting for him, accounting for all his residents' whereabouts. None of them had made a complaint. He forwarded the information on to Jeremy.

His next order of business was assigning the new residents different tasks based on their abilities, and after that he needed to look over the plans for expansion. They would need more land if they were going to accept more people.

Applications were still coming in, especially after the recent interview. Different types though: military leavers, others that were fed up with their country's system, people who'd tried to get into things like politics and not been very successful, and a large number of artists, writers and musicians, too. Normally they'd be the kinds of people he'd reject, but he found himself considering the military applicants as well as the artists who seemed to be like Anya.

Around mid-morning Jeremy phoned. He'd managed to discredit two of the four complaints against Sherdan, but the mayor had got wind that Jeremy was helping him and his hands were now tied. The mayor was playing dirty.

Sherdan couldn't help but be impressed. He hadn't expected the mayor to be intelligent enough to throw these kinds of things his way.

After setting up another interview for the following Wednesday, Sherdan finished off his work and went back to his house. Anya was sitting in his favourite chair in the study. He tried not to be annoyed.

"You were on the news again today," she told him.

"I was?"

"Yes, a very tasteful piece about your desire to help people make their lives better."

"Sounds fairly accurate." She smirked. "You don't think so?"

"With you, Sherdan, there is always more than meets the eye."

"Likewise with you. For one, I am surprised you are still here. Are you not missing your friends and family?" he asked.

"There's still something I'm meant to do here, something God wants me to do, though I know you don't believe in my God."

"What are you meant to be doing here?"

"I still don't know yet."

He did not know how to respond and let her carry on reading.

Sherdan checked his emails after dinner. Ellie's father had accepted his request to come visit the following weekend. Anya continued to lounge in his study as if it was her own home. He found her highly distracting, as he tried to work.

"Are you going to work tomorrow as well?" she asked.

"Why?"

"Tomorrow's Sunday."

"I work every day," he explained.

"I was thinking that it might be fun to do something together in the afternoon."

"Do you have something in mind?"

"There's a theatre show I'd like to see."

"I've got an arrest warrant out on me."

"That didn't stop you appearing on the news."

"True... okay, we can go to the theatre." She smiled and kissed him on the cheek before leaving him to his work. He frowned. She had only shown affection because he had given her what she wanted. It did not make him feel any more confident in her willingness to cooperate.

The arranged outing, and the peace and quiet as a result, helped Sherdan be very productive for the rest of the evening. He filed more paperwork with the government, in preparation for Wednesday's announcement.

CHAPTER 19

Travelling to the theatre impressed Anya. The police were still at every barrier so they had to be driven via Sherdan's emergency tunnel. She'd been awed by the secret entrance set-up and likened it to the bat cave.

She was also ecstatic over the tickets he'd acquired. They had the best box to themselves. Sherdan had never enjoyed spending money as much as this, and it wasn't entirely Anya's reaction. Some of the fun was taking time away from his work and forgetting about it. He'd been busy almost every minute of every day since Hitchin had first told him the prophecy.

When the production finished, Anya turned to Sherdan with a very large grin on her face.

"Can we go get dinner?"

Not a single part of him could refuse. He nodded as she slipped her hand into his. When they had settled back into his car he asked the chauffeur to take them to Bath, to the sea food restaurant he often went to. When they arrived he ordered for her, treating her to lobster and champagne.

Over two hours later he requested the bill. He handed his card over to the waitress without thinking.

"Oh, Dr Harper? Dr Sherdan Harper? Aren't you the one blocking off the land in Bristol?" the waitress exclaimed. Sherdan swore under his breath.

"Please keep your voice down, ma'am," Anya asked, but it was too late. Other people had heard and were turning to look at him and his companion. He finished paying as fast as the waitress would allow, grabbed Anya's arm, and walked for the nearby car.

They had both just climbed inside when several police cars pulled up outside the restaurant. They watched as armed police poured out of the vehicles.

"That was close. I'm sorry." Anya turned to Sherdan.

"It's okay. I think we should go back now."

She nodded her agreement as they were driven past the police cars pulled up on one side of the road.

Sherdan didn't relax until they were safely back in his house. It was already in the news online that he'd been seen with a woman in Bath. Thankfully there hadn't been anything but a description of Anya. She'd be in a lot of danger if they identified her.

They both agreed that, although it had been a fun Sunday, they'd be better off not repeating it. Sherdan had Nathan keep an eye on the news to make sure nothing else was found out about Anya. Despite her objections, he spent the rest of the evening working.

The next few days followed in a haze of work. Sherdan hardly saw Anya, and completely forgot about Hitchin's request for her to have more tests done. He also forgot about seeing the newest batch and figuring out their new talents. He had far too much work to do in preparation for the future.

Tuesday evening broke the monotony. The police had patrolled the perimeter for many days and in doing so had found a few particular spots where the emitters hadn't quite closed off the area. They'd also figured out that it was only around the perimeter and of a set height.

Several helicopters flew over and air-dropped a raid squad right into the centre of the facility at the same time as two squads came in at both of the weak points they'd found.

Sherdan mobilised the entire security team in seconds. He'd expected something like this eventually and rushed over to the command bunker using his private tunnel. All the residents were advised to stay indoors and, within five minutes, only the security team and police were moving in the entire area.

With help from the many cameras, Graham soon had the police located and he fed the information to the guards. They split into four teams. Two headed towards each squad that had broken the perimeter and the other two teams came at the central raid squad from both sides.

By the time Sherdan was in the command room, the first security team had informed the police to the south that they were trespassing. The police had taken cover and pulled out their guns. The guards knew not to fire on the intruders unless absolutely necessary, but they also kept to cover and aimed their guns back anyway.

A few minutes later the guards reached the police on the north-east edge of the site as well. The same thing happened. The guards informed the raid squad that they were trespassing and everyone took cover.

Sherdan authorised each guard team to sneak forward to gain the upper hand and disarm the police. This happened without any issues in the north-east.

The guards snuck around until the police had been cornered. The police soon put their guns down when they realised they were out-manoeuvred and out-manned. Sherdan sat down to wait. His men were well-trained, and the response to the inevitable police reactions had been a long time in planning.

He watched on the cameras as every gun, and all spare ammunition, was confiscated by his security. They then escorted the squad back the way they had come, before placing another emitter to block the gap in the perimeter.

While this was happening, the two teams in the middle, very near Sherdan's house, were still trying to circle the largest police squad, and the guards to the south were trying to disarm the police they'd backed into a corner.

There was one younger police officer to the south who, despite having three guns pointed at him, refused to stand down and put his own weapon on the floor. In his panic, he fired.

The bullet left the gun as it normally would, but slowed dramatically three feet away from the man it was aimed at. It fell to the ground less than six inches from him. The officer shot a few more times, but the same thing happened.

After that the whole squad surrendered. If their bullets were useless they weren't going to risk their lives any further, as Sherdan had expected. The squad was treated to the same routine as the first. Sherdan smiled; this was easy work so far.

Everyone in the command bunker then focused on the final squad and sent the two successful security teams to help. The police had moved in the direction of Sherdan's house, in a very wary manner. Without the cameras, the guards would have found them very difficult to track.

With everything running so smoothly, Sherdan felt no concern. He could sit back and watch, needing only to add the odd few instructions in the ear of his commander.

As orders were fed to them from the eyes in the command room, the twenty strong team of guards soon formed a closed perimeter around the eight policemen, although the police were still unaware of any pursuit. The officers crept along the street towards the target house, using cars and house corners as cover.

The security team were right behind the police, following the example of how to sneak set before them, but doing it that little bit better. In front of both parties, more guards snuck closer, not as fast as the following guards but equally as confident. Their faces were grim but their movements sure.

For the first time, Sherdan interjected. He ordered a few security guards to enter his house through the back garden and ensure the police didn't get near Anya, nor see her there. He didn't want anything to happen to her.

Sherdan briefly wondered if inviting the mayor into his home had been a bad idea, but he put the thought from his head. Dwelling on past choices did no good. He would deal with any consequences as they arose.

He watched as the police came within a few hundred metres of his front lawn. The security guards were another three hundred metres behind them and closing. The guards in front slowed so they could concentrate on staying out of sight and closing the gaps between them in their approach to the target house.

Everyone in the command bunker agreed that the best place to flank the squad was his front lawn as the police came up to the building itself. The home was set back from the road and houses either side, so the guards could be out of sight for longer and appear from more directions at once.

"Anya, are you anywhere near a radio?" Sherdan asked into the nearby microphone. He was contemplating asking again, or sending a guard to find her, when the same frequency crackled into life.

"Sherdan, is that you?"

"Anya, you're in danger."

"What kind of danger?"

"There are men with firearms advancing on the house. I have extra security in the front of the building but there may be wild fire."

"I'm in your study currently."

"Move towards the front of the house but turn left instead of right and walk to the end of the hallway."

"But it's a dead end."

"No it's not." Sherdan got up from his seat in the command room and went through to his rest room so he wasn't overheard.

"Where do I go now, Sherdan?" she asked, when there was a delay in instructions.

"You have a mirror in front of you?"

"At the end of the corridor?"

"Yes, that's the one. On the back, left hand side of the frame, there is a button, push it."

"Okay, found it. What does that light mean?

"It's an eye scanner, look into it. I added your retinal pattern a week ago."

"Already done. Do I just follow this wherever it leads?"

"Yes, and please hurry." Sherdan opened his end of the tunnel and took the steps down two at a time. He rushed along until he could see her up ahead. She had done as she was told and jogged along. Now she looked pale and was out of breath. He took her hand and walked back towards the compound with her.

"What's happened?" she asked in between gasps for air.

"There is a raid squad. They have guns and have already shot at one of my guards."

"What are they after?"

"Me."

"Thank you for letting me know." She squeezed his hand. "I know you could have disappeared had they reached you, but I didn't want to risk you getting hurt."

She smiled but still didn't look happy. He'd worried her and it would take her a while to recover.

Even though she was already tired, he marched her along to the compound, requesting an update as he did.

"They've not engaged yet," the radio informed him. He didn't let go of her until they were in his safe room at the command centre.

"Stay here, please. This might not be pretty and you'll be safe here." She nodded and sat down in the nearby chair, still clutching the walkie-talkie in one hand.

Sherdan flicked his attention to the camera screens on the far wall as soon as he was back in the command room. The front man in the police squad was only a few feet away from the garden, and the guards were all still undetected. No one spoke as everyone watched the monitors.

When the first officer reached the front door, all the guards behind rushed forwards, their hand-guns aimed at the police squad. The security guards around the sides of the house followed quickly, but the police panicked. Before the security inside could show themselves and completely surround the police, they fired their weapons.

"Keep calm, men," Graham called into the microphone. They managed to keep their heads and didn't return the fire. Instead, they walked slowly towards the officers.

When their ammo had run out, the police all stopped. Their mouths hung open and their gun hands dropped to their sides. No one was harmed.

The security kept advancing, telling the police to surrender and allow themselves to be escorted off the premises. The other two teams of guards soon joined them to assist.

At first, the police seemed happy to cooperate. All but two

had their hands tied and were being moved off when one of the final two officers elbowed the nearest guard and followed it with a punch to the face. The police officer didn't achieve anything else as he was tackled to the ground by another three guards. They were all marched off the enclosed site.

Sherdan didn't leave the command room or inform the residents that everything was dealt with while the men were still on his land. He waited until they'd been shoved past a road barrier and the emitter blocking the path was reactivated. As with the other two squads, all their weaponry and ammo had been kept.

"That should send a good message. Well done, security. You performed perfectly." Sherdan handed the microphone back to the security commander and told him to finish everything off. He went back to Anya in the adjacent room.

She stood up as he entered, her face full of concern.

"It's okay. One of our security may have a broken nose, but considering that an hour ago twenty police were here with loaded guns, I think it went very well."

"Will they try again?"

"Possibly. Keep this radio with you, in case, and come here straight away if it does." She nodded. They went back to the house the same way they'd both come. "Oh, and please don't mention this tunnel to anyone. Very few people know it exists. Not even Hitchin does. Only you or I can use it."

"My lips are sealed."

CHAPTER 20

Sherdan stayed with Anya until very late that night. She'd been shaken by everything that had happened and didn't want to sleep. Now that he knew she'd been having nightmares he wanted to make sure she had calmed before he left her. Even once he'd gone to his own room he left the door ajar to hear if anything disturbed her again.

Whether she slept well or not, nothing woke him until his alarm went off. He stayed with Anya at her request, working in his study rather than the command room. She sat near him and read, trying not to disturb him.

In the afternoon he had to leave her and sneak out of his facility to travel to London again. Anya asked if she could come too, but he refused. He didn't want to put her in danger yet again. He didn't add that he wanted time to think.

Sherdan had been a lot more panicked the previous day about Anya than he'd expected, and wanted to keep her safe from the British government. She'd captured his heart even though she continued to keep him at a distance. She'd show the odd sign of affection but wouldn't allow him to do anything that would imply a romantic attachment of any kind.

He'd finally gone to the medical ward in the morning. The three from the previous batch were there, along with all the new ones. He'd still not been able to see a single power in any of them, and right before his eyes someone from the new batch had turned the water in their cup to ice.

Sherdan's power should have shown him that at least a few moments before, but it hadn't. When it hadn't worked on Anya he'd not been that concerned; she had a different enzyme. But it should have worked in the ward. It should, but it hadn't, and he had no clue why.

There would be problems if the powers stopped working or faded over time. However, both he and Hitchin had been sure that the change wasn't reversible, though for short periods it could be inhibited.

He had to put it from his mind, despite his worry, and focus on his next interview. The same TV channel as before was interviewing him again.

Sherdan allowed himself to be led through the same routine of make-up and preparation. He even had the exact same slot on the program.

He grinned as he thought about his announcement, especially when the security he'd brought with him informed him the police were already at the studio. They wouldn't get to him in time, not with the rambling building he was in.

Within seconds of thinking this, he was directed up onto the stage to take his place ready for the interview.

"Thank you for coming again, Dr Harper." Emma turned to him with a polite smile on her face.

"Thank you. I talked of surprises last time I was here. I actually have one I'd like to talk about." Sherdan took control straight away.

"What would that be?"

"As of now, the area of private land owned by myself and the residents in my facility is an independent country."

"I'm sorry, Dr Harper, I don't quite understand. How can it be an independent country?" She looked at the camera and off to her colleagues at the side, confused and obviously hoping they would feed her information via the scrolling text screen.

"Well, it's quite simple, really. Anyone who owns land that has a permanent population and a means of negotiating on a diplomatic level with other countries can declare that fixed land independent. I have done everything required on behalf of all my residents, and we are now an independent country called Utopia."

"Have you been planning this from the start?"

"Yes, close enough to the start that it might as well have been."

"Are you still accepting applications?"

"Yes, of course. They will become applications for citizenship, followed by everything else we were offering before."

"Legally, isn't being recognised as a country very difficult?"

"It can be, but I think we've satisfied all the official criteria and, with our technology, people will have trouble stopping us."

"That brings me on to some rumours. Am I right in thinking there has been at least one attempted raid on what is now your country? The police are denying it. Is it true or not?"

"Yes, late yesterday evening twenty police managed to make it through our perimeters. Most via a helicopter. Our guards managed to escort them all back out again with very minimal harm. I believe there were only a few bruises and wounded egos, despite the police opening fire when unprovoked."

"I imagine that it won't be repeated?"

"No. Anyone caught trespassing, unless they're military and the country of origin negotiates for their return, will be prosecuted by our courts for breaking the law as would any other country in the world."

"Thank you, Dr Harper."

Sherdan smiled as he took a different route out of the studio, bypassing all the police waiting for him to try and arrest him yet again.

He had help from some of the TV personnel with his escape route. Many people thought he was a hero, especially with how the police were treating him. The authorities were chasing their tails, as far as he was concerned.

He hurried his driver to get him back to his new country as soon as he could. He needed to monitor the reaction to his announcement and could only fully do so from his home or compound. His phone could only do so much, and there were a number of possible outcomes, the most violent being if the UK tried to send the army to invade. If they did so before he got back he'd be very angry.

Ten minutes later his phone rang. Graham greeted him from the other end.

"Sherdan, sir, the army are assembling at each one of our barriers. At the moment they seem to be waiting. The Prime Minister of the UK has phoned. He wants to speak to you."

"Tell him I will speak to him as soon as I get back. Let me know if the military make a move and warn all the residents to stay inside and prepare their shelters until we know what response we'll get."

"Yes, sir."

"Oh, and get Nathan to inform the woman in my house. Have her shown where the spare bunker is in my house."

"Of course, sir, anything else?"

"I'll be back as soon as I can be." Sherdan hung up and ran his fingers through his hair. He then encouraged his chauffeur to drive faster and to head straight to the safe house with the tunnel.

He drummed his fingers on the armrest while he waited. He needed to do something. Flipping open his laptop he connected it to the internet via his phone and requested more information via email. Within minutes he'd received a reply.

The army are still waiting. They've not said anything to the guards. I've had the security equipped with the larger guns from the armoury, and they are manning each barrier to show we mean business. We are waiting on your return, Nathan.

Sherdan sighed and sat back. It appeared that the Prime Minister did want to speak to him before taking any serious actions. It only made him feel a little better, however. He wanted to be back.

Half an hour from Bristol his phone rang again.

"Sir, we've found out that the police are checking every car coming into Bristol to try and find you."

"Tell Scott to get the train ready."

"Already done, sir. It's the only way in, currently."

Sherdan informed his driver to head to a small yard off the track in Saltford, a little village off the edge of Bristol. He smiled to himself. The police were always a few steps behind.

When the car pulled into the deserted yard there wasn't any sign of the train yet. He got out of the car and let it head to Bristol without him. The train pulled up less than five minutes later. Sherdan hopped straight into the driver's cabin and shook hands with the driver.

"We are sorry for the delay to this train. There was a signal fault, but we should be in Bristol Temple Meads in less than ten minutes," Scott said to his passengers. He then handed Sherdan a uniform and a fake pass, to look like an employee. Another car would pick him up outside the station and take him into his country.

He shook Scott's hand again when they arrived and slipped him a cheque for two thousand pounds.

"Cash it quickly. If it doesn't work, let me know."

Scott nodded and they went their separate ways. Sherdan moved with the people through the station in a similar manner to Anya over a month before.

His heart rate increased when he used his employee pass to get through the barriers, but only moments later he sank into the back seat of the new car. Nathan had the driver's seat.

"Home as quick as you can without drawing attention to us." Nathan nodded and drove through the quieter than normal streets of Bristol. Sherdan sighed as he walked into his house, less than twenty minutes later.

"What's going on?" Anya demanded as soon as she saw him. He kissed her full on the lips, taking her by surprise, and then grabbed her hand.

"Come with me." He led her down the tunnel to the command bunker in a very similar manner to the night before. He explained about the army along the way. She'd watched the news report so she already knew about Utopia and his announcement.

"Does this mean I'm a citizen as well?" she asked. He

smiled.

"Not really, more of a refugee. We're not officially recognised as a country yet either."

"How long will it take?"

"It depends what the UK does and if the UN decides to recognise us as a country."

Sherdan asked Anya to stay in his safe room again before entering the main command area.

Everyone was already at their stations and monitoring the perimeter and skies. Sherdan went up to Graham and got him to pass on any information that he didn't already have.

The screens on the end wall all featured similar pictures. His guards patrolled every entrance into the country and the British army sat less than thirty metres away, stopping anyone coming in or out. They had guns and dogs, as well as armoured vehicles at the major exits.

The soldiers just sat and waited. They stopped anyone coming too close, but other than that they simply made their presence known. Sherdan told the guards not to engage them in conversation, and then focused on his residents.

The commander had made an announcement requesting them all to stay indoors, except in an emergency. He had also asked them to prepare their bomb shelters, just in case. As far as Sherdan was aware, they had all obeyed.

Sherdan's final order of business was returning the phone call from the Prime Minister. He'd left a number for Sherdan to phone back on.

He picked up the nearby headset and put in the numbers. There was an audible click after only a single ring.

"This is number ten, Downing Street. Who is calling?"

"This is Dr Sherdan Harper. The Prime Minister called me almost two..."

"Wait just a moment, Doctor." Sherdan was put on hold. He sighed as he waited. This conversation wasn't going to be easy.

"Dr Harper. You made it back safely." The PM, Mark Jones, broke the silence.

"Yes, I did. Despite some futile attempts to stop me."

"I received your letter and watched your interview on TV.

Very impressive. I must confess that I didn't really believe the letter until I saw you on the news and had a report from the police."

"I am always very serious when it involves the wellbeing of my citizens."

"I understand. It's their wellbeing I'm concerned for, as well."

"Did the police report you were given have much detail concerning the recent arrest attempt?" Sherdan asked.

"No, it was only meant to give me an overview."

"I would highly recommend you make sure you have the full report of that before you make any decisions about me and the other people here."

"Why don't you tell me yourself?"

"I'm afraid that would take too long."

"Well, I would like to request that you stop this fight for independence and allow me to consult with your residents on what they really wish for."

"I won't stop. If it helps ease your mind, I can forward the document I have signed by every one of my citizens as I offered to do in my letter?"

"Forgive me if I don't take your word for it. I have the British army surrounding the area you have blocked off. I again suggest that you stop this fight for independence and allow me to consult with your residents. I will request the army assist me if necessary."

"Before you do, I strongly suggest you dig deeper into what happened with the failed police raid. I'm very determined, and force will not dissuade me."

"Dr Harper, I'm warning you."

"I can forward some of the camera footage if you wish? In fact, to prevent you risking the lives of all those troops, I think it best to do so. I have your personal email address." Sherdan began tapping away at the computer in front of him.

"How on earth do you have that?"

"That's not important. I've sent you some of our footage of the police raid. I'd also like to add that, as a country, I will consider it an act of war if you send troops into my land."

There was silence for a while. The prime minister was obviously watching the video.

"Thank you for sending this over, Dr Harper. I will continue this conversation with you tomorrow, if that's convenient?"

"Of course. It's always convenient for me to help the world see Utopia as a new, valid country." There was only a click in reply to this final statement. For now there would be a stalemate, but Sherdan had the upper hand. The Prime Minister hadn't even been properly informed. Knowing your enemy was one of the first rules of warfare, and so far everyone kept underestimating Sherdan. They were making it easy on him.

There was an excited buzz in the command bunker after the phone call. They had only heard Sherdan's side of the conversation, but it had been enough for them to work out that Mr Jones hadn't got what he wanted.

They all waited for another ten minutes, watching the perimeter cameras to see if the army did anything. They didn't.

"Sherdan, we've just had a message from one of the Conservative MPs," Graham called across the room. "Mark Jones has called an emergency cabinet meeting."

"Good, tell me the second they decide on something. Send the MP some money." Sherdan tapped away on the computer some more, scrolling through a few more cameras. He didn't think anything else would happen that evening and called for silence in the room before pressing the intercom button for every house in Utopia.

"Thank you for your patience in this trying time. We now feel that it is safe for you all to move as you wish again. We would recommend caution, but I have spoken to Mark Jones concerning the presence of his army and for now he is assessing things. We'll know more tomorrow. We do not expect to be attacked or raided at this time. Thank you again for your patience."

There was applause from the room as he turned the intercom back off. He gave out a few last instructions on when and why to disturb him through the night and handed the reigns back to his security commander.

CHAPTER 21

The moment Sherdan had left her, Anya stepped to the other side of the bed and activated her power. Her clothes dropped to the floor, out of view of the door so at a glance they wouldn't be noticed. She contemplated going into the control room after him but realised that now was also a good opportunity to check over her test results for herself.

She walked through the door and went towards the lab. She only got lost and had to backtrack a few times, before she found Hitchin's lab.

On the way, she moved out of the path of people whenever they came towards her. Not only did she not like the feeling of walking through something, but she wasn't sure if other people would feel her moving through them as well.

Annoyingly, Hitchin was in his lab when she got there. He had several machines going and Anya assumed that he was making more enzyme. She went over to his computer. The monitor faced away from the area Hitchin worked in and with all the noise from the machines any sound of her keystrokes would be covered.

She nudged the mouse, getting rid of the automatic screen-saver. Hitchin's login bar came up. His user name was saved and already there. She frowned. Passwords had never been her strong point.

Her first try was 'password' but expectedly it told her she had only two tries left. Her second attempt was 'Steven'. Sherdan had told her it was Hitchin's middle name, although Hitchin often told people he didn't have one because he thought it common and boring.

Anya hesitated over her third try. It was her final attempt before the computer locked her out of the system for a while. Throwing caution to the wind she typed in 'Sherdan' and hit enter.

'Access Denied' flashed up on the screen for a third time. Rather than disappearing as it had the previous times, it stayed with a five minute timer. It had already counted down a few seconds.

Not wanting to sit and wait until it finished, she wandered around the room. It didn't take long for her to be drawn to the whirring machines. There were hundreds of test tubes full of a pale pink liquid. On each one she saw a little label with 'ENZ351' on it.

Suddenly the password clicked in Anya's head and she rushed back to the computer. Hitchin still sat undisturbed at the other side of the room, absorbed in checking things with his microscope. The timer had over a minute left on it, but watching it count down made it feel even longer.

She tried really hard not to tap her fingers or breathe too loudly while she waited. The last thing she needed was for her impatience to disturb Hitchin.

Eventually, the computer allowed her back to the login screen. With her breath held she typed in the enzyme's code. She smiled as the computer desktop appeared before her eyes.

For a moment she stared at it. She had a Mac, like a lot of the creative people she knew, and hadn't used a computer with Windows on it for many years. She pressed the start button and typed 'results' into the search bar. Lots of files came up so she tried 'Anya'. Finally, only her folder came up. She opened it and looked at the contents.

There was one document file, three scanned pages, and a picture. She started with the three scans. All of them were paper documents of medical reports.

The first seemed to be the blood test she'd had. It listed what she'd had tested and the unexpected results. Most of it was codes and things she didn't understand, but at the bottom were a few notes about the presence of a different enzyme.

She raised her eyebrows when she read that it had faded out of her blood samples. She soon flicked to the next report. It was the same template and most of the numbers, codes and ticked boxes were the same.

Her eyes scanned through the notes on the bottom. They were almost identical to the first, expressing surprise at the enzyme disappearing so quickly.

The final scanned document was a request for more tests. There were several ticked to be done but none of them had ticks in the completed boxes. At the bottom were two words, 'Patient refused'. She smiled.

All the while she had flicked through the files she had forgotten about Hitchin. He coughed, making her jump. She knocked the mouse and it clunked against the keyboard. He turned towards her and for a brief second she panicked that she might be visible again. Thankfully he soon went back to his work.

Being more careful, she closed the scanned reports and previewed the picture. It was an enlarged image of a sample of her blood. The enzyme had been circled but it wasn't something that interested her. Neither was the final document; it reiterated what Hitchin had put in the notes of the blood test but no more.

For a while Anya was angry at finding Sherdan had lied to her about the first blood test. Both of them had obviously worked. She really didn't like how manipulative he could be when he wanted something.

He really made it difficult to know what to think. The friendship between them, if it could be called that, was so volatile she felt confused most of the time. He evidently wanted to keep her safe but she suspected it was only because of his own plans for her. Plans she had no intention of honouring unless God approved them.

She didn't know what to do next. Anya had found what she'd come for but didn't feel like leaving yet, so she moved the mouse back to the start button and clicked. She browsed what was there, including the recent documents. The five she'd just opened were in the list, as well as some test results for other people.

One entry just had Hitchin's name as the title. She hesitated before clicking on it. The document popped up to reveal his diary. She had to put her hand over her mouth to stifle a gasp.

Anya closed it again, her conscience wouldn't allow her to read it. The temptation to see if she were mentioned was strong. She had wanted to know what the vision concerning her had been for ages.

She jumped when Sherdan's voice came through the intercom thanking everyone for their patience. It dawned on her that if they were all safe now Sherdan might be able to go back to the room she'd been left in.

Anya sprinted back out of the lab through the closed door and towards the safe room. She needed to get back and put her clothes on before he walked into the room, or he'd know she had been sneaking about. There was no time to be careful about other people. She ran through them all without looking back.

When she reached the room, she realised she could have just run through walls in a straight line rather than along the intricate maze of hallways. She mentally slapped herself as she pulled her underwear on.

Her jeans were awkward to get on when she couldn't see her own hands and legs so she had to completely deactivate her power. She prayed no one would come in until she was decent again.

She'd just yanked her top down over her stomach when she saw the door handle turn. She sat on the bed and looked towards the door as it was opened as if she'd been there for ages and the sound had disturbed her.

Sherdan walked in and smiled at her.

"For now, we are safe. Are you tired?" he asked when he noticed she was sat on the bed.

"A little. Is it all right to return to the house now?" He nodded. She got up and waited for him to open their secret exit. Before he could, they were disturbed by Hitchin. He seemed surprised to see Anya there and hesitated over what he'd been intending to say. Sherdan waited.

"Sherdan, I was wondering if you have time to see the latest test batch? We think another has developed a new talent but we are unsure exactly what it does."

"I'll come tomorrow morning. Keep them in the ward."

"As you wish." Hitchin's eyes flicked to her before he left. Anya smiled when she realised he had been turned down in preference for her. By the look on his face, it wasn't normal for Sherdan to say no.

When they were back at the house she suggested movies and hot chocolates. She didn't really expect a yes. He'd been working a lot lately and would probably need to work some more. To her surprise, he not only said yes, but let her choose the film. He really had turned Hitchin down just to be with her.

She queried why he hadn't done what Hitchin had wanted once their film was finished. For the first time ever he didn't seem to want to answer.

"I've been working very hard lately and I may be very busy in the future. I thought you'd appreciate the company."

"I do, thank you. What do you think will happen next?"

"At this point, one of two things. We'll get what we want and be recognised by other countries and the UN, or England will try and invade and claim our area back."

"Won't that put a lot of lives in danger?"

"With our defences, hopefully not."

"You mean to resist then?"

"Of course. Where would be the sense in going this far if we didn't resist being reclaimed?"

Anya didn't know what to say.

She didn't approve of his plan at all, but she could understand why some did. For a long time many people had been fed up with the choices politicians gave them. He had presented people with another, alternative, option. It was something different, even if no one knew exactly what yet.

She only wished they'd see God could provide what they wanted. God was the 'different' they were searching for. The Western church left a lot to be desired, however, when it came to God, and their traditional and often boring way of making being a Christian appear. It made her feel equally as sad that churches in the West often attacked each other for their differences as well. She'd never understand why people couldn't be nicer to each other.

Sherdan was hope to people and, for the first time since she got there, she was seriously considering doing what she could to help him. She really didn't like how he went about his goals, however. The blood tests were a perfect example.

If she did decide to support him, she knew not to admit it to him. He'd read too much into it and think they could get married, or something similar. Thankfully, he'd not mentioned that lately. It worried her that he might do something drastic if she kept resisting him.

CHAPTER 22

Sherdan set his alarm an hour earlier the following morning and asked for an update on the emergency cabinet meeting less than five minutes after opening his eyes. They'd adjourned the meeting very late in the night, to continue the following morning. He ate breakfast while getting ready to leave, and woke Anya to tell her he was going.

"Already?" she asked through blurry eyes.

"Yes. Keep a radio with you at all times. I don't know what might happen today." She nodded and laid her head back down on her pillow.

He went straight to the command centre. The night team were still there and they looked tired but relaxed. There wasn't anything new to report. Mark Jones was still inside the cabinet meeting, and they hadn't stirred for a few hours.

"Have our request for recognition sent to the relevant official at the UN," Sherdan ordered as the first call of duty. If he could get the UN involved quickly, it would increase his chances of getting England to accept what he'd done. As soon as the first task was completed he phoned the government in Ireland.

"The Prime Minister, please."

"Who's calling?"

"Dr Sherdan Harper, Prime Minister of the newly formed country, Utopia."

"One moment please," the woman informed him. He had to wait almost half an hour before the Irish prime minister took his call.

"Dr Harper, this is quite a surprise."

"I wished to personally inform you and your country that, despite our relatively exclusive view to how we operate, we're open to diplomatic relations with the Republic of Ireland."

"That's a nice gesture, so it is. Am I right in understanding your country is the one that's claiming independence from the UK?"

"Yes, we're a small country currently. My residents and I are very determined to be recognised as such."

"I understand. I'll have to talk to my ministers here. We'll be in touch."

Sherdan thanked the man and said goodbye.

He spent the rest of the morning contacting the governments in as many different European countries as he could. Very few of the secretaries would actually let him through to their leaders. One or two didn't even know who he was. He tried to explain and get them to believe he wasn't a prank caller.

By the time Sherdan stopped for lunch he felt exhausted, so he went to his private room to take a break for a few minutes. It jogged his memory about Hitchin asking for him the night before. He'd put it off for as long as he could, but would have to tell Hitchin his ability had gone.

With a sigh, he trooped through the building on his way to the lab. Everyone stayed out of his way. He had a permanent frown fixed to his face. Hitchin noticed it too and put down the folder he carried as soon as he saw Sherdan. Neither of them spoke for some time. Hitchin knew to wait when Sherdan looked like this, and Sherdan still didn't have the words to say what he wanted.

"I think my abilities are gone. They've not worked since Anya arrived... At least, I don't think they've worked since then," he finally got out. Hitchin frowned.

"That's not possible."

"It shouldn't be."

"Let's do some tests to be sure."

"I don't have time for many."

"We'll start with the faster ones, then." Hitchin guided him over to the other side of the lab. They started with the simplest of tests, and Hitchin took three samples of Sherdan's blood. He put the pots aside and labelled them so he could identify them later, then led Sherdan towards the MRI lab to check he still had increased activity in the correct areas of his brain.

Before they reached the room, Sherdan's radio called for his attention.

"What is it?"

"The Prime Minister called for you again."

"Okay, keep him on the phone. I'll be right there." Sherdan left Hitchin without even saying goodbye. He went back to the command centre as fast as he could.

"Good afternoon, Prime Minister."

"Dr Harper."

"How did your emergency cabinet meeting go?"

"You seem to know a lot about my doings."

"I like to be informed."

"Well then, you'll appreciate me telling you that, unless you open up your barriers and give up your attempt to form a country, we will send in the army to do so for you."

"Did you not see what happened to the police?"

"We don't think you'll endanger the people there with you and, if you do, you will prove that you don't have their best interests at heart." Sherdan couldn't help but laugh when he heard this.

"You really believe you've got me backed into a corner? Well, good luck to you. I will not be opening up my barriers." Sherdan hung up.

Graham already had his radio in his hand, informing the guards of the expected attack. Once he was done, he also told the residents, while Sherdan contacted Anya. She seemed reluctant to leave his house even when he stressed the danger she was in.

As he talked to her on her way over, he watched the screens. The army were no longer sitting around with nothing to do. Ranks were forming and vehicles were being started up.

Graham scanned the radar for signs of the military in the air. RAF Lyneham wasn't far away, and was the number one site for establishing temporary bases. They also had a lot of planes at Lyneham and Brise Norton. He soon saw the blips on the radar that indicated planes on a flyover trajectory, probably with the intention of dropping troops. He informed Sherdan straight away.

Everyone in the security team was alerted and prepared. They'd increased the number of security guards over the last few days. There were over a hundred in total now, and all had been put through very thorough training.

As they were being deployed, Anya arrived at the command facility. She'd brought a book with her and curled up on the bed. Sherdan promised to check in on her regularly but she didn't appear to want to talk. He soon left her to go back to watching the TV screens.

Each guard carried the same shield device as they'd used when the police had shown up. There was also a shield attached to each residential shelter, the command room, and one large one that encompassed the whole country and shielded the country from outside forces.

No bullets or weaponry could penetrate from outside. Only the weaponry each soldier brought in with them could cause any damage. Not even grenades could harm people.

Sherdan watched on the cameras as the soldiers tried to advance through the barriers. The guards didn't even acknowledge them as they walked into the barrier, went dizzy and retreated. A few tried to push on, having been trained to keep going and obey orders. They soon lost control of their bodies and had to be pulled out by their comrades.

Shortly after, the first few troops parachuted into the country. The guards watched them approach long before they landed, and snuck in groups to surround the expected landing points. The soldiers rose to their feet to find many guns aimed at them already.

Each soldier was moved to one of the various safe houses to be imprisoned and the guards went straight back to work on finding more. Less than a third of all paratroopers made it past this initial net. Still, none of the troops had got in from the streets.

Sherdan sat in the command room with a very large grin on his face. Graham issued instructions behind him as he watched and waited. His pulse felt a little elevated, but his worry was not apparent to anyone else.

The guards were fed information from the command room to help them go after the remaining soldiers still loose. Four of them had managed to group together and there were another twelve scattered in different areas in ones or twos. All of them moved in the direction of Sherdan's house. It almost made him laugh out loud.

Despite their tactics being flawed, they were wiser than the police officers from two days earlier. Sherdan noticed they moved faster and more confidently than the police had. They also regularly checked behind themselves, making it difficult for the guards to sneak up on them.

Ten minutes later only two of the sixteen soldiers had been stopped in their tracks and escorted out of the way. The four moving down the high street were the ones of most concern, especially when they were joined by another two soldiers the guards hadn't circled in time. If the group got too big there would be the risk of gunfire and related problems.

The smile on Sherdan's face disappeared and he sat up a little more, his eyes never moving from the far wall, while he listened to the orders being given around him. Very occasionally he spoke out and gave a command of his own.

Thankfully, the second the soldiers spotted a guard up ahead they stopped. A large group of experienced security members then closed in on them, ignoring the warning shots and yells they were given. All six soldiers moved to the best defensible position nearby, a civilian house.

The guards rushed over as fast as they could, but all six made it inside before they could be stopped. Again, the soldiers fired warning shots.

"Move inside," Sherdan said into the radio in his hand. It would not be good if the troops found the shelter for the house and the people hiding inside.

Five men rushed around the back of the house as another seven went in the front door. Gunfire erupted. Nothing could be seen on the cameras, only the sounds could be heard over the radio of one of the guards.

Almost ten minutes later the guards emerged, escorting the six officers; with their hands tied and weaponry confiscated. Sherdan was gaining a very large weapons cache at a very low cost.

"The family weren't even found. We've checked on them. They're all just fine; alarmed by the gunshots but otherwise nothing wrong," one of the guards informed Sherdan.

"Well done. Keep up the good work, all of you." Sherdan beamed. No one harmed and only eight soldiers left to detain. As this very thought ran though his head another soldier was surrounded by six guards and restrained. Only seven of the initial sixty to go.

The guards knew what they were doing and were well practised. Even when bullets came flying towards them they did not flinch. Sherdan had never seen a more decisive and bloodless battle between two armies. Despite all the weapon fire, no one had been hurt.

He continued to watch as the last soldiers were rounded up and put with the rest. The security team made it look effortless. As soon as they were done they waited for further instructions. Sherdan had them stay on duty until the rest of the soldiers outside gave up trying to get in.

All the while the command room had been focusing on the air-dropped squads, there had been activity on the edges of the country.

Several units had decided to try driving in and had fired up the tanks. They drove forward to a certain point and the tanks slowed to a stop. They still revved, but went nowhere. The soldiers couldn't even get them to reverse out of whatever they were stuck in. Before long, all of them were abandoned and the soldiers went back to their waiting.

A few minutes after that the whole area was back to the way it had been before. Except for the moved tanks, everything was just the way it had been before the attack.

CHAPTER 23

Sherdan picked up the phone and tapped in Mark Jones' number. He went through the same hassle of having to get approval from the first voice on the phone before he could get through to the Prime Minister himself.

"Dr Harper! Have you phoned to surrender?"

"Quite the opposite, to negotiate on the release of the sixty British soldiers I have in my prison cells. I'm intending to keep the tanks, however. Also, I'm considering the attempted attack as an act of war."

"Excuse me?"

"Shall I phone back in a few hours when your army has bothered to inform you of their failed attempt? It really was rather pathetic. I did–"

"That won't be necessary, Dr Harper. This country does not negotiate with terrorists and that is exactly what you've become." The Prime Minister hung up on him.

"Have our prisoners spread out between our safe houses, and fetch those tanks," Sherdan ordered. The tanks would be moved to face outwards at the same exits they were currently stuck in.

The soldiers watched helplessly as three guards walked out towards each tank. The two on each edge walked forwards, emitters in the rucksacks on their backs. The middle man got into the tank and drove it into Utopia, turned it around and aimed it at the very troops who had been using it only hours before. This was repeated at every main entrance.

As each vehicle was put into position a small cheer went up in the command room and the atmosphere improved. People smiled, sat back down and relaxed after all the standing and rushing around.

Less than three hours after the first soldier had tried to enter Utopia, the battle was over and the victor was clear. The British army was four tanks and sixty guns down, and Sherdan had gained it all with no injuries and no extra cost.

When it looked like there would be no follow-up attack, Sherdan had the residents informed and went back to Anya. She had stayed, her legs tucked up under her, reading the entire time, but she looked pleased to see him.

"Is it over?"

"For now. It may start again at any point. The Prime Minister wasn't interested in backing down just now."

"How bad was the first attack?" The look of concern on Anya's face shocked him. She cared more than he expected.

"Not bad at all. Most of the strike force couldn't make it in and the few that sky dived were quickly rounded up and locked in separate cells. No one was hurt. They could try much worse and we would win easily."

"Well, I hope that's the last. Putting people's lives in danger, no matter how low the risk, is wrong." Sherdan didn't bother responding. He felt worn out by the day and didn't want an argument.

The afternoon had managed to push all thoughts of his tests with Hitchin out of his mind and he had arrived back at the house with Anya before he remembered that he needed to go back to the lab. He sent Hitchin an email to let him know they'd try again the following day. He'd explain why when they met.

Anya didn't say much their entire evening together. Sherdan sat with her, but soon found himself drifting towards work. The UN had replied to his application for recognition as a country and were requesting even more information. They also had recommendations to speed the decision and help it in his favour.

Most of the suggestions were obvious things like contacting

officials in nearby countries and displaying openness to discussion and diplomatic relations. Laws also needed to be in place and all sorts of diplomatic positions needed filling.

They thought his population was a little low, but Sherdan had plans to increase that. Many of the previous applicants had contacted them in some way, requesting to be considered for citizenship as well as the training program. Everyone that had was moved to the top of the waiting list.

Several news reporters had also requested to enter the country and do pieces on his progress. Sherdan would use these opportunities wisely, and scheduled in a satellite link-up with a news studio for noon the following day.

The rest had all received written statements in reply to their requests. He definitely did not have time to be interviewed by all of them, but hoped they would at least think him cooperative.

He also wanted the British people to hear what their government were doing in the people's name. He didn't think all of them would be happy with the attack, and he intended to stir as many of them up about it as he could.

His two MPs in each of the three major political parties had fed him the reaction to today's discussion in the House of Lords. There had been an outrage that troops had been moved in so soon, especially as videos of the police raid had been leaked and all the MPs had seen how ineffective they had been.

Sherdan watched the late news, knowing most of the focus would be the raids on Utopia. The reporter went through all of the other reports about the rest of the world in the first ten minutes of the show.

The police raid was the first focus on Utopia. The leaked footage was aired. Sherdan laughed when he realised it was all the camera feeds he'd sent to Mark Jones. Someone must have got hold of it after that.

Anya joined him to watch, noticing what the videos were of. She exclaimed out loud when the police fired on a guard and all the bullets fell to the ground. He delighted in the look on her face. He intended to explain, but the news reporter reappeared and continued his piece on Sherdan, informing anyone who didn't know about the recent claim for independence.

They followed everything up with footage from outside the barriers that day, showing all the soldiers' failed attempts to get in and, finally, a clip with the tanks being taken and turned on their own army.

"If the government had seen the leaked footage of the earlier police raid, which is now all over the internet, it comes as a surprise that they tried such measures with the army." There was a brief pause as the reporter waited for this to sink in with the audience.

"There's been no confirmation that our government has tried to negotiate with Dr Harper on his stance, or to find out what the residents living inside the new country want."

Sherdan beamed. The news reporter had not only referred to the area as a country but obviously didn't approve of the guns-blazing approach Mark Jones had taken. He had been brave enough to say so on air, which would enforce the public's ability to say what they really thought.

Anya still looked shocked. She'd not known about any of the technology Sherdan had to defend the country and people with.

"You're practically unstoppable."

"With enough numbers, we would be stopped. As a country, we are very small. The mayor caused me a lot of problems and forced me to declare independence sooner than I'd originally planned."

"Is it all the abilities that make the technology possible?"

"Yes, it's how all of this has been possible." Anya stared off into space, her eyes still wide. "Now do you see why so few lives are in danger?"

She nodded absentmindedly. It was clear she hadn't fully absorbed everything she'd learned.

"I wish to create Utopia here on earth. A new Eden. You can be my Queen. You only have to say yes," he offered, realising how much he wanted it as well. She looked at him, her eyes sad. He took her hand.

"Oh Sherdan, if only it were that simple."

"Do you not see that it's inevitable?"

"No, I don't." She pulled her hand back out of his. "You're

powerful, yes, but don't underestimate the feelings of other people. Don't underestimate their desire to be different and greedy either."

"Anyone who doesn't join us will eventually perish."

"So you will kill all those who oppose you?"

"I won't let anyone stop me."

"Careful, Sherdan, people will get hurt. And one day it will be someone you care about."

Anya kissed him on the cheek again and said goodnight. She had not mentioned her God but he knew she'd been thinking of Him. He hadn't got cross with her this time, however. It made him feel sad more than anything else. He wanted her, of all people, to understand him.

Sherdan went back to his work. He didn't want to sleep yet, and a very interesting email had come through. Someone unknown was offering him a very large sum of money for the shield devices each guard wore.

He spent the next hour trying to figure out where the email had come from, not that he had any intention of ever sharing the technology. It seemed to be Russia, but he wouldn't be surprised if they were only trying to make it appear as if it had come from there.

Sherdan replied, politely saying no. His technology was the biggest advantage they had. He needed that advantage.

At three in the morning, Sherdan went to bed. He checked on Anya on the way. She slept soundly, looking every bit an angel in the moonlight from the window. It took a long time to tear himself away from her to go to his own room.

CHAPTER 24

"Sherdan, are you there, sir?" the radio squawked, breaking through Sherdan's dreamless sleep. At first he couldn't place what had disturbed him. "Sherdan, sir, please respond." He grabbed the radio.

"I'm here. What is it?"

"We're being attacked, sir. You're needed in the command bunker." He was out of bed before the sentence had been finished.

"On my way."

He hurriedly yanked his clothes on and ran into Anya's room, noticing that it was still dark outside. Even though he wanted to leave her in her peaceful sleep, he shook her awake. As soon as she saw the concern on his face, she sat up.

"We've got to go."

She grabbed the dressing gown he handed her and got out of bed. His eyes went straight to her bare legs but she didn't notice.

"Is it another attack?" She looked at him expectantly. He nodded while she stuffed her feet into her slippers and followed him.

"The residents have all been informed, sir," the radio came to life again.

"Have it announced several times. Many will be sleeping deeply," Sherdan fired back to the command room. He took

Anya's hand as they rushed down into the house and toward the secret passage.

She yawned as she hurried along beside him. It wasn't even six yet. Sherdan had a headache from such little sleep but he felt wide awake. The adrenaline had got rid of the dozy feeling he'd had when he first woke up. By the time they were in the compound, the same had happened to Anya.

She tried to follow him into the command room but he pushed her back and shook his head. He didn't have time to explain to her why.

The cameras were a haze of coloured thermal scanning images. One of the assistants was doing a third intercom announcement while Graham, not even fully dressed, was already passing orders to the security team.

More transport planes had flown over, dropping almost one hundred soldiers. That had been a quarter of an hour ago.

As they had done the first time, the guards were rounding up as many soldiers as they could as each one landed, but they didn't even catch a third this way. Sherdan's men rushed around as best as they could, but in the dark, with very limited help from the command room, they struggled to see the soldiers.

To make it harder, the troops didn't all head towards the same destination as they had done before. Instead, they all went towards six separate, easily defensible locations, meaning the groups of soldiers got larger more rapidly.

Half an hour later, only ten more soldiers had been stopped and taken to one of the five prison areas. Sherdan couldn't help but get angry at the circles the soldiers ran around the guards. He banged his fists down on the desk in front of him a few times.

He knew he had to change strategy.

"Nathan, have the prison buildings go down to only eight guards each. Lead the rest to help capture the enemy," Sherdan said into the radio. Having eight in each would be enough to defend against the biggest soldier groups so far.

"Done, sir," Nathan replied a few moments later.

"Thank you. Send each new squad of guards to the nearest house the soldiers are trying to get to. I want you to take your team towards my house. There's eight closing in on it, and only the two men inside currently."

"Is Anya there, sir?"

"No, she's safe here with me, but I would still prefer my house to remain untouched."

"I understand, sir. On my way."

The soldiers took their time travelling to Sherdan's house, as they were more cautious in the dark. They were only just at the front lawn when the first few guards came to join the security already inside.

"We're there, sir. Should be enough of us to keep your house safe now."

"Thank you, Nathan." Sherdan sighed with relief. He had not been sure it was his own men coming up to the house from behind.

They needed a better way of telling their own guards apart from the soldiers on the night time thermal cameras. At the moment the command room had to check it wasn't guards they were looking at before telling them where to go. Twice now they had surrounded their own men. Sherdan almost threw the microphone when it happened a third time.

The soldiers near Sherdan's house began shooting the second they saw the security coming out the door towards them. They had soon emptied their ammo clips.

"They are all drawing knives and other close-combat weapons. Please advise, command." Nathan said, shortly after.

"Keep your distance. Another squad is closing in from behind. They will surrender soon." Sherdan replied. He didn't want anyone to be hurt, unless absolutely necessary.

What Anya had told him the night before came back to him, making him frown. If she ended up being right, their relationship would go backwards again.

"If they move to attack, shoot for the legs rather than allow yourselves to get hurt," he added. It was the first time he'd ever told them retaliating was allowed. He hoped no one lost their heads.

"Only if there's no alternative."

Thankfully, the eight enemy combatants soon realised that

knives wouldn't help them against the thirty-plus team of guards that were hemming them onto the lawn of the house. They surrendered.

Nathan and the rest of the squads moved in to slap wrist bindings on each of them but one soldier hadn't finished putting his knife down. He lunged out at the nearest guard, Nathan. A responding fist soon knocked the idiotic man to the ground.

After swearing, Nathan apologised. He only had a scratch down his right arm but he immediately got ordered off operational duty to report to the medical section. The captured men were taken to the nearest prison, along with three more stragglers the guards picked off along the way.

As it got a little brighter, the guards headed for the next target: nine soldiers in a civilian house not too far from Sherdan's.

The house had a small group of young adults locked in an outside shelter. They'd radioed in to say the soldiers had not realised they were there, but Sherdan didn't want to give the invaders the chance.

The guards ran over under cover until they were only a few metres away. Forty of them stormed the house, again to weapon fire from the soldiers. Sherdan was listening to this happening on the radio when Graham called to him.

"Sir, there are more planes on the radar coming our way. Lyneham again."

"They'll drop more." Sherdan frowned. If they dropped another eighty soldiers his security would be outnumbered. He grabbed the microphone for the country-wide intercom.

"The UK government is trying to overwhelm us with numbers. Any man between the age of twenty-one and fifty who wishes to help defend please safely make your way to the nearest prison facility. Do not come alone and do not engage any enemies."

All the people just rescued instantly requested to help. At the guard houses they were fitted with shield devices and given easy to use hand guns, loaded with sleep darts. Each one was then partnered with one of the trained guards. Hopefully it would give the illusion that they were trained security but they wouldn't need to do anything.

Sherdan made a mental note to accept more military-type applicants and get more security trained. This was only the second attack of who knew how many, and they already ran the risk of being overwhelmed.

As soon as the guards had captured the soldiers within the house, Sherdan had them scatter and look out for new paratroopers. The growing light would aid them.

While the guards dealt with the new soldiers as best as they could, the residents who wished to join all slipped over to the nearest security hub. With the soldiers already on the land in centred pockets and the rest still in the air, the citizens all managed to move without meeting any resistance.

Just in case, Sherdan had two of his command team focus on watching the residents on the cameras to help keep them safe. The last thing he needed was his citizens getting hurt.

Sherdan was surprised at the number of people who responded. Over three hundred turned up at the five security buildings; there weren't enough personal shields to go around. Everyone that could be protected was sent out. The remaining fifty eight stayed at the secure centres to help lock up all the incoming prisoners.

With all the extra man power, as well as the new light of day, the task soon got easier. As with the first attack several days ago, the soldiers were captured in ones and twos and locked away.

By eight there were almost two hundred soldiers being held. There were still another forty-three loose in four separate locations. Sherdan had the men split into two and pick off two more of the groups.

One group of eleven were taken without a fuss. They hardly even used their weapons, as it was soon apparent doing so wouldn't work. The second group proved more stubborn.

They were holed up in one of the civilian homes, and the young child in the cellar had cried and alerted the soldiers that there were people under the house. The soldiers started prising the door open. The family radioed it in and the guards all raced into the building.

Sherdan gritted his teeth as he stared at the three cameras focused on the outsides of the house.

The family were safe; a little panicked, but safe. It had been close; too close in Sherdan's mind. He had the guards head straight for the other two buildings occupied by soldiers, even though another set of planes had appeared on the radar.

Sherdan noticed the soldiers with dogs on the edges of the country didn't even bother trying to get in. They were waiting for the people inside to let them through, once they'd secured locations in Utopia. They would have a long wait.

As the planes flew overhead and dropped the third and largest load of troops, Sherdan had the guards clear the shelters in all the homes that had been rally points so far. The last two sets of soldiers had all tried to go to the same six fixed places. He figured the third would do the same.

He smiled when the guards managed to re-secure the final location and take the owners to the nearest safe shelter. Hopefully it would ensure they remained unharmed. At the least, it would give them some company during the attack.

As before, the security spread out across the whole country, following soldiers in the sky to capture them as they landed. This third wave was even bigger than the first two had been, but the extra help still meant half the soldiers were captured and neutralised before they could really move.

They parachuted down and were surrounded before their feet had even hit the floor, often being pinned inside their own chutes.

Sherdan then had the guards move straight to the nearest of each of the six suspected destinations and wait inside to capture soldiers.

The command room finally calmed again and people sat back down instead of rushing between desks and monitors, including Sherdan. The soldiers were followed on the camera as they walked into buildings full of guards who had their guns aimed and hand ties ready.

Rather than move, the soldiers were held inside as more paratroopers arrived. It was the most effective strategy yet. Less than fifty minutes had passed until the additional enemy combatants were safely locked up.

Congratulations were echoed everywhere, and a buzz of excitement spread as it approached nine. Sherdan even took a moment to check on Anya, who had got into the bed and looked fast asleep.

Despite there being no more immediate danger, he didn't allow any of the guards to stand down yet. Each wave of fresh soldiers had been just over an hour after the previous, and there were still a few more minutes to go before a fourth group could appear.

He watched over the radar himself this time, eager to see if the RAF sent any more. The rest of his command team milled around and took a break, passing croissants and cups of orange juice around to anyone who wanted them.

Several minutes passed. Sherdan was about to order everyone back to their normal tasks when dots appeared on the radar again. Everyone sprang to life; the guards watched for parachutes and the commanders manned their stations.

They waited for the next assault, but it didn't come. The planes flew over a few times, each pass a little lower than the one before, but no soldiers emerged. Less than ten minutes later Sherdan was watching the dots on the radar turn back the way they had come.

It appeared this battle was over. With reasonable ease, they were yet again the victors. When everyone had patted each other on the back and praised the guards on the radio, Sherdan got back to the running of his country.

There were some changes he wanted to make: he wanted more personal shields as well as a much larger military division of his own. He had not liked being outnumbered, and how close the soldiers had come to discovering the civilians.

The ideal solution would be to stop the troops parachuting in, but until there was an ability that helped, short of putting emitters everywhere to hinder soldier movement ,there wasn't anything they could do.

Sherdan had everyone informed that the attack had finished and normal working life could begin. As soon as he was unneeded he went back to Anya, who had been woken by the public announcement.

She yawned and blinked a few times. Although she didn't say anything, it was evident from the look on her face that she was getting weary of the constant assaults. He hoped the residents didn't agree with her.

This time he didn't bother phoning the Prime Minister again. If the attacks were going to stop they would call him, and until then, Sherdan wouldn't release the soldiers with all the information they had gained, for them to pass it on to their superiors.

There was also the noon satellite broadcast to prepare for. What he said would make waves among the British public. He prepared some notes back in his study, then went through applications, checking for people suitable to go on security.

A new group of acceptance letters was sent out for a fresh set of residents to join them on Monday. They would all have to be secretly brought into the country, but that wouldn't be difficult. They had planned for the possibility.

Anya went to the living room to watch the TV whilst he turned the study into a mini broadcast centre and video link with the news. Ten minutes later the news started. Sherdan watched as they went through all the other pieces. They always left the most important report until last.

A lot of the footage from the night before was shown again and the reporter told everyone about the latest attack. Sherdan was introduced and his face was shown to the millions of people watching. As usual, he was thanked for his time.

"Please tell us what has been happening at your end during the attacks?"

"Not very much. The British military have tried to invade us twice now, simply because we've refused to recognise our land as part of the United Kingdom. Despite the attacks, no one has been seriously hurt on either side. All the soldiers that parachuted in are now in our prisons."

"So the attacks have been completely ineffective?"

"All they've done is fill our prison cells."

"What do you intend to do with those captured?"

"When the British authorities have stopped, and agreed to

accept Utopia as a country, we'll let them all go home."

"And if the attacks continue?"

"The soldiers will remain unharmed as prisoners of war. However, we don't like being at war. All we want to do is live our way. Our no-harm policy seems to be making people think we're weak. Therefore, every time we are assaulted, we'll expand our borders by ten square metres, taking more territory, for every soldier sent and weapon used."

"Won't that harm people?"

"Not physically, no. However, we will act in a way that shows we mean to be listened to and respected."

Sherdan wasn't able to say any more. The news reporter cut him off and the show ended. He'd said enough, however, and knew it would give people something to talk about.

He went back to the applications. The government would try to invade again, and Sherdan would extend the perimeter, taking another chunk of Bristol. Then the new citizens arriving would all have somewhere to live.

CHAPTER 25

Later that afternoon Anya disturbed Sherdan. She had been watching TV since before the broadcast. He put down his laptop and followed her. The Prime Minister was doing a speech outside number ten.

"Dr Sherdan Harper is nothing more than a terrorist." He paused to look up from his notes before looking back at the podium. "This country doesn't negotiate with terrorists. We will use the full force of the British army to re-open the closed-off area of Bristol and rescue the people this madman is calling his 'residents'."

The journalists in front of the podium shouted questions at him, but Mark Jones ignored them all. He went back inside his house and shut the door. The speech was short and to the point; there would be more attacks.

"The UN will put pressure on him not to attack once we're recognised. As will other countries," Sherdan told Anya. He wanted to reassure her.

"If Utopia is recognised." Anya sighed. She went back to her book. Sherdan sat and watched the news channel a little longer.

When he went back to his study he radioed the command bunker and told them to be prepared for another attack. The commander acknowledged the information but Sherdan noticed the weariness in his voice. After three attacks in four days, the people were tired and it would only get worse for the next few days.

He spent the rest of the evening preparing a speech for the residents. He only spoke to Anya when they ate. She didn't say much and had been subdued since the second assault. He knew he had given her a lot to think about.

There had also been a lot on Sherdan's mind so it didn't come as a surprise when, later that evening, his head throbbed with a large headache. He rubbed his temples. He also had to see Hitchin for more tests, but everything non-life-threatening would have to wait until after the expected attempts at invasion.

Anya came through to say goodnight as it passed midnight and the following day began, but she got no further. The country was under attack again. He took her hand, looking apologetically at her, and led her to the command bunker.

She stayed silent during the walk, reinforcing Sherdan's worry that something was wrong. He couldn't deal with it at the moment, however.

He was about to leave her in his private room at the command centre as a loud explosion sounded somewhere above them. She flinched and ducked, looking up as if she expected the ceiling to fall on her.

"It's okay, the force field will have detonated it outside and prevented anything from flying in at speed and causing damage," Sherdan reassured her. She didn't look convinced and just curled up back on the bed again, her eyes pointed upwards.

He frowned and rushed into the command bunker. The look he gave the people in there stopped everyone in their tracks. He wanted answers.

"Nothing has been damaged. The shield worked," the nearest worker said.

"Good. Keep track of what is being sent our way so we can expand our borders as required," Sherdan replied.

"Yes, sir!"

He nodded and went to his station. It took him a few seconds to focus. The reduced sleep and added pressure were taking their toll on him.

The explosions continued to be heard overhead and he could

not help thinking of the woman waiting for him in the nearby room. He hoped she could get some rest with all the noise and mayhem.

He watched the screens, although little could be seen on them. The darkness made it harder to organise their defences so they had to be extra careful. Thankfully, so far, there didn't seem to be any paratroopers.

The aircraft overhead quickly dropped bombs and flew back to their starting airfields. Other than a small amount of debris, the bombs had no effect on the country. Their shield kept everything safe and all the bombs detonated far above the tops of the homes.

By the early hours of the morning the air raid had stopped. Up rolled more tanks. The explosions flashed just outside the shields, and when the smoke cleared the only damage they could see was to the UK Army's own barriers.

The shields had not only blocked the incoming projectiles but deflected the blasts back towards the source. One tank which had driven up only a few metres from the barrier set itself alight with the first shot. Sherdan smiled as Graham and a few others laughed out loud.

When the attack finally ceased, he noticed spirits had lifted amongst his command team. They had watched for three hours as the UK Army had done nothing but waste money and make noise. No guards had been needed, and the only concern had been the debris building up on the ground.

Sherdan ordered everyone to get some rest and leave the clean-up for the morning. Residents would need to be careful in the meantime, but only to not trip over any of the bomb parts that had fallen through the shield after detonation. None of it could hurt anyone now.

He went to his private room to find Anya asleep, as he had expected. She looked very peaceful, on her side, her hands tucked up under the pillow her head rested on. He wasn't sure he had the heart to wake her. Instead, he poured a drink and sat down.

It still surprised him that she remained with him. She had the ability to leave, and would probably be a lot safer if she did.

She had also given him no indication she wanted to progress a relationship with him.

He sighed. He was unsure of his feelings for her and he didn't like it. Except for one or two occasions, he'd always had everything he wanted. There had been one student who had rejected him back in his earlier days at the university. Sandy had dated the astrophysics professor, Paul Carmichael. He had been older than Sherdan and not quite so well-groomed, but that evidently had not bothered her.

He just could not work Anya out, no matter how hard he tried. For the first time, he didn't even know if he wanted something, let alone if he would achieve it.

Sherdan didn't move when he had finished his drink. He continued to stare at the puzzling girl, tucked up in his bed. Slowly, he drifted off to sleep, thinking of Anya and Hitchin's prophecy.

He remained asleep in the chair until he felt a hand stroking his cheek softly.

"Sherdan," Anya whispered. He opened his eyes to look into hers. She smiled and stepped away. The bed was unmade, and she busied herself making it neat again.

"What time is it?" he asked.

"Gone nine. Hitchin turned up half an hour ago but said he'd email you. Why didn't you wake me?"

"I intended to. I fell asleep."

"What time did the attack stop?"

"Not until the army realised it was doing no damage at all." Sherdan smiled as Anya stopped what she was doing.

"They were bombing you. How was nothing blown up?"

"Our shields. They stopped anything but the debris getting through."

Anya's mouth fell open and she blinked a few times, completely lost for words.

"They can detect the velocity of projectiles trying to pass through them. The faster they travel the more it seems like a wall is in the way. The bombs they just dropped couldn't cope with the forces stopping them so they exploded on impact with it. Anything that remained then passed through the shields to fall on the ground," Sherdan explained.

"I don't understand. If it's based on speed, how are the soldiers who try to walk in stopped?"

"There are two parts to the shield system. The second part stops anyone who doesn't have the enzyme from being able to pass. You wouldn't be able to go through it even though you have an ability, as your enzyme is different."

"No one was hurt then?"

"No. No one from our country. I don't think any UK soldiers were hurt either."

"Your country."

Sherdan raised an eyebrow and blinked. It took him a moment to figure out what she meant. He nodded, stopping her from explaining. He didn't think he wanted her to tell him she didn't intend to stay and be his queen. They'd been around that circle already and he didn't want to say anything which might make her leave.

He opened the secret door for her to go back to his house but did not follow her. She'd distracted him enough from his job. His citizens needed him to focus on them and their needs.

The big tasks for the morning were cleaning up the streets and working out the process to expand their country borders in retaliation. Not only did they need to work out exactly how much they should expand by, but also where.

Sherdan didn't want to take territory he couldn't easily defend. He also didn't want to upset the British public too much. He'd be making many of them homeless and something like that would need to be done as delicately as possible.

He started with the clean-up process. Bomb remains were littered all over the area. The army had chucked a great deal of explosives at them. Ninety percent had been over the old university area, part of which housed their command centre, but there was hardly a street without some cleaning to do.

The guards were enlisted in the tidying. He wanted the residents to feel like everything was under control. They would have been scared by all the noise through the night, and the sooner their world returned to normal the better they would handle the immediate future.

Sherdan was pleased he had thought to write a short speech already. He quickly modified it to suit the aftermath of the last attack and pressed the intercom button.

He delivered a short, comforting message, reassuring the residents that he knew what he was doing and that they still stood strong and unharmed. He even got to mock Mark Jones a little for his incompetence.

When Sherdan was satisfied that his country was all tidy again he allowed his officers some room to breathe and retreated to his rest room. There, he finally checked his emails.

Hitchin had emailed, as Anya had informed him. The contents were no surprise; Hitchin wanted him to come in for more tests. Sherdan marked the email to reply to it later. It still had to wait.

He also had an email from Ellie's father. He hadn't travelled down to see his daughter, not believing it to be safe. Instead, he demanded his daughter be returned to him. Sherdan smiled to himself as he wrote his reply.

Every good reason not to allow Ellie to leave was now presentable. Not only was it unsafe for her to go but the British army were highly unlikely to let her. There was even the possibility they would take her in for questioning and she'd be in even more danger.

Sherdan didn't expect this to pacify the father at all, but he sent the message anyway. He spent the rest of the day working out what buildings he wished to take as part of the country.

He needed more space for all the people arriving on Monday. He had two days to find room for all of them. Only a small amount of housing remained free within the borders, as previous expansion had been done very slowly and covertly, using many different company names and representatives to hide that one person was taking over the whole area.

They also needed to be careful not to annoy too many British residents. At the moment they had support from the general population and he didn't want to lose it until they'd been officially recognised as a country. It would be a delicate operation and needed to be started as soon as possible.

Sherdan had already partially planned for this moment.

Many months earlier, he'd written a set of instructions to ensure the act of taking more territory went as smoothly as possible. Nathan had been asked to lead the operation to start with and had been briefed on the subject more than once. He had an enormous amount of patience and people warmed to him quickly, so Sherdan felt he was the perfect choice.

Although he would never admit it, Nathan was the closest thing he had to a friend after Hitchin, and he wondered if it might be because of the man's ability. He could hear a lot of Sherdan's thoughts and therefore knew him better than most other people got the chance to.

Once he'd finished poring over the map of the area and pinpointing where they were to expand, he took his suggestions to Graham. He wanted a second opinion about the defensibility of the area, as they had to use their shield emitters wisely.

It took another two hours to go over everything with his command team before Sherdan was happy with the preparations. They agreed to get started first thing the following morning and give everyone what would hopefully be another good night's sleep so they were fresh for the challenges the task might present.

Sherdan went back to his retreat to pack up and go home. He hesitated, noticing that the paperwork he'd left behind had moved. He frowned, not sure who could have been in the room.

He was just about to collect everything up when the door opened. A gust of air ruffled the documents on the table as Hitchin walked in.

"I know, I know. I need to come for more tests." Sherdan held his hands up.

"That's not why I'm here." Hitchin smiled. "I've had another successful batch of recruits. They're all alive and have developed powers. One in particular is very interesting. All animals come to her when called. They seem to understand her."

"All animals?"

Hitchin nodded and Sherdan finally gathered together all his loose paper. He had an extra spring to his step all the way back to his home.

Anya was in his study. She hardly acknowledged his presence but continued drawing in a note book.

He had no idea where she'd found either the pretty, flower-patterned sketch book or the box of sketching pencils which lay open beside her. He frowned but she didn't notice.

Sherdan sat down opposite her, but she still didn't say anything so he watched her draw. Her pencil flicked almost effortlessly across the paper in quick, gentle lines. He couldn't see what she was drawing.

"You left the compound?" he asked. She looked up, confused. "To get your art supplies."

"No. Nathan found these for me."

"Nathan?"

"Yes, your security guard. He noticed I was bored and, when I told him I was an artist, he had some materials fetched for me."

"You talked to my guards?"

"Of course. Both they and I are alone here all day. I talk to them frequently... Will you be here tomorrow? It's Sunday and I always miss company most on Sundays."

"I have things to do tomorrow. We are claiming new territory." Sherdan smiled as Anya looked at him again. She bit her lip.

"What are you going to do?"

"Take new territory. We were attacked," he explained.

"What about the people living there?"

"They'll have to move. It's an unfortunate consequence but it can't be helped."

Anya frowned again and went back to her drawing. Sherdan sighed. She didn't approve and, surprisingly, it bothered him. It seemed no matter how much time passed she didn't soften towards him and his plans.

Sherdan contemplated taking some more forceful measures, but everything he could think of would drive her to leave instead.

"Why are you still here?" he asked, breaking the silence again.

"I don't know. I don't really want to be, but I don't feel like I can leave yet."

"I cannot stop you. You can leave when you wish... Of course, I'd prefer you not to."

"It's not you stopping me." Anya smiled very briefly before resuming her picture. Sherdan couldn't get her to say much for the rest of the day. He gave up after dinner and returned to his work instead.

CHAPTER 26

Anya lay awake for many hours that night. She wasn't happy and had been having increasingly worse nightmares. She still felt afraid that Sherdan would revert back to being nasty again.

He often got angry when she expressed her disapproval and also grew frustrated at the way she kept him at arm's reach. Her feelings about him were still mixed up. He attracted her, that was for sure, but she didn't like his personality as much. He thought too much of himself and disregarded her opinion too readily. She wanted more respect from a potential life partner.

The last few days of attempted invasions and bombings only made her feel even less safe around Sherdan. She didn't understand the technology he had and imagined the compound being invaded at any point. It made her feel stuck between two powerful forces, and she couldn't decide who she wanted to win, if she wanted either to.

When everything was calm and Sherdan reminded her that he had originally forced her to stay, she hoped the British army would sweep in and save her. When the country was under attack, she prayed for Sherdan's defences to hold and for no one to get hurt.

She sat up in bed, tucking her knees up and wrapping her arms around herself. The room was so familiar to her now that she had begun to forget the details of her own house. She could generally picture it, but little items and particular things which made it her home had faded.

She closed her eyes to try to picture the bedroom better, but after a few minutes flashes of her torture came into her head instead. The constant flipping between two extremes was taking its toll on her emotionally. Combined with her nightmares, she felt more drained with each passing day. She also felt more tempted to let Sherdan have things his way. It might make her feel safer.

Anya blocked this thought from her head right away. It would do her no good to be his wife. Only God could ensure her safety and He only promised safety for her soul. Sherdan would only put her in more danger.

She got out of bed and went to her window, praying for God's peace as she had done the last five nights. Tears flowed down her cheeks. She didn't understand why God wanted her here. All she knew was that she had to endure it for as long as it was required of her, but that was no easy task.

When she finally felt tired enough to sleep she got back into bed. Within five minutes she had slipped into a dream...

She sat in the middle of an all too familiar room. She was, thankfully, unchained this time. As she got up Sherdan came in. His eyes blazed and she took a step back, catching her breath. It wasn't normally him but the guard instead.

Sherdan advanced on her and she backed up until she could go no farther. He pinned her up against the wall with his own body. She could feel his heart beat against her own. His significantly calmer than hers.

He didn't hurt her and she didn't struggle. Her eyes never left his as his expression softened. As time passed, her fear faded and still neither of them moved. Finally, he bent to kiss her but stopped as a noise came from outside.

The door slammed open against the wall and in rushed three men with swords drawn. They advanced towards her and Sherdan. She shrank back even further, thinking they had come for her. They hadn't. They marched towards Sherdan, who also backed up, afraid.

Anya didn't know what to do. She felt frozen to the spot and could only watch as each step brought the three men closer to Sherdan. Feeling pushed from behind, she rushed to the middle of the room and in front of him.

"This man is under my protection. Leave now," Anya felt her mouth say with a voice unlike her own. They laughed and continued, ignoring her and trying to walk past.

She thrust her right arm out sideways, catching the nearest soldier in the kidneys. As she swung her arm back she grabbed his sword hand and pulled back his fingers.

He dropped the weapon and it clanged onto the hard floor. Anya watched as her arm reached out to pick it up and she swung around, slicing the throat of the same man. Blood sprayed out as she moved to the next two. They hesitated. They hadn't believed her threat any more than she had.

She seemed to know exactly what to do and soon dispatched both of the soldiers to follow the first into the next life...

Anya woke up, breathing heavily. She had never had a dream like it. The idea that she might be able to defend herself had never occurred to her, and to act in such a violent manner in defence of Sherdan disgusted her.

Her stomach heaved as she ran to the bathroom. Thankfully, she reached the toilet in time for the second spasm which removed her evening meal from her stomach. She shivered violently, kneeling on the floor for the next few minutes as her brain tried to process the odd dream.

She had felt herself do things as if another was in control of her body, at the same time as knowing exactly what doing each of the martial arts moves would feel like. It played through her head again as vividly as it had moments before, but she still couldn't understand why she would ever do anything like it, or why she'd protect Sherdan.

A part of her despised him for everything he had let his guards do to her and for all the manipulative conversations he'd followed that with. But it was only a part of her. On occasions she found herself thinking about life by his side. She assumed it was something like Stockholm syndrome, but couldn't feel peaceful either way.

She decided to see what God said about violence and killing

in the Bible and picked up the copy Sherdan had let her have. Flicking through it didn't help at first. There were plenty of wars in the Old Testament, but that wasn't as relevant. She was only one person, not a nation.

Instead of reading any more from the Old Testament she moved to the New Testament and Paul's letters. He'd often been persecuted for his faith and talked about both his trials and the trials of many of the other disciples.

She scanned through, looking for relevant passages and stopped in Romans. There was a section in Romans 12 titled 'love in action'. The last line said, "Do not be overcome by evil, but overcome evil with good."

She stopped breathing as she stared at the section. God expected her to overcome the evil situation by being righteous. She'd been awful to Sherdan and suddenly felt very guilty.

It was important she didn't let him control her but, while she remained and God wanted her there, she knew she needed to be better at showing Sherdan kindness. She was struck with the thought of how far her kindness and goodness should go and the idea of her defending him didn't seem anywhere near as absurd.

The martial arts still baffled her, however, as she'd never studied it in the slightest. She had to ponder further over why she might have dreamt it, but her eyelids drooped and stopped her confused thoughts until morning.

Sherdan had gone to lead his team in taking more territory long before breakfast, so Anya ate alone and, as she'd been doing every day, she put the twenty-four-hour news channel on. It gave her more information on Sherdan's plans than he did.

Already the focus of the reporter was the new country. Sherdan's teams had already begun warning people in the area that they were going to have to leave. Many still hadn't been out of bed when the guards had arrived. The army tried to stop them but it seemed that barriers were all covering the new area as well. Sherdan had been thorough.

The cameras got as close as they could but were still a long way off. Anya could tell they wanted to interview the residents but many were already busy, packing up their belongings. A lot were in shock and seemed to be working autonomously. A few stood on their front lawns, unable to think coherently.

Many of the guards were lending a hand. Anya was surprised at how amicable everything was. It seemed most of the people losing their houses understood there was no point in arguing, and the kids seemed to think the day was a great game, a far more exciting way to spend a Sunday morning.

The army and news reporters watched as several hours passed. The people all packed their possessions into the crates they were provided with. The crates were slowly stacked into cars, and by midday the first few people were ready to leave, although they were mostly students who had less to pack.

Anya couldn't believe the heartlessness of the whole thing. Many of the women cried at having to leave their houses, especially when a large amount of the furniture was being left behind.

She could hardly tear her attention away from the news. As people left the area, the reporters finally got their interviews and new footage was shown on the TV.

The people interviewed struggled to articulate how they felt and many just cried. Anya was moved to tears by them at several points.

When there were still people leaving and packing long after dinner had been and gone, Anya grew restless and turned the channel off. She could not watch anymore.

She went to pick up a book but found she had read all the modern ones that interested her. Sherdan had forbidden her touching all his old, first-edition books, so she wandered through the house until she found herself in the security room.

All four of the security team were there. Nathan and Julie were standing in the open space. None of them had noticed her so she hung back and watched, curious.

Nathan was instructing Julie on something Anya couldn't hear. The next thing she knew the two began sparring. Nathan was evidently the better of the pair and the instructor of the other.

Anya gasped when Nathan landed a blow and hit Julie. All four guards turned to her. Only Nathan smiled.

"Good evening," he said.

"Good evening. I'm sorry, I don't mean to pry... I just... I..."

"I was teaching some self-defence. Do you wish to join in?"

"I... You'd teach me?" Anya's eyes went wide. She hadn't expected to be offered lessons in martial arts.

"I'm teaching already. Another one of you wouldn't make much difference."

"I'd love to learn." Anya beamed but looked nervous all the same. She took a few steps into the room before hesitating. She had no idea where to begin.

Nathan sent her to fetch some more suitable clothing. She almost didn't go back, but after the dream she knew she couldn't say no. She just hoped that she'd not have to use it, not really use it, at least, but she didn't think it was a coincidence that Nathan had offered to teach her less than twenty-four hours after she'd dreamt about it.

Before she could back out, Anya rushed back to the security room. When she arrived she noticed that both Julie and Ed were gone. Nathan got up as soon as she walked into the room.

"Oh, I'm not getting in the way, am I?" she asked.

"No, not at all. It only takes two of us to do our duty when people are in the house. One to watch the safety of the residents and one for the exterior." Anya looked puzzled. "You're here so I'm still doing my job."

She finally smiled, put at ease by Nathan's eagerness and reasoning.

He encouraged her to come and stand out in the open and ran her through thirty minutes of warm-up and basic exercises. She was already out of breath and exhausted by the time he had finished.

"You'll need to bring your fitness level up to get good at a martial art. You'd be surprised how tiring fighting is." Anya nodded at him. She wasn't sure she could speak. He started by showing her the very basics: how to stand and protect herself.

She did her best to concentrate, picking up the gist of his requests quickly. Calmed by his gentle instruction, she soon lost track of time. He'd shown her some basic blocking movements and almost two hours had passed.

He stopped teaching and bowed towards her. She copied his

movements.

"Thank you. I enjoyed that," she said as she straightened back up

"You're welcome. You're a fast learner. Have you done anything like it before?"

"Not at all. I don't even know what you've been teaching me."

"Oh, just some karate. Mostly the defensive side of it."

"Well, thank you." Anya smiled.

"Would you like to learn some more? We can continue at the same time every day, or in the last hour of my shift in the morning, if you'd like?"

"Morning would be better." Anya didn't want Sherdan to get upset that she was spending time with his guards instead of him. He always worked in the mornings so would be a lot less likely to miss her.

She thanked Nathan again and went back to the study. It was almost midnight and there wasn't any sign of the master of the house. He'd been at the compound for over sixteen hours.

The news still focused on Utopia and the day's events. The Prime Minister had presented another speech, late in the evening, saying he considered Sherdan's latest move an act of war.

Anya laughed when she heard this. They were already at war. The attacks had seen to that. She also noted that to be at war both parties had to be countries. Sherdan had gained ground in that regard.

She found herself being swayed in Sherdan's direction and disapproved of how her own government were handling this. Brute force evidently wasn't going to stop Sherdan or his people.

It amused her that the army had been unable to do anything but watch all day. They'd tried to save face by helping the people kicked out of their homes but they couldn't get anywhere near people until they were let out by Sherdan's men. He was in complete control.

The Utopia security team used the emitters as a sort of double gateway, opening up one gap after the other, moving the leaving people out of the way but keeping all of Sherdan's citizens safe at the same time. It impressed Anya.

She gave up waiting for Sherdan at two in the morning and went to her room. Her body ached a little as she climbed into bed. She prayed she'd get a good night's sleep and not have any more nightmares. She felt exhausted. The day had been fraught with nervousness as she watched the happenings on TV and, with her karate lesson to finish the day, she felt a lot more tired than usual.

CHAPTER 27

Nathan was just the right man to head the first few hours of the day's plans. He had joined the security teams on the ground as soon as he'd finished another night shift at the main house. He was tired but knew Sherdan had entrusted him with an important mission. People would need to be kept calm and the guards would need to be as polite as possible.

Nathan had an advantage none of the others had. Thanks to the enzyme, he could tell what people were thinking. He could also project his own thoughts into someone else's head as if he had said something to them. The first of these two abilities was perfect for pre-empting the reaction of people to being asked to leave.

As soon as his usual guard shift was over he reported to the guard house nearest the strike area. There, a team waited for him.

"Right, men, we need to be polite but efficient. We're representing this country on one of its first diplomatic missions and we want to give a good impression." Nathan smiled at his men. Everyone filed out to do their duty.

Eight men had backpacks on. The army wouldn't realise they carried emitters for the shields and barriers in them. The soldiers would be pushed back as the guards advanced.

The eight fanned out along the perimeter side that was being expanded and began walking towards the edge. Nathan kept everyone else close behind.

They were careful to miss the housing, walking between them so the emitters didn't reach any farther than the brick walls of each house, ensuring they would just push back the army. They wanted the people within their houses to continue sleeping.

A few rows of houses near the compound had already been evacuated by the army when the soldiers had first arrived. This only made Nathan's job easier. They would be readily available for any new residents.

In the cover of night, the guards advanced on the resting soldiers. They soon shrunk back, feeling the effect of the moving barriers. The retreat was a shambles as the men rushed to get away from the unseen advancing walls.

Nathan smiled as his team took over the British barricade and abandoned defences. Everything was running smoothly, and only the odd barking of a dog in the distance showed their progress had been noticed by anything other than the army.

Sherdan urged Nathan on from the command bunker, evidently excited. He in turn encouraged his own men forward.

After an hour had passed, the entire targeted area was under their control. Each guard with a backpack was stationed to form a new perimeter, keeping the soon-to-be refugees within the area and the army out.

As soon as everything was secure and just how he wished it, Nathan led his security team to the first few houses. He split the groups into four and had them knock on the nearest doors. He waited and watched from a central location.

He concentrated hard on listening to each conversation as the doors were opened. The first was a little girl who had beaten her parents out of bed. She ran to fetch them, evidently a little scared.

The second door revealed an older mother. She had two teenage sons. The pair of men at her door launched into their rehearsed speech about who they were and why they were here. She started crying, which finally attracted the attention of her children.

Nathan projected instructions to the guards on how to handle the situation, reminding them to stay calm and as non-threatening as possible. They asked the worried mother if she had anyone the family could go and stay with, until her insurance paid out. She nodded, brightening at the thought of insurance covering the financial side of things.

There was a possibility the evacuee's insurance wouldn't cover the house against being taken like this, but that wasn't a problem Nathan could address. He just had to get them all to leave as quickly as they could.

The third people to answer were equally amicable. They had been expecting to be moved from their houses anyway and were already partly packed. The three University girls went to sort their remaining possessions and phone their already worried parents to let them know they'd be coming home very soon.

Nathan had the groups that were done move on to the next houses. So far so good.

"Two houses packing. Only two hundred or so to go," he said into his radio, reporting to Sherdan.

"Thank you, Nathan. We'll need to pick up the pace to get them all out by nightfall," came the reply.

"Yes, sir. I suggest sending in the extra men. We'll need some help. There are quite a few young children." Nathan waited, listening to the parents at the first door. The father was trying to argue with the guards.

"They're on their way. Give me a report in half an hour." Sherdan's voice commanded.

"Yes, sir," Nathan replied, only half listening.

"Tell them they have until midnight tonight to be packed and ready to go or they'll be removed without their possessions, with force if necessary," he sent into the head of the guard. He soon heard the guard repeat it to the irate father. The soldiers walked away to the next door before any more could be said.

The father contemplated following but his wife tugged on his arm and instead they retreated inside. Nathan sighed with relief. He wanted this to go well.

As the sky grew lighter, and each successive door was knocked on, Nathan grew more and more tired. Each new house presented a fresh reaction, and with the extra security there were eight to concentrate on at a time. The remaining guards did useful things, like taking the people crates to pack into.

The single mother even made use of one of the male guards to help her load her car with the packed boxes as they were done with.

An argument soon broke out when an old lady, living alone, tried to go around to a friend's house and tell her what was happening instead of packing her own things. Nathan sent a more mature female guard over to explain to the resident why she had to go back to her own house.

He lingered nearby as he listened to their conversation. The poor old woman had been very intimidated by the men and their uniforms. Sending another woman to deal with the situation did the trick and she soon allowed herself to be walked back to her house.

"Make sure Annie hears it from you and not one of these big oafs. She's a nervous one. They'll scare her," the old woman added. Nathan smiled when his guard assured her that her request would be granted.

"Well done," he whispered into the guard's head before switching his focus elsewhere.

Three hours later, just over a third of the residents had been informed and other than one house everyone was packing and sorting through their possessions. The army had tried to get into the area a couple of times but hadn't succeeded. Nathan had a headache and knew he couldn't keep using his ability much longer.

"Stay another hour if you can manage it. Use your power sparingly," Sherdan requested. Nathan did as he was told, hoping the hour would pass without mishap. He only had to make it to half ten and he would be relieved from duty.

The occupants of the house currently troubling them did not seem to be there. Nathan's men knocked on the house three times before he gave the order to knock the door down. No one was inside but the house looked like it had been lived in.

"Sherdan, we've got a house with no occupant. If the fridge and laundry is anything to go by, there should be," Nathan radioed.

"What number is it?"

"Thirty-seven."

"Okay, we'll check the address. Leave it alone for now."

Nathan sighed. This job wasn't easy and his headache only got worse as the hour progressed.

The first person to lash out at a guard did so with only ten minutes of the hour to go. Nathan rushed over to the scene, as did a few other guards.

The man had punched the soldier when he'd been informed of the ultimatum. Thankfully, the guards soon had him restrained and sat down. Other than the blood flowing from the guard's nose there was no harm done.

Nathan had the two men separated, just in case tempers flared, removing the guard from duty to get himself checked out. He thought it better to be careful where this kind of thing was concerned.

"I'm sorry that today's news has upset you."

"Too right it has. You've got no right ter take our houses," the middle-aged man replied.

"Sherdan warned the British government that he would do this if they attacked."

"That don't make it right!"

"No, but it's our only way of retaliating without risking civilian deaths. We don't want anyone to get hurt."

"We're gettin' hurt though. You're takin' our houses."

"We wouldn't be doing it if we could think of a better option."

The man hung his head. The fight had gone out of him. Nathan felt sorry for the balding man, but he had a job to do. "You should find somewhere to go for the meantime and then enquire about your insurance, if you own the house."

He received a nod in response but that was it. He had the guards let the man go and everyone backed off to give him time to think.

Nathan, very thankfully, finished his shift. Sherdan sent another guard to take over from him and he didn't waste time, leaving to turn towards his own home. He lived in a small house not too far from Sherdan's, in case he was needed.

The walk back didn't take long, and he was soon climbing the stairs to his room. He removed his uniform and climbed into bed. It was gone one in the afternoon so he would have less than five hours before he would need to be up for guard duty in Sherdan's house. Before he settled down to sleep he reached into the top drawer of his bedside cabinet and pulled out his Bible.

CHAPTER 28

Sherdan sat in his chair at the command centre. He thought everything was going well, if a little slower than he would have liked. He watched the screens at the end of the room as he usually did. It didn't give anyway near as much information as he wanted but for now it was the best they had.

As the guards were busy, Sherdan didn't want to interrupt and slow them down. He tapped his fingers impatiently and let his thoughts drift to Anya. She'd repeatedly requested his company, then hardly said more than a sentence to him at a time.

He drifted in and out of his thoughts while watching over the developments of the day. Several times Graham interrupted his daydreams just as they were drifting to his imaginings of getting Anya into his bed. She was an attractive young woman and occasionally he really could not help thinking of her like that.

His command room wasn't the best place to be thinking those thoughts, however, so he made more of an effort to steer his mind back to his work when he had been interrupted for the third time. He thought of all the weird things that had happened since she arrived instead, and what it might mean.

The first time anything weird had happened in his life was back when he'd known Sandy and Professor Carmichael. Then he had put it down to science that was yet unexplained, but now he found himself wondering if he had been too closed to possibilities. So many more weird things had happened since Anya had arrived that he wondered if he had to rethink his earlier interpretation of those two as well.

Graham soon interrupted his brain's meanderings on that score, too. There was work to monitor and, even though Sherdan was doing very little, his opinion was needed on most of the decisions.

The day was long but Sherdan went home satisfied. Everyone who needed to had left. The students who hadn't been in their house when the evacuation had started had turned up at about three in the afternoon.

Sherdan had managed to have them moved into the area as another family were leaving. Interestingly, all three of them had requested to join the program rather than be kicked out. They were studying graphic design at Bristol's second university: the University of the West of England.

It made Sherdan stop and think for a bit before he gave an answer. They reminded him of Anya, especially when they said they were studying something artistic. As the after-effect every thought of Anya had, he found himself feeling more compassionate and he eventually said yes to their request.

When he got home it was almost four in the morning. He was glad that none of the new residents were arriving until the following afternoon. He checked in on Anya on his way to his room. She didn't look peaceful at all.

Her face poured with sweat and she was curled up on her side with her knees drawn up against her chest. She gritted her teeth, evidently in pain. Sherdan rushed over to her to wake her up.

"Anya, you're having a nightmare."

She sat up with a jump, disorientated. He perched on the edge of the bed as she started crying into her hands. She didn't look at him or even acknowledge he was there. After a moment's hesitation he sat beside her, put his arms around her and pulled her into a hug.

"It was just a bad dream, you're safe now," he whispered. She sobbed against his chest as he stroked her hair. He waited for her to stop and calm down while he enjoyed having her so close to him, although the reason behind it pained him greatly. He'd never felt anything so bitter-sweet.

As her crying ceased she pulled away. She seemed ashamed to be seen like that, and neatened her hair with her hands.

"Is it more nightmares about what happened?" he asked. She nodded. "It won't ever happen again, I promise. You really are safe now."

Sherdan tried to look her in the eyes to reassure her, but she wouldn't meet his gaze. He knew she didn't really believe him.

"I wouldn't have allowed it, had I known you like I do now. Had I known how important you are."

"I'm only important to you because of Hitchin, and I don't believe he's right. I definitely don't like the way he talks about me." Sherdan looked away. He didn't want yet another argument. "I'm sorry, I just don't believe you, but thank you for waking me and checking I was okay."

"You're welcome. I don't like to see you upset. I mean that."

"I don't hate you for what happened, but I'm not sure I belong here."

"I've told you that you're free to go."

"Would I be free to go if I wasn't able to walk out without you stopping me?" she asked. He paused and looked away, seriously considering his answer.

"If I knew you weren't happy here, then, yes, I think you would, even if it made me sad doing so." He looked deep into her eyes as he replied, hoping she would believe him. She smiled but looked away.

"There's no way to know for sure now."

"I'll let you rest," he replied and got up. The divide between them was so large sometimes even he doubted Hitchin could be right. He made a mental note to run the vision by Hitchin again and check that he had interpreted it right.

When Sherdan's alarm went off at seven, he immediately turned it off and rolled over, falling fast asleep again. Less than three hours' sleep was just not enough. Anya woke him at nine. Her concerned face was the first thing to come into focus properly.

"You overslept," she said as if it explained why she was in his bedroom with nothing but some flimsy pyjamas on. He grinned at her.

"I'm not sure I mind if you're what I wake up to." She blushed and went to leave. "How did you sleep after I left you?"

"Well... Thank you." Anya left, but before he could follow, Graham called for his attention on the radio. He didn't sound happy. Sherdan assumed he had called several times and it had woken Anya too.

"I'll be right there. Give me a few more minutes."

"Yes, sir," came the relieved reply. Sherdan sighed. He had so much work, and all he really wanted to do was spend time with Anya before it was too late and she left.

He said goodbye to his distant companion and walked out of his house. Breakfast would have to wait.

A few last minutes' preparations were needed before he could go meet the new arrivals. The recruits were joining today, despite government warnings to stay away and threats of arrest for anyone seen with Sherdan. Therefore, he felt it necessary to go meet them all and escort them personally into their new country.

His commander fidgeted while Sherdan ran through some of the day's plans. Sherdan was intending to leave him in charge of the country while he was gone, although he had already expressed concern over it.

"Are you sure this is wise?" Graham asked half an hour later.

"Of course. It shall be fine."

"Last time was a close thing, sir. I'd hate for you to get caught."

"I won't. I'll have a team with me." Sherdan left the command room before Graham could say anything else.

He went straight back to his house and into his car. His chauffeur drove him through his usual tunnel and out into what was now a separate country. The driver travelled all the way to Bath and dropped Sherdan off at the Bath Pavilion.

On entering the building, he was snuck behind the scenes before any of the people milling about noticed him. There weren't many there yet but there would be soon. They'd all been invited elsewhere and were being brought here by his own people, to make sure the British government didn't know anything about it.

Sherdan stood on the other side of the curtain, watching the people gather. It took almost half an hour and everyone was served drinks while they waited. There weren't quite as many as had been invited but that was to be expected. The way things had gone the last few weeks, he understood that the Prime Minister's ramblings would have put some of them off.

He had to wait for almost an hour until one of his team came up and told him that everyone who intended to come had arrived. Sherdan allowed them a few minutes longer to make their way through to find seats and drinks.

When he stepped through the curtain silence immediately fell and every eye fixed on him. He smiled and walked right to the centre of the stage. Every little fidget and awkward cough could be heard by Sherdan, as well as every single one of his deliberate footfalls.

"Good afternoon, everyone. I sincerely thank you all for travelling here, many of you a very long way. It means a lot to me and my residents that you all wish to join us, despite the slander and lies being spread." Sherdan smiled and paused as he looked around at all the eager faces. They trusted him to give them a better life than the one their current government had given them. They wanted change, something different. His heart swelled. He could give it to them.

"As you are aware, it is currently not very easy to access your new home, Utopia. We'll all be leaving here very shortly to head there. You will all need to move quickly and efficiently and go where you're asked. Of course, for anyone still unsure about joining, now is the time to say so. It is quite possibly a one-way trip."

Sherdan smiled again and jumped down from the front of the stage as the first wave of applause broke out. People soon began to come up to talk to him but he simply encouraged them to follow.

He walked to the front door with a wave of people behind

him, like he was a prophet leading his followers, and got into the stretch limo which pulled up outside. The few people right behind hesitated before the chauffeur waved them into the car. The first seven piled in and sat down around him.

The second the car started he struck up a conversation with his fellow passengers. First impressions were so important. He was treated as a celebrity at first. All of his companions were shy and nervous but he soon put them at ease.

They were understandingly apprehensive about the journey and what would happen to them, but Sherdan did everything he could to reassure them that they would be okay. There was safety in numbers and they were adding significant numbers that day: over one thousand.

Sherdan put all their fears to rest in the hour-journey that ensued. They had all been driven north to a small, private, desolate railway station. Today, however, the station was very much active and used. A magnificent steam train stood puffing a great plume of smoke into the otherwise quiet air.

There were murmurings amongst the arrivals as they saw the train. Many long, luxurious carriages had been attached to the steamer. Each carriage had wine and nibbles aboard, as well as very comfortable seats.

The passengers soon came flowing aboard and Sherdan alighted in no particular hurry. It would take a few moments for all the cars to arrive and everyone to be seated.

A hostess service was already on board, passing people drinks and encouraging them to remain in their places until the train started moving.

As each carriage filled up, Sherdan moved through, greeting people, shaking hands and making small talk. Many of them had relaxed, finally feeling safe and taken care of. Sherdan was thanked repeatedly for being there, despite the risk of capture.

He smiled as the train started moving and their journey to Utopia began. There was a railway station in Bristol which had a back entrance leading into Utopia. The army were checking each train carriage as well as the people exiting the front of the station, but they couldn't get past the platform to the rear entrance thanks to Sherdan's emitters.

With the train being a privately owned vehicle, and only registered to pause there for a moment to let another train go past, no one would even expect people to be arriving on the train.

Sherdan had only moved a third of the way through the people when the train began to move. From that point people got out of their seats and started milling around. He soon found himself surrounded.

"What's it like, running a country?" a bright-eyed young woman asked him.

"Difficult. There are lots of rules, and people to keep happy, but it's rewarding. Every day I get to see my decisions making a positive difference to my citizens." Sherdan smiled. It was just the kind of question he'd been hoping someone would ask.

"You actually think it makes a difference?" a man in his fifties piped up.

"Of course. I can see the difference in my residents already. They're happier now they have a greater sense of purpose, coupled with the security I can provide.

"This security, you've obviously got some fancy new technology. What is it?"

"It's true, we do possess some equipment the rest of the world doesn't own yet. I probably shouldn't go into too many details right now as it will be covered in your information seminars tomorrow."

At this answer, several looks of awe spread over the faces of the people listening. He thought he'd get a reaction from this but it was even better than he had hoped.

"Without giving too much away, it was developed right here in the heart of my little country by a man not too dissimilar from yourself, Mr Jameson. A man who thought the best of life had passed him by."

Mr Jameson smiled and shook Sherdan's hand. Everyone murmured amongst themselves as Sherdan moved on down the carriage to some fresh faces and new questions.

He could hardly wait until he was back in his country with all the new residents. They would have quite an impact on the United Nations in persuading them to recognise Utopia as a new country.

On top of all the immediate benefits, there were also all the new abilities the people would gain. The smiling, excited people around him would soon become eager workers and helpers, making his country stronger and taking them closer to the end target.

The train journey flew by as Sherdan talked with all the people around him. Many were of a similar age to him. People who'd had jobs their whole lives and got nowhere in life. He'd given them so much hope, and they were grateful for it.

CHAPTER 29

The hostess encouraged people into their seats as Sherdan moved to the front of the train. He would need to change into a driver's uniform and leave with the driver. He didn't want to raise suspicion too soon.

The driver was none other than the man who'd picked Sherdan up on his last train journey. He would come with them this time. His family were aboard the train and also joining them.

Sherdan had soon put on his new uniform and was standing with the chauffeur as the train pulled up. He couldn't help but smile at what would happen over the next few minutes. So many people were going to be surprised.

The train pulled to a stop in the station and Sherdan jumped down. He glanced around before hurrying towards the back entrance. As he did, he could hear other people beginning to disembark behind him. The hostesses on the train would also act as guards for everyone following him.

He pulled a radio out of his pocket as soon as he crossed the border of his land.

"I'm back. Proceed with the plan," Sherdan commanded. He stepped out into the road as his usual car came sweeping up. It drove him straight to the command bunker, where everything was being coordinated.

His men would already be overseeing the arrival of the new residents. He was eager to head up the task before getting back to his home and Anya. He'd not seen her properly for several days and he found himself missing her even though it saddened him that she was so distant.

He snapped himself back from his thoughts of Anya as his car stopped and his chauffeur opened his door. There was work to be done and he had a responsibility to all those eager, happy people he had met today.

The smile on his face was broad as he walked into his command room. It remained fixed as Graham filled him in on what had happened during his journey. He could see everything that followed on the screens. Rows and rows of people walked into his country, while the army just stood and watched. They could do nothing.

It only took half an hour for all the new residents to arrive. They were driven to their new homes, where they were given the evening to settle in and explore their new country. He'd had welcome packs made up for each new home, and the guards were out on the streets, patrolling the new areas especially.

Sherdan stayed in the command room even though he wasn't needed. He expected the army to attack again after what he'd done. There was no doubt that if taking the houses had made the Prime Minister angry, sneaking in almost one thousand UK citizens would tip him over the edge.

If he had any sense he wouldn't attack Sherdan again, as it would only lead to more of the same, but Sherdan didn't expect him to think like that. They would attack again, he was sure of it.

While he was waiting, Sherdan went to see Hitchin. It was gone five in the afternoon but he knew Hitchin would still be working. The labs were his second home; perhaps even his first.

Hitchin was with the latest residents to take the enzyme when Sherdan arrived so he waited for his friend to finish. He didn't have to wait long. Hitchin was not the kind of person to ever keep someone like Sherdan waiting.

"So, shall we go do those tests now?" Hitchin asked, before Sherdan could say anything.

"If it's all right, I'd like to talk over something else first?" Hitchin raised his eyebrows but motioned for his friend to continue. "Will you go through your second vision with me again, the one concerning Anya?"

"Of course, if you wish." Hitchin went to his desk and unlocked the top left drawer. He pulled out a small journal and came back to Sherdan with it. "I have it here, I wrote it down so I wouldn't forget anything important."

"Tell me it again." Sherdan smiled trying not to show his anxiety or doubts. He didn't want Hitchin to realise he wasn't sure of the whole thing, although he had no idea why he was so uncertain.

Hitchin repeated the whole vision again in pretty much the same way he'd told it the first time. Sherdan sat, listening and hoping it was true. He was more concerned about winning Anya than he was that his ability had gone, although Hitchin was evidently more worried about the tests and soon turned the conversation back to that subject.

"The good news is that you're the only one who seems to be losing their ability. It doesn't appear to be wearing off for me or anyone else from the earliest groups."

"So I'm an anomaly?" Sherdan asked.

"There's no way to know for sure yet. It's possible that whatever gave Anya her power is having an effect on you, if it was something in your house, perhaps. Without a working sample of her blood it's hard to say. It could just be that you're overworked and tired."

Sherdan smiled as he nodded his understanding. He felt relieved that at least it only appeared to affect him. Everyone else was growing in their abilities. More tests would reveal what was wrong.

As Hitchin had requested last time, they went straight for an MRI. While he was lying, being scanned, he thought about all the things Hitchin had told him in the last hour. Anya had them both confused, even if Hitchin didn't want to admit it.

She kept claiming everything was her God. Whatever it was that had brought her to him and given her an ability, despite her not taking the enzyme, it seemed to want her to have the upper-hand and wasn't going to allow him to control her.

He had only one option open to him. He'd have to win her over the old-fashioned way, with romance.

Hitchin wanted to do further tests after the MRI, but before Sherdan could let Hitchin study his brain further they heard the sound of an explosion. They were being attacked again.

Sherdan leapt up and ran towards the command centre without even saying goodbye to the scientist. The assault he'd been expecting had finally come. The radio in his pocket called for him just before he pushed open the door and walked into the command room.

"Bombs and missiles, no paratroopers yet," his commander said swiftly. Sherdan nodded and went to his station, awaiting further information.

The rest of the evening flew by in a haze of bombings. As usual, the army was completely ineffective. The only problem that arose was calming the new residents who got scared.

A few of them left their houses and refused to go back inside until Sherdan dispatched a security team to help calm them down and get them back to a safe place. The patrols had stopped only half an hour before the attack.

By the time Sherdan could leave his duty station and go back to his home, and Anya, it was almost midnight. He didn't expect her to still be awake. As normal, his work was getting in the way of spending any time with her. He knew it had to be this way, but his heart felt heavy nonetheless.

He went to pour himself a drink and take half an hour to unwind before he slept. He could sit and think of ways to endear Anya to him.

He had just got comfortable in his favourite chair when he heard the soft pad of familiar feet on the carpet. He looked up to see her in the doorway.

"Good evening. You've been very busy," she said. He smiled.

"I've had a lot to do. I think the worst of it has only just begun, however." Anya nodded. "I'm sorry. I've left you alone a lot."

"That's okay, I've been watching what you've been doing on

the news."

"Have they said much?" he asked. She laughed and nodded.

"Yes, I've found out more about your plans watching TV than you've ever told me."

"I like to surprise people."

"Maybe. I think that you're not used to trusting people."

"You're probably right."

"So what's next?"

"More of the same. While they continue to attack we will continue to expand. I hope the UN will recognise us before it gets too out of hand. Our case is stronger now we have both extra ground and over fifteen percent more citizens," Sherdan said, being truthful with her.

"Well, I best get some sleep and let you do the same." Anya walked towards the door.

"Stay," he called. She stopped and looked at him expectantly. "I'm not tired yet and I'd appreciate some company."

After a brief pause she came to sit near him. There was a silence as she simply sat still and waited. He racked his brains for something to say to her.

"How is your art going? Do you still have everything you need?" he asked. She hesitated before nodding.

"It's going well, thank you for asking."

"Good. I know it's hard for you to be here. If there is anything else you need or want to make things easier just let me know." Sherdan smiled as she looked up at him.

He'd surprised her and he hoped it had a lasting impact.

"Can I see some of your work?" he said. She nodded and went over to his desk. He hadn't noticed before now that her sketch book was lying there. She passed it to him and sat back down.

He grinned at her as he opened the first page. On it was a relatively simple sketch of a vase of flowers. They were roses, but the petals looked like they were melting and dripping onto the surface below. He flicked to the next page where there were just a few doodles of patterns and single items. He recognised one of them as being the pattern on the ceiling in his dining room.

The third page held his attention for some time. It was a winged man standing on the edge of a cliff. Sherdan wondered if it was deliberate that it looked like him from behind. He wanted to ask her who she'd intended it to be but couldn't bring himself to do so.

"Do you like them?" she asked. He looked at her to see her sitting forward. Her eyes darted to the pad and back to his face. He smiled.

"I do. You're very good," he reassured her. She grinned. "Do you do portraits?"

"I... I've done some a long time ago as part of art school. People aren't very easy, though."

"Would you consider drawing me?" he asked, suddenly.

"I'm not sure. I've not tried to do someone's portrait in a professional capacity before."

"Well, it's only a whim of mine. I doubt I'll have the time to sit still and let you draw me for as long as you'd need."

"You expect to continue being so busy?"

"Unfortunately, yes. I'd like to try and spend more time with you, however." Anya blushed a little. "I enjoy getting away from work and talking to you."

"All work and no play kind of thing?"

"Something like that, but I really do like being with you. I'd appreciate it if you'd consider helping out with the country while you're here."

"In the command room?" Anya asked.

"No, probably not. I only have my experts in there. It helps keep things simpler, and it would actually put you in more danger," Sherdan lied. It wouldn't put her in danger unless someone outside the country thought she knew things, but he didn't want her in the command room. She was an artist and didn't belong in that kind of place.

She nodded and the conversation ended. She didn't ask where he had meant. He didn't really know anyway. He only mentioned it because he wanted to give her a reason to stay and be happy here.

He handed the pad back to her and thanked her for the

privilege of seeing inside. It occurred to him that he might be able to look at her previous artwork on the internet. He felt sure he would find something online as she said she'd been making a living from it.

They then talked about the news and the outside reaction to the recent things Sherdan had done for a few minutes, before Anya yawned. He wanted to ask her questions but he realised it would be better to let her sleep. The nightmares he'd caused were making her tired.

"Will you tell me more about what's in the news tomorrow evening?" he asked as she got up to sleep.

"Yes, if you wish."

"Very much so. It helps a lot to know what people of influence are saying, and I can only spare so much time to find out myself."

"Then I'd be delighted to do so for you," she replied. He got up and hugged her. She looked shocked but allowed it, although he wasn't sure why he'd suddenly felt like doing so.

When he let her go, she stood in front of him with her eyes downcast. There was an awkward silence while he watched her fidget.

"Well... goodnight, Sherdan."

"Goodnight, Anya. Wake me if you have another nightmare and need some company."

She hesitated, then left. Sherdan went back to his seat and poured himself another brandy. He felt like he'd made a little progress but not very much. It would take a considerable amount of time to get her to trust him.

At least now he had a very good, work-related reason to talk to her for a little while each day. He would do his job better knowing what was being said about Utopia and himself in the public sphere and get to show Anya he cared at the same time.

The important thing, over the next two or three weeks, would be to make himself special to Anya in some way. He didn't entirely know how to do that but knew someone who would. Sherdan put down his empty glass and wandered through to see his security team.

"Nathan, have you got a few minutes to come to my study?"

"Of course, sir." Nathan leapt up and followed Sherdan back to the room he'd come from. Sherdan offered him a drink and a seat. He declined the first but took the latter.

"What can you tell me about Anya, Nathan?" Sherdan got straight to the point while pouring himself a third drink.

"Anya, sir?"

"Yes, I want to romance her, let her know I care about her, but I want her to think I'm genuine and none of my usual... methods... are working."

"Do you genuinely care, sir?" Nathan looked uncomfortable saying this but Sherdan was pleased he was so frank with him. He thought about the question for some time and sat down as well.

"I believe I do, at least I care for her more than I normally would care about a female. I'm not used to feeling particularly attached to anyone, however."

"She's a Christian. She'll expect to be respected as such. You might start by listening to her about exactly why and what she believes. It will help her see you care for her as she is and that you're not trying to change her into something else," Nathan explained.

Sherdan didn't know whether to feel disgusted or agree. Nathan was right, but that didn't mean he liked the suggestion. So far he'd only told Anya that he thought her beliefs were stupid and it wasn't the most endearing of attitudes.

"I don't have to believe in it too, do I?" he asked.

"No, I wouldn't expect anyone would believe that was genuine, but being a little more open couldn't hurt. She's an adult with a sensible mind. There's got to be something important in her decision to believe in the Christian faith."

"Well, open is something I can finally say I am. There have definitely been some things that even stump Hitchin, but I don't think I believe in all this maker nonsense. Christians refute so much of the proven science we have."

"Just ask her to explain some things about her faith. You might be pleasantly surprised."

"Any other suggestions?" Sherdan waited as Nathan looked thoughtful.

"I think she's bored and lonely. Your time and company would do a lot to help her. She also has a soft spot for animals, more so than a lot of people. I'd consider getting her a pet while she's here. It would give her companionship. Maybe a cat; they're lower maintenance and Anne likes them too."

"Thank you, Nathan. I think that's a good start."

"You're welcome, sir. If I think of anything else I'll let you know." Nathan got up before he finished speaking. Sherdan waited for him to leave and continued to think over what he'd been told. He didn't like the idea of talking to her about God, but he could spend a little more time with her, and surprising her with a kitten would be easy.

He got up from his chair and went to his laptop straight away. He sent an email to the girl who could talk to animals and requested for her to find him a particularly affectionate kitten. He told her it was for a friend of his who was missing the family she'd left behind in Britain and he wanted to make her feel less lonely by giving her the cat.

With a much lighter heart, and a fresh plan, Sherdan headed upstairs. It was gone four again. He checked on Anya, who appeared to be sleeping better, before collapsing into his own bed.

CHAPTER 30

Anya hadn't known what to make of Sherdan that evening. Her heart had skipped a beat when he'd asked to see her artwork and two more when he'd requested a portrait. She'd almost said yes before it occurred to her that, with a possible case of Stockholm syndrome, incorporating him into her artwork would be bad for her.

She hoped he accepted her excuse. It had only been half true. She wasn't very practised at painting or drawing people. Practice would be good for her, but she didn't think Sherdan would appreciate it if it wasn't really good. She didn't like that kind of pressure.

She felt her muscles ache and complain as she climbed into bed. Earlier, she'd had a second martial arts lesson with Nathan. He'd insisted she was picking it up quickly. As soon as she had warmed up, he went over all the blocking he'd taught her the day before and then followed it with some new moves. Her fitness let her down, however.

The following day's lesson was similar, although thankfully, she ached less than the previous two days when she was released from the teaching. She put it mostly down to getting a better night's sleep than she had for a while. She'd been thinking of her art before bed, thanks to Sherdan, and it gave her the emotional release she needed.

That morning, she'd almost had to wake him again as he overslept his alarm for the second day running. Something inside her knew that wasn't like him. It was obvious he had been working too hard lately and couldn't keep it up. She felt sorry for him.

The second request he'd made of her bounced into her head. He'd been very interested in what she'd seen on the news. She could keep watching and reading to find him info. It would help him make informed decisions, but it wasn't helping enough to make her feel like she might be doing something wrong.

She took his laptop through to the sitting room and turned the TV on. She'd have the twenty-four hour news channel in the background while she read through the online news reports. If she finished those she'd start reading relevant blogs by influential people.

Anya felt really good when she'd made several pages of notes. The news was full of reports on the influx of residents to Utopia and Sherdan's seemingly unstoppable progress. Even the retaliatory attacks were considered a waste of time by the news in general. All they did was provoke Sherdan.

At noon, she watched as Sherdan's people expanded their territory again in response to the attempted invasion the night before. As the next few hours of events went by, the news team began interviewing people. Almost everyone was suggesting that the army stand down and negotiations should begin.

To her surprise, the European Union were planning an emergency meeting for the following day. Sherdan hadn't applied to them for recognition within Europe, just to the UN. So far the UN board had not given any indication either way.

It gave her a greater sense of purpose to be doing something with her time, and she found the day passed much faster than they had felt like in previous weeks. She'd enjoyed finding out the public's opinion on Sherdan. He had a lot of support among the general population but a lot of politicians didn't like him.

She had to eat dinner alone, as she had often done recently, but she was heading back to the sitting room to continue her work when Sherdan arrived back.

"Good evening," she said as she walked towards him. She

stopped as she noticed he was carrying something small in his arms.

"Good evening. I have something for you, to help with the loneliness." Sherdan held out the tiny little ginger kitten towards her. She gently took it from him as it mewled at her.

"I think this is the fluffiest kitten I have ever seen," she said, unable to help but smile.

"You like it then?" She nodded. "Good. I hoped you would. When someone said this little fellow needed a home I immediately thought of you."

"Thank you. He's beautiful." Anya kissed the top of the kitten's head and stroked it. It elicited a second meow before it began to wriggle in her hands. She gently lowered him to the ground and let him go.

"There you go. Now you can explore your new home." The kitten gently took a few steps forward, sniffing at the unfamiliar surroundings.

"What do you want to call him?" Sherdan asked as they watched him explore.

"I... I'm not sure..." she looked thoughtful. "Antonio. The guy who voiced 'puss-in-boots' was Antonio."

"Very well. Antonio is your gift. If you leave at some point you're also very welcome to take him with you. In the meantime, I have already let Anne know to put food and a litter tray out for him in the kitchen."

She nodded, still watching the kitten as it crawled around underneath one of the chairs. Suddenly she looked straight at Sherdan. He smiled at her as she hugged him. She wasn't sure why, but she'd always wanted a cat. Now she had the cutest, fluffiest one she'd ever seen.

When she stopped hugging him she went straight back to watching Antonio explore. He'd now made his way to the doorway into the sitting room and she followed the little creature. Sherdan wasn't far behind.

"Before I forget, I made notes today on what I saw, seeing as you were so interested yesterday."

"Perhaps you can tell me about it all while I eat something. Have you already eaten?" Sherdan replied.

"I've already had food but I can sit with you in the dining room if you wish?"

"No, that's not necessary. I'll have food in here with you and our latest arrival. That way we can watch him together as well."

Sherdan sent for Anne and sat down on the sofa beside Anya.

They laughed together at the kitten's antics as he tried to get up beside them and play. He got his claws stuck in the side of the sofa and found he didn't know how to fully retract them. As such, he stuck to the side, unable to go up or down.

She lifted him off, set him down beside them both and stroked him, as Sherdan reached out to do the same. Their hands brushed against each other until she pulled hers back. Her cheeks flushed red as she thought of all the film scenes where the same thing happened. She stared at the kitten, trying to recover before she had to look at him.

Thankfully, the awkward moment was relieved when Anne brought in dinner for Sherdan. He had to stop stroking Antonio to take the tray and place it on his lap, giving her a moment to compose herself.

She fetched her notebook from a nearby chair and skimmed through it to remind herself of some of the things she had read and heard that day. The notebook was fuller than she expected and she had taken in a lot without realising. Sherdan had long finished eating by the time she'd told him everything.

"And what do you think of what I'm doing?" Sherdan said when he realised she'd finished.

"I... What do you mean?"

"You've told me what politicians think, governments and the general population. What do you think of my actions?"

"I think that what you've done is impressive. I'm just not sure whether it will work in the long term. People are often so far from perfect. I fear that even with the best of efforts to change governments, your country will be no better than everything that's come before."

"That's no reason not to try."

"Perhaps not, but there is also the enzyme you've all been taking. Eventually someone with less honourable intentions will take it and use the ability they gain for ill."

"Perhaps, but I don't think so. Hitchin's vision says otherwise."

"You already know my opinion on that." Anya sighed. Sherdan couldn't see the error of his ways and was so closed in terms of what he thought.

"You know we're both as closed-minded as each other. Maybe we could both do with being more open?" Sherdan suggested as he got up.

He left the room to take his tray back to the kitchen, leaving Anya to feel indignant at his assertions. She felt tears sting her eyes and sat back, shocked at her own emotions.

She resolved to turn the subject back to more amiable conversation the second Sherdan came back, but it was some time before he walked into the room again. When he did, he had two bowls of chocolate ice cream.

"Anne informed me you hadn't eaten any dessert. I fancied ice cream. It's got chocolate brownie chunks in it." She took the peace offering gratefully and smiled. Chocolate went down well with most women and she was no exception.

They ate in silence, until they were both finished and had put their bowls down. The kitten had provided enough of a distraction as it continued to get used to its new surroundings that the quiet wasn't awkward. She'd never have expected someone like Sherdan, with all his antique furniture, to like the idea of a pet.

"Did you do any artwork today?" he asked, stirring her from her thoughts.

"No, I spent the day researching people's opinions for you."

"Thank you. It will help me going forward, but please do draw... and anything else you'd normally do. Don't feel you have to do what I ask. I'd rather you did whatever made you happiest."

"Actually, it did make me happy. I really enjoyed researching." Anya smiled in reassurance to Sherdan. She could hardly believe how nice he was being to her. A part of her expected him to change back to the controlling version of himself at any moment, however.

"I have some more work to do, but I'd appreciate some

company while I did it, if you want to join me in the study?" Sherdan asked. She thought about it for a moment, considering saying no, to stay and play with the cat, which had climbed up onto the coffee table.

"Yes, I can draw from in there as easily as here," she replied instead. It had plagued her conscience that she'd not been kind enough. Being in the same room as him would do her no harm.

She followed him into the study and picked up her pad and pencils. When Sherdan had sat himself in his usual chair and put both his laptop and documents nearby, she sat down where she could glance at him without him noticing too much.

A smile spread across her face when Antonio followed them. He evidently didn't want to be left alone. He soon settled down by her feet and curled up against the leg of the chair.

She flicked to the next spare page in her sketch book and began to roughly sketch Sherdan's outline. It took her quite a few minutes, as she didn't want Sherdan to notice her staring at him. Thankfully, she managed to get his outline done before he looked up from the document he was reading.

"I'm sorry, I'm not talking much," Sherdan said.

"That's okay, I don't talk much when drawing either, and the sooner you're done working the sooner we can do something more fun." Sherdan smiled at Anya before picking up his pen and going back to the document. He made notes while she slowly drew him.

Half an hour later she had a picture of him she wasn't that impressed with. Sketching him from one side was helping in some ways but not in others. No matter how hard she tried, she couldn't get his mouth right.

He soon reached for his laptop and placed it on his lap, completely changing a lot of what she'd drawn anyway. Flinging her pencil and pad down, Anya gave up and sighed. Sherdan looked up at her but she avoided his gaze. She didn't want to disturb him from his work.

Instead, she got up and went to the nearest bookshelf to read the covers of the many books Sherdan had. She wasn't surprised to see 'The Origin of Species' by Darwin. It occurred to her that she'd never even flicked through it.

Her hand reached out to pick the book up before remembering she'd been forbidden from touching his older paper books. Another sigh escaped her.

"You're bored," Sherdan said, making her jump.

"A little. I don't really leave, ever. The house I mean. I'm in these four walls daily." Sherdan looked thoughtful.

"Give me a few minutes to finish this." He went back to his laptop and tapped away at the keys. Anya patiently went to stroke her kitten. It mewled as she started running her hands over its very soft fur.

It made her heart feel a little lighter as she knelt, making a fuss of the gift he'd given her. She decided then and there to have Antonio up in her room when she went to bed. It could keep her company and might even provide enough of a calming presence that the frequency of her nightmares would reduce.

Suddenly, Sherdan got up. He paused for a moment, lost in thought, before snapping back and looking straight at Anya.

"Take Antonio through to Anne in the kitchen and ask her to look after him, then go up to your room and fetch some warm clothing and shoes." Anya nodded and picked up her cat, snuggling it to her. It didn't take her long to head through to Anne, who seemed to be expecting the kitten. A litter tray and food were already laid out for him. She placed him down in the tray so he knew where it was and thanked Anne for being so prepared.

It took her a little longer to find warm clothes. She didn't have much in the way of warm clothing and she couldn't decide between two jumpers at first. When she realised she'd been gone over ten minutes she grabbed her coat and shoes, and rushed back to Sherdan's study.

He still waited for her there and smiled as she walked into the room.

"So what are we doing?" she asked.

"You'll see. Come on, get your shoes on." She did as she was told, feeling unexpectedly excited. She'd been cooped up so long that whatever Sherdan was planning, she thought she'd enjoy it.

As soon as she got to her feet again he took her hand and led her out of the study. He didn't explain anything, but she didn't complain.

CHAPTER 31

The smile plastered on Sherdan's face said everything as he waited for Anya to come back. He'd just told Anne and had a small picnic thrown together to put in his car. It contained mostly wine and nibbles. He'd also informed his security that they were going out.

He didn't have to wait too long before Anya came back and he led her to his personal car. He had a two-seated Jaguar that he used to drive for fun when his country wasn't so isolated. It had stood in his garage ever since. At last, it would get some use.

Sherdan opened the door for Anya to get in. The small picnic basket was already in the boot, along with a blanket, for him to surprise her with later. As he thought of this his grin grew even wider.

Nathan activated the tunnel switch from the security desk for them and Sherdan drove them down his escape route and out into the heart of a Bristol suburb. Neither of them said anything until they were out on the road.

"Have we just illegally crossed a country border?" Anya asked.

"Yes. I suppose we have. Does it bother you?"

"I'm not sure. I know it ought to, but it feels more... adventurous, than wrong."

Sherdan nodded. He could hardly believe his luck with Anya the last two days.

Since he'd decided to try and convince her of his feelings the more traditional way she'd been increasingly more cooperative. It had been a very easy two days so far, although he hadn't actually finished his work for the day. Once he'd had this idea, he had dropped everything and would need to return to it later.

He drove towards Bath and then slightly south into a quiet little village called Southstoke, before parking his car and helping her out. As he pulled the blanket and basket out of the boot, Anya gasped.

"When did you get those?"

"While you were in your room. Now, I think it's this way... I've got a torch. Here, do you want to light the way?" She took the torch Sherdan offered.

"Where are we going?"

"There's a little look-out that's very pretty, either night or day. It's not far, but well worth visiting." She nodded and walked with Sherdan, lighting the path for both of them.

They walked through a kissing gate onto a farmyard track that led off and up-hill. After less than five minutes' walking, Sherdan veered off through an open metal gate.

The trees on that side had opened up, showing them that they were high up on the side of one of Bath's hills, overlooking a valley.

He led her around a mound in the grass to a semi-circular stone bench built into the hillside. Rather than sitting on the cold stone, he spread the blanket on the ground in front. After positioning the basket within his reach he sat down and lent against the pale stone.

Anya was staring out at the night in front of them. It was a clear night, so a full set of stars could be seen. He waited for her to finish taking in the view. When she turned to see where he was, he patted the blanket beside him. Her eyes lit up as she came to sit down.

"What if someone comes and recognises you?" Anya said, a moment later.

"It shouldn't be too busy here. The chances are slim, even if anyone comes along."

"Good. I'd hate for you to get arrested." Sherdan didn't know what to say and reached for the wine and glasses. He poured some for both of them without even asking if she wanted any. He made sure he only half filled his own glass. He didn't want any accidents when he drove her later.

They sat drinking the wine and enjoying the food. They didn't eat a lot, but it was nice to pick at the grapes, cheese bites and chocolate-covered strawberries.

"Thank you for not leaving yet. I think my life would be all work and no play if it wasn't for you."

"Then I am glad to be of assistance," she replied. "You do work very hard."

"I have citizens to look after. They're counting on me to make their lives better."

"You really want to help them?"

"Of course. I want to make the world better. I know you don't like all my methods but I do have my reasons."

"I know. I understand more than when I arrived. I'm sorry I was so awkward the first few weeks." Sherdan almost choked on his wine in shock. An apology was totally unexpected.

He poured her some more wine to recover and looked out at the sky. It occurred to him that she didn't know his power had disappeared roughly the same time as hers had appeared, but he couldn't bring himself to say anything.

"Have you been practising your ability at all?" he asked, trying to lead them to the subject.

"A little. I can now mostly control switching between the two states, being just invisible and also being able to pass through things. I can't keep it up for too long though; I have to concentrate."

"Does that mean you can suddenly appear again?"

"Yes, usually just after an hour has passed."

"That's not bad. Many of the residents struggle to use their powers so long so soon into their training."

"Really?" Sherdan nodded and noted the look of satisfaction on her face. "I'm also learning karate. Nathan's teaching me."

"Good. With your ability, that's a useful thing to learn."

"You approve?"

"Very much. It will help you keep safe, especially if you do leave."

"Nathan says I'm picking it up quickly." She beamed. He was pleased. She'd found something to amuse herself with while he was gone.

The more she did what she enjoyed, the more likely she would stay. It would take years for karate to be beneficial to her in a real situation, but he wasn't going to burst her excited bubble.

Sherdan snapped out of his thoughts when he noticed her shivering. She'd finished her glass of wine so he swallowed the last gulp in his and began packing everything back up. He didn't want her to catch a cold.

Anya lit the way back as soon as they were ready to leave and they were soon back at the car. He felt a little exhilarated from the danger of being out on British soil, but they'd seen no one the entire time, not even a dog walker.

"Thank you," Anya said as Sherdan started up the car. "I really liked that place."

"You're welcome. It's one of my favourites. I almost considered setting up Utopia in Bath but it wasn't practical enough. Bristol had so many more things in its favour."

"Well, hopefully soon you can have all this silly war stopped and be allowed back here."

"We shall see. It may never be possible." They lapsed into a silence which lasted all the way back to the house. Normally Sherdan didn't like silence but it felt different with Anya. He felt comfortable being quiet in her presence. She said a lot with her body language and, at the moment, she was very smiley and content.

They walked back into the study and he found himself hugging her. He said goodnight as she yawned into her hand. She wished him the same, then pattered off to leave him to his work.

It had only just gone eleven so he wouldn't be as late to bed as he had been most of the nights recently. He would need to push his thoughts of Anya out of his head, however, as they would be very distracting. She'd made him a very happy man that evening and given him hope again.

When he picked his laptop up he found an email from Hitchin. He'd looked over Sherdan's MRI and not found anything wrong. He wanted to do more tests, as Sherdan expected, but he was beginning to think it was just fatigue stunting the ability. At least, that was the most plausible explanation so far.

Sherdan spent the next few hours planning the growth of his country and how they would build bomb-shelters for the new homes. Not all the latest residents had somewhere safe to go if more soldiers were air-dropped in.

He also briefly looked at the new abilities. He had a small team working on coming up with some kind of air defence which kept planes out of his airspace but didn't harm anyone.

At two in the morning he went to bed. He had to be in the command room at an earlier time the following day. He really hoped he'd get some kind of lie-in at some point soon. He wouldn't survive on five hours or less sleep each night for much longer.

The next two days were a blur for Sherdan. He'd contacted the UN again to try and get them to recognise his country. There still wasn't anything which gave an indication either way. The European diplomats were still discussing things in their emergency meeting.

Sherdan hadn't submitted for any more tests yet, preferring to spend time with Anya and Antonio, who were now inseparable. The little kitten went with her from room to room and curled up with her, or encouraged her to play, whenever she was still.

He'd thanked Nathan for his ideas as well as teaching Anya the martial arts. So far the combination of time spent with both men and the pet was having a good impact on her. She had been smiling a lot more and she'd told Sherdan she'd had two nights in a row without nightmares.

He hadn't managed to tell her about his ability disappearing yet and he hadn't wanted to bring up her faith since he'd called her closed. Now that everything had improved so much, he didn't want to argue with her.

There hadn't been any attacks on Utopia either, which was unexpected. He hoped it meant a step forward in his plan, but the Prime Minister hadn't returned his last two phone calls so Sherdan couldn't tell for sure yet.

Anya greeted him very enthusiastically on Thursday evening when he arrived back home, hugging him as he walked into the study. Neither of them had eaten yet, despite it being after seven, so he led her through to the dining room before she could say anything to him about her day. He noticed Antonio got up and padded silently after them.

"There was a lot about Utopia in the news today," Anya blurted out, practically bouncing in her chair with excitement.

"What was said about us?"

"The European Union has decided we're not a threat and have advised the United Kingdom to stand down and negotiate." She beamed. Sherdan didn't know whether to feel more pleased that the country was making progress or that Anya had said 'we' and included herself as part of the country.

"That's brilliant news. That should make the Prime Minister think twice."

"On top of that, UN members have started to speak out and say Utopia should be considered a country."

"Good. Hopefully we'll get official recognition soon, then."

Anya told Sherdan everything else she'd learnt that day while they ate. She'd spent most of the day on the net and had a whole wealth of information. He couldn't help being impressed.

"When are you going to let the world know about your abilities?" she asked as they want back to the sitting room.

"Soon, but not until we're established as a country." He sat down at his usual end of the sofa and waited for Anya to join him. She picked up Antonio and plonked herself down right next to him instead of the opposite end of the sofa. He put his arm up on the back of the sofa behind her in response.

They watched some TV like that for the next hour or so. Sherdan didn't want to do or say anything that might make Anya move away. He liked having her relaxed and so close to him.

When there wasn't anything left on TV either of them wanted to watch, Anya flicked it off. His arm was still on the back of the sofa.

"What would you like to do? We still have a few hours," Anya asked.

"I'd like to show you something, if you're interested. I've got a particular opera I like on video. It's not as good as seeing it performed but since I have to be careful going out it will have to do."

"Sounds wonderful." Sherdan didn't hesitate to get up and find the relevant disc. He put it on and returned to his position beside her.

He'd picked another opera, knowing how emotional it had made her seeing the last one. She'd been a delight to spend the evening with afterwards as well. Hopefully he could recreate the atmosphere this time, too.

The opera was Madame Butterfly; very sad, but hopefully easy for her to relate to. It had the desired effect, and Anya's eyes weren't dry by the end. Sherdan handed her a tissue as he pulled his arm a little closer around her.

"I'm sorry, the music was just so moving," she said, once she had dried her eyes.

"Don't apologise. That's why it's one of my favourites. It makes the very depths of a person respond."

"It's beautiful."

"I'm very glad you liked it." He looked down into her upturned face and held her gaze. They smiled at each other before she dipped her eyes down. He could sense her nervousness but she didn't pull away or even turn her face from him. He hesitated. He wanted to kiss her and he thought in that moment she might finally be receptive but, now it came to it, he felt unsure of himself.

Anya stood and picked up Antonio again. It took all Sherdan's self-restraint not to swear out loud. He'd missed his chance.

"I should get some sleep. It's late." Anya smiled half-heartedly and quickly left the room. It had only just gone midnight and was about an hour before she had been going to bed recently.

He stayed sat where he was for a few minutes, wondering what had gone wrong. Maybe he'd been too quick. It hadn't been long since he'd first started trying to put the effort in with Anya again. He resolved to go a little slower but he definitely wasn't giving up yet.

Sherdan sighed and fetched his laptop to carry on working. He had yet another email from Hitchin reminding him to come in for more tests and informing him of all the new abilities that had developed. As usual, he wrote all the new names in his book.

The list of enhanced people was growing nicely again and there hadn't been a single death lately. Admittedly, they'd been a lot more careful about who they gave the enzyme too. Having a much larger pool of people to choose from meant they'd been able to reject any they thought might die.

Sherdan ignored the nag for more testing and went about the rest of his work. He was doing a live TV broadcast the following day from his study.

He still didn't intend to reveal the abilities and enzyme, but lots of news teams wanted to interview him about taking more land and sneaking in so many more people. Utopia was completely unstoppable, and not a single person had been harmed during the entire war.

There was also the issue of all the soldiers they had locked up. They still lived in the cells at the guard buildings he had dotted all over the land. The cells were almost full but, so far, no more soldiers had attacked.

Something would have to be done with them soon, however. Several had started trying to escape. While none had succeeded, escapees would tarnish his otherwise perfect reputation.

Sherdan dealt with as much work as he could manage before his eyelids drooped and he caught himself falling asleep on the sofa. He shut down his laptop and got up. His thoughts automatically returned to Anya. He really felt a little lost with her and wasn't used to feeling this way where women were concerned.

CHAPTER 32

Anya didn't leave her room for breakfast while Sherdan was about the following morning. He went over to the compound with a sad weight on his heart. He'd have to hope she was more open again that evening. Women were so fickle.

There was plenty of work to do, however. The shelters at all the newest occupied houses were being built and installed. Sherdan also expected some kind of response from the UN after Anya's news the day before.

He had a live link to the BBC news just after six that evening so he could get a full day's work in before he needed to be back in his own study. He hoped Anya wouldn't stray out of her room while it was happening. There wouldn't be time to tell her about it before hand.

The morning passed uneventfully and he soon took a break to grab some lunch. Hitchin joined him, a little unexpectedly.

"I know you don't like being studied, Sherdan, but we really need to do some more tests. People are beginning to wonder why you don't come and identify the new abilities in the growing number of residents who still don't know what they can do." Sherdan sighed but knew his friend was only telling the truth.

"I'll come next week, I promise."

"Very well."

Hitchin stayed where he was sat, despite not saying any more. Sherdan waited, not sure he wanted Hitchin to say anything else but not wanting to offend him either.

"How's everything going with Miss Price? Has she agreed to marry you yet?"

"Not yet. I think things have improved but something holds her back. Her beliefs, I think."

"Hmmm... that would be tricky. Can you not get her to see that it's in her best interests to do as she's told?"

"She's a headstrong girl," Sherdan said. "I'm sure it won't be much longer. If anyone can succeed, I can."

"I'm sure she'll see sense soon, as well. After all, it's a definite result." Hitchin finally got up and left. Sherdan hadn't been entirely truthful with him. He didn't want Anya to just 'come to her senses', but to actually love him. He wanted more than he'd ever wanted from a woman before.

The first conversation they'd had regarding Hitchin's vision sprang to mind. His presumption of winning Anya had been so arrogant. He thought he'd be impossible to refuse and hadn't really known what it was to love someone. He was learning.

At first he'd only wanted her to do as he demanded, but it no longer seemed enough to have a woman do as he wished. Now he wanted a woman who really thought similar things as important as he did, someone who wanted to be at his side.

With this thought, Sherdan went back to work. Hitchin hadn't cheered him up at all. Instead ,Hitchin had only shown him how different falling in love had made him. He threw himself into his work with more energy than normal, practically making Graham's job obsolete. Two hours later he'd given himself a headache.

Shortly after four that afternoon a phone call came through for him. The UN had decided to approve the request for recognition as a separate country. While officially the Queen of England owned the land, it was an old law, and the UN thought there was enough weight behind Sherdan's request to disregard that problem.

They added that they felt it was important Sherdan not take any more land, however, saying it only weakened his political position with his neighbours. Sherdan didn't particularly care. He had what he wanted. The UK would be forced to treat him with more respect than they had recently.

Less than ten minutes after he got off the phone, the UN announced the decision publicly. The whole world knew he had succeeded. Sherdan immediately addressed his country.

"I have brilliant news for you all. Utopia has officially been recognised and accepted as a member of the United Nations. In celebration of this, there will be a street party and ball a week today. Congratulations."

There was a sound of applause from the command room when Sherdan took his finger off the intercom button. This was another very important day for his country. So far, with the exception of Anya, everything was pretty much going to plan.

Sherdan had another phone call before he could do anything else. The President of America, who had ignored him after his first attempt at opening diplomatic relations, now wanted to speak with him.

"I've only a moment, but I wanted to say congratulations on achieving membership in the UN. I think we should talk about trade and other such things between our countries."

"Of course, Al, I'm sure we can discuss things like that over the coming weeks. Shall I have someone get in contact with one of your cabinet to begin discussions?"

"That sounds good. I look forward to hearing from you."

Sherdan smiled as he put the phone down. He was highly unlikely to trade them any of the things they probably wanted, but they didn't need to know that yet.

Many similar calls rolled in from various diplomatic figures across the world. All of them were congratulatory, with an undertone of visitation or trade. He had something they all wanted.

He had to cut short the last of the calls and request Graham take any more as he headed back to his house for his live news interview. He'd only just sat down where Anne had set up his satellite link when he was introduced.

"Sherdan Harper, you've become quite the icon today. How does it feel to gain recognition as the leader of a new country?"

"It feels very good, considering the opposition we've faced. We've also been working hard on relations with other countries and are in the beginning of all sorts of agreements with many of them."

"What do you plan on doing next?"

"It depends on the British government, really. At this point we'd like to negotiate a ceasefire with the UK and concentrate on forming a working political system. We will continue to retaliate as we have been if things stay as they are, however."

"Do you intend to give the homes you've taken back to the original owners?"

"Possibly. Some of them. Definitely not all. A lot are now inhabited by my own citizens. As I said, I wish to negotiate a ceasefire, and giving land back is something I expect to be a part of that."

"And what about the soldiers that are considered 'missing in action'?"

"All of them are safe and will be allowed to return home as soon as we're at peace with the UK."

"Do you intend to divulge any of your technology now?"

"We intend to keep as much of it as possible to ourselves. For the most part, we just want to get on with our lives in peace."

"Thank you again, Dr Harper." Sherdan nodded before he was cut off. He looked up to see Anya in the doorway. She'd been listening to the whole thing. She smiled.

"So are you a Prime Minister or a King?" she asked. He smiled and chuckled.

"Neither, yet. I have my views on the best form of government. You already know about that, however."

"I do. I happen to agree with them in principle."

"Only in principle?" He noticed she had her kitten curled up in her arms again.

"I'm not convinced you'd be as benevolent as required."

"What would you prefer to be?" he asked, changing the subject back to her first statement.

"I don't understand."

"I want you to be my wife. Which would you prefer? Queen

perhaps?"

"That's not what I meant."

"I can make you anything you want to be right now."

"The only thing I want is to be free." Her eyes flashed in anger. He shook his head.

"I'm not trying to upset you, Anya. I love you. I want you to be happy."

She sat down, all the anger dissipated from her. She let Antonio go and watched him play on the floor for a moment.

"Can I come to the party and ball then?"

"You can, if you are staying. It would be dangerous for you to be seen with me and then to leave here."

"I don't see how."

"It just would, Anya. Please, can we not argue about everything?" She looked away from him. He'd upset her yet again, but he felt hurt too, and she never seemed to see that.

"I'm sorry. I don't really want to argue either. I'm just fed up of being stuck here."

"No one is keeping you here. If you're really not happy with me, then please leave and go somewhere you are." She turned her face back towards him. A tear slowly ran down her left cheek and it pained him to see her like that.

"I can't leave. I'm... I don't even know if I want to. I just feel like I'm trapped in limbo. I can't live properly here and I don't feel like I can leave."

"I don't understand what's forcing you to stay." Sherdan continued to watch her cry. "I want you to stay and be my wife, but above that I want you to be happy, wherever you are. Will you let me try and make you happy here, at least?"

She wiped away her tears and shrugged. He got up, went to her and took her by the hands, pulling her to her feet. As soon as she was standing he embraced her in the biggest hug he had ever given anyone and didn't let go for some minutes.

When they finally parted she appeared calm again and even gave him a small smile. He took her hand and led her to the sitting room. He went to the kitchen and got Anne to bring their dinner through to them there.

Having meals in the dining room was something he normally

insisted upon, but lately he had been slack. He wanted Anya to feel relaxed more than he cared about such concepts anymore.

He kept conversation focused on small things, like soon-to-be-released films, while they ate. By the time they'd finished dessert she seemed a lot brighter again. She evidently liked talking about films and actors. She knew much more about them than he did. He didn't usually have time for them, although he enjoyed them when he did.

After dinner the topic progressed to books which had been made into films. Sherdan felt on more familiar ground. He often read, especially since purchasing a kindle.

They talked for ages, comparing their opinions. She preferred the Narnian books to the films. He preferred Lord of The Rings as a book and she as the films. There wasn't much they agreed on, as usual, but it was an amicable conversation.

The ended their evening together much happier than they had begun it. Sherdan felt relief when Anya left him to sleep, although he still felt confused about her indecision. She acted like she didn't want to be here, but didn't leave, even when offered the opportunity.

For the next few days Sherdan avoided all serious topics of conversation with Anya. He didn't think it would do either of them any good. She allowed Sherdan to get closer to her again, but if it felt like they might kiss she soon retreated. No matter how hard he tried, he couldn't get past that final wall she'd put up.

There were no more attacks on Utopia either, and diplomatic relations were beginning with many countries, although the UK had not spoken up yet. Sherdan had called the Prime Minister again a couple of times but, just like with Anya, the walls were still up. The army still patrolled all the borders and they still had an active arrest warrant out on him.

There was nothing Sherdan could do but wait and keep trying, hoping both Anya and the UK would thaw soon.

CHAPTER 33

The nightmares had greatly diminished since Anya had been given her pet, Antonio. Sherdan had surprised her with the gift but it had been the perfect choice. It had almost torn down her guard completely and she'd had to remind herself that Sherdan had tortured her for several days.

Several times now he had said that he both loved her and wanted her to leave if it would make her happy, but no matter how many times he said it, she couldn't decide if she believed him. His words were still as fresh to her as the moment he'd said them.

Anya wasn't sure how she felt about him either. She had considered leaving several times recently, before she did something she regretted and got herself in too deep.

Every time she told herself she was leaving, she'd have the same dream again about saving Sherdan's life. Thankfully, it didn't make her throw up anymore.

God evidently wanted her to stay. She hoped she could bring herself to leave when it finally came down to it. The longer she stayed the more she felt attached to Sherdan and his country's fate.

There had been one moment when she'd almost allowed Sherdan right under her skin. She knew that couldn't happen. He wasn't why she was here, and she would have to leave at some point soon. She couldn't have a relationship even if she wanted one.

Anya sat down with a thud, surprising herself at thinking seriously about being with Sherdan. Before today she'd denied any desire for anything of the sort. She'd put any feelings down to some kind of saviour complex over his timely intervention of her interrogation.

Her thoughts were so muddled. She couldn't think of anything to do but pray and hope she could leave soon. Her feelings could be worked through in her own home and church, safe from Sherdan's unhealthy effect on her.

She absentmindedly stroked the kitten beside her as she prayed. Strength and focus would be important until her task here was done, even if she still didn't know what that was.

Her karate lessons were going well. Nathan had taught her a lot in a short space of time. They'd gone through all the blocks so many times that Nathan now struggled to land a blow. She had then begun learning attacks, but she wasn't as good at those yet. Her punches were very weak, although her kicks weren't too bad.

Nathan had suggested she try sparring with her ability turned on. In her half-way stage she'd be invisible but be able to strike back at an assailant if needed. If she thought she was going to be hit she could move into the full state of her ability and any blows would go through her.

She'd turned down his offer to practice this as she'd not felt completely comfortable fighting him naked, even if he wouldn't be able to see anything. Also, she didn't know if she would be able to keep herself invisible and concentrate on karate at the same time. His suggestion had merit, however, so she'd spent a further hour each day practising alone whilst invisible.

Another Sunday passed, with her still away from her church, and another week began, leaving Anya feeling down again. She knew she'd need to leave soon. She finally felt like her time here was coming to an end. It still felt like something needed to happen first but, as the week began, her feelings of expectancy grew.

She could hardly focus on her karate Tuesday morning and

did very little in the way of research for Sherdan. The public opinion on him hadn't changed much lately anyway. People mostly thought he was amazing. The houses he'd robbed people of were almost forgotten already.

He joined her earlier than normal that evening, but looked even more tired than he usually did. He grinned at her and went straight to his laptop. She came and sat nearby.

"So what's the plan this evening?" she asked, expecting him to suggest something, as he had for the last week.

"I'm too busy this evening. I didn't get enough of my work done."

"Why ever not? You've been gone since seven."

"I... Hitchin had me in the lab a lot of the day." She raised her eyebrows. "I needed some tests... it seems my ability has disappeared. Hitchin is the only other person who knows, however."

"I won't say a word. How will this affect your country?"

"Hopefully it won't. It seems to just be me, and it also appears that there is no discernible scientific reason, but we don't have the results from all the tests yet."

"Oh. I will let you work then." She got up to go, feeling sorry for him.

"Please stay. At least until dinner. Tell me about your day."

"Nothing really happened. I've been practising my karate, and my ability, but not much else."

"Keep practising, it's good for you."

"What kind of work do you have to do?" she said, changing the subject back from her to him.

"I have to work out some trade agreements with some of the countries that have asked to trade. I don't want to give them any of our advanced technology so I'm having to come up with other things we have to offer. Trade will be important to us; with some of them, at least." Sherdan looked thoughtful for a moment. Anya thought it sounded rather tedious but let Sherdan continue.

"Also, a few countries want embassies here. Finally, there's the ball in three days."

"I'd like to come to that."

"I've already said. If you are staying then I think you should come."

"I'm not sure I am staying, and even if I were, I have no dress." Anya got up and walked away to inspect the books. She'd looked over them so many times before, but the familiar names soothed her agitated mind. A part of her considered saying she'd stay just to go to the ball but she couldn't lie.

She lost herself in thought until Sherdan made her jump. He had stopped working and come up behind her. He took her right hand in his and turned her to face him.

"I want you to stay. Be on my arm at the ball, in front of my whole country." She looked away and then back again. "Stay."

"I don't know if I can."

"Do you want to?"

"No... Well, maybe. I can't decide." She couldn't lie but hated that he'd asked her. "I have things I need to do back home."

"So do them and come back. I'll even drive you myself."

"It's not that simple."

Before either of them could say anything else Anne popped her head through the doorway and told them dinner was ready. Anya immediately tore her hand away from Sherdan and went into the dining room. It gave her a moment to compose herself.

She'd come so close to giving in and saying she'd come back. He made her head spin and she was very grateful when he had to carry on working after they had eaten. It gave her some respite from his attentions.

She deliberately fetched her bible and sat reading it in the same room as him. It wasn't something she'd done before while being with him. He'd made such a mockery of her beliefs that she hadn't wanted to draw any attention to it, but it seemed like a good idea now.

The whole evening Sherdan said very little. His work absorbed his attention and she often looked up to see him frowning over it. A part of her wanted to help him. His workload was obviously too much, but she'd already got herself far too attached to him and his country to offer any more assistance. Enough was enough.

CHAPTER 34

Sherdan poured himself into his work that evening. Every time he pulled another few bricks out of Anya's walls she retreated from him or got angry. Now she'd started reading the Bible in front of him and the message was clear: she wanted him to back off because she was a well-behaved Christian girl who didn't get involved with the likes of him.

Anya went to bed at her usual time and Sherdan sighed with relief. The evening had been horribly awkward. He'd actually done more work than he needed to because he hadn't wanted to stop and have to force another conversation with her.

As soon as he was alone, he got up and poured a drink. Tonight he needed it. He sat and thought over his problem with Anya for another hour.

He felt like they were getting close to a tipping point and, if he didn't have her won over by then, she would leave forever. Sherdan knew he needed help again so he went to call on Nathan's advice.

Nathan was as quick to join him in the study as the last time.

"What can I do for you, sir?" Nathan said, taking a seat but refusing a drink again.

"I need more help with Anya. The kitten worked very well but I'm not all the way there yet."

"How did talking to her about her faith go?"

"I've not done so yet. I don't really know where to begin," Sherdan explained.

"Ask her what convinced her to become a Christian. If you can understand why she chose that faith she'll be less confusing to you in general."

"Maybe. I don't know if I can talk to her about what she thinks without arguing. She sat here with her Bible all evening to show me she thought her moral opinions to be more sound than mine."

"Had it occurred to you that she may have read her Bible in front of you because she wanted you to understand it meant a lot to her and she was hoping you ask about it?" Sherdan looked at Nathan as if he'd been slapped and he had to stop himself responding in his anger. The guard was just trying to help.

"She wants to come to the ball on Friday," Sherdan said, changing the subject.

"So let her come."

"I don't want to put her at risk."

"At risk of what?"

"If she comes, people will know she's been here. If she then leaves, the British government might capture her and torture her for information. I promised her that would never happen to her again."

"With her ability, she could just walk out. Just like she can here," Nathan pointed out.

"I didn't think of that."

"Does Anya know of your reasoning?"

"Not exactly, no."

"Then I'd explain it to her and give her the choice," Nathan said and got up.

"That's it?"

"It sounds like most of your troubles are caused by not communicating with her properly. Talk to her. If you still need help after that, I'll be more than happy to sit down with you again." Sherdan nodded and let Nathan leave.

He poured himself another drink as he mulled over their conversation in his head. A lot of what Nathan said made sense and, whether he was right or not about her reasons for reading the Bible in front of him, it was worth talking to her about what she believed.

With a resolution in mind, he finally got some sleep. He needed to stop getting such late nights. It was the early hours of the morning again. Hopefully, Hitchin would have some good news about his ability the following day, and he would also make some more progress with Anya.

Sherdan was woken up before his alarm by none other than Anya. She still wore her pyjamas and had a slightly tear-stained face.

"I had another nightmare," she told him, as if it explained everything. He went to get out of bed to hug her before he thought that she might not want to see him in just his boxers. Instead, he patted the edge of the bed. She shook her head.

"I just wanted to say that I was sorry I was so argumentative yesterday. I'm finding everything that has happened in the last six weeks very difficult."

"That's okay, I understand. I've not always done much to help," Sherdan glanced at the clock and noticed his alarm was going to go off in less than five minutes. "Why don't we talk about this later? I'm needed in the compound shortly."

She nodded and left, leaving him unable to follow. He hastily pulled on some clothes and went through to her room. She'd got back into bed again but she was sitting rather than lying.

"Are you going to be okay?"

She nodded at his concern.

"I've got a karate lesson in an hour."

He reluctantly left her and headed over to the compound. Hitchin awaited him in his easy room. He smiled at his friend, who appeared much happier since Sherdan had let him run all his tests.

"How is everything?" Sherdan asked.

"We have a delightful new batch of test subjects... perhaps one female in particular. Quite the bright young lady. I may train her as an assistant."

Sherdan recognised the familiar twinkle in his friend's eye. This particular woman had evidently caught his eye for more than professional reasons.

"I'm here to let you know that all your tests came back perfectly fine. You don't even seem to be fatigued enough to explain it. I can only assume it has something to do with Anya," Hitchin continued.

"So, if Anya stays, I won't get my ability back?"

"Not necessarily. I won't know for sure unless I can find out what gave her the ability she has."

"Fair enough. I'll bring her in for more tests as soon as I can make her see it's necessary."

Sherdan went into the command room to get away from Hitchin before he could continue talking about Anya. She wasn't going to be made to do anything. He was still determined to win her over properly and had a couple more things he could try.

He'd sent an email with Anya's measurements to one of his colleagues. They were picking up a ball gown for her today. That evening he would present it to her.

For the majority of the day, Sherdan had to deal with the American President. The Americans were demanding some of his defence technology in return for becoming allies. He wouldn't let them have anything they still used regularly so he instead tried to offer them some of the country's other advances, something that affected less military matters.

There had been other breakthroughs in medical treatments, as well as food production thanks to studying the abilities and how they worked. Parting with things like that would benefit whoever received it but not increase any potential threat to Utopia.

The Americans believed they were a powerful enough country that Sherdan would give anything to be allies. They were wrong. America had very little to offer them, and other countries were willing to be amicable for less.

Sherdan repeatedly said no until the President got so cross he slammed the phone down on him. He left his diplomat, Sharon, to continue trying to deal with it while he got on with other work. His work was never finished.

It was gone eight before he got away from the compound.

Anya wasn't anywhere downstairs so Sherdan rushed up to his room to check on the dress he'd had Anne smuggle up for him. It was a gorgeous, deep-blue, floor-length ball gown.

He picked it up off the bed, where it lay, as he heard a rap on the door frame behind him. Anya gasped as he turned around. She stood there with her hands over her mouth.

"Yes, it is for you," Sherdan said as he held it out to her. She didn't take it.

"It's gorgeous, but I haven't decided if I am staying."

"I know. I'm letting you come to the ball, if that's what you wish to do."

"Really?" Her eyes lit up.

"Yes, but please understand, if you leave it could put you in danger, being seen here, with me."

"I know. I appreciate your concern, but I'd like it to be my choice, just like leaving or staying should be." Sherdan nodded and walked towards her to place the dress in her hands. This time she took it. She held it up against herself.

"You'll look gorgeous in it."

"Thank you." She beamed and scurried off. He slowly walked out into the hallway. Her door was shut so he waited outside. He didn't have to wait long before she flung the door open and came out wearing the dress. She twirled.

"So what do you think?"

"It really suits you." She spun again, obviously pleased. "So will you come to the ball with me, then?" Sherdan asked. She stopped spinning and paused for a moment.

"Yes. Yes, I think I will."

"Really?" He took her hands and pulled her towards him. She nodded and his heart beat faster. He wrapped his arms around her in another embrace but she pulled away after only a few seconds.

"You don't want to crease it. Let me get changed again."

She rushed off before he could reply and shut her door on him again. He chuckled to himself and went to find some food. Anne had gone home earlier than normal, as it was one of her sons' birthday.

It was his turn to be surprised when he walked into the

kitchen. Two trays were already laid out, ready, and a casserole and some roast potatoes were in the oven. He noticed there were ten minutes left on the oven timer. Anya came up behind him as he stood, unsure what to do.

"Anne assured me you liked sausage casserole so I made one for dinner."

"Umm... thank you. I have to admit it's quite unexpected."

"I thought I might as well. Anne said she had to go, but you weren't back yet."

"Thank you. I don't think I've ever had a woman, other than my mother or housekeeper, cook for me." She blushed at this and busied herself tidying the kitchen to cover her embarrassment.

Sherdan was touched by the effort she had gone to and hoped it was a sign their evening would go well. He planned on trying to talk to her about her faith, if he could find a way to bring it up. It could wait until after the food, however. He intended to enjoy her company and her cooking.

They ate right there in the kitchen, sat on stools at the breakfast bar, which was something Sherdan had never actually done before. He didn't spend that much time in the kitchen so he'd allowed Anne to design the room how she wanted it.

Anya finished eating first, evidently hungry from waiting. He wasn't far behind, enjoying the meal she had made him.

A smile lit up her face when he had cleaned his plate and put his knife and fork together. It had been delicious.

"Thank you. You're a good cook."

"Not really. I know how to make one or two things well. It's good to have a few dishes that can be cooked well," Anya replied, her cheeks flushing red again. He laughed at her sound logic.

"The way to a man's heart is through his stomach." He got up and went to her, took her by the hand and led her through to the living room. They sat side by side on the sofa, with her hands in his, for some time. She blushed a lot but didn't pull away.

"Has your God said anything lately about why you're here?" he asked and then frowned. It had come out sounding a little harsher than he had meant it.

She pulled her hands away from him.

"I'm sorry. I didn't mean it like that. I am trying to understand."

"Understand what?" she demanded.

"I know your faith means a lot to you. I love you. I want to understand you and your beliefs better."

"Oh... I... I don't really know how to explain it entirely."

"You said God told you to come here and has said to stay. Did he literally speak to you?"

"No, I don't know if God literally says things out loud. For me, it's more like thoughts that come into your head, combined with feelings. It feels 'right' to do as God asks."

"And He's asked you to stay here?" Sherdan asked.

"For now, I think so, yes, but I will have to leave at some point."

"Why?"

"I will need to go back to my church."

"But you are here now. Did God say why?"

"I'm not sure. I had a dream but I didn't completely understand it." Sherdan nodded. "So I'm waiting here until I know why." He reached up a hand and stroked her cheek.

"I am very glad He asked you to stay longer. I would not have known the feelings I have now."

"I'm glad I'm here too, but I don't think I can stay. At some point I will have to go, Sherdan." She looked away. "I'm sorry." He lifted her chin back up.

"But you are here now, and God wants that."

"Yes, I am here now..." Whatever she had been about to say was lost as he lent forward and pressed his lips to hers. When he pulled back to look at her she followed and kissed him again, more passionately than he'd expected.

He smiled as he wrapped his arms around her and pulled her even closer.

"I love you," he whispered. The words sounded so foreign to him but, in that moment, felt so right.

"I... I love you, too." He kissed her again, wanting to show her the delight and joy her words stirred in him.

He had dreamt of this moment on several occasions but the reality was so much sweeter. His fingers caressed her cheek as his lips touched hers again and again.

After many minutes she pulled away. Her eyes shone and she smiled in a way he had never seen before. She breathed heavily and had a brightness to her he liked. He remembered the only other time he had seen her like this. It had been right after she had gained her ability, but before they had fallen out.

"You do know I can't... Before marriage I'm not meant to..." He put his finger up against her mouth.

"I understand. We don't have to go that far. I've... Well, there have been many women I have rushed into bed with and I do not want us to be like that. We can go much slower." She nodded her gratitude and he pulled her in close to him again, studying her features.

She blushed at his intense gaze, making him chuckle.

"Are all Christian girls so delicate and shy? You're perfect. Had I known, I would have found one of you sooner." She frowned. "I'm teasing. I've never met anyone like you and I am really not used to feeling like this, about anyone."

He shrugged. His feelings couldn't be easily explained and it frustrated him a little. Without hesitating, she settled back against the sofa back and pulled his arm around behind her so they were cuddled up close.

They talked of happy subjects like family memories and silly things they did as children, whiling away the time. Occasionally he would give her another kiss, as if he couldn't believe she was reciprocating.

Neither of them mentioned the future and where they would go after that evening. He couldn't bring it up in case she still said she intended to leave.

Sherdan didn't know if he believed in her God but, in that moment, he prayed anyway that He wouldn't take Anya away from him. He'd found his little piece of heaven and he didn't want to lose it.

CHAPTER 35

The evening passed at a rapid pace before Sherdan's eyes. He didn't want to stop being with Anya. He was neglecting all the work he needed to do in favour of talking to her and he didn't care.

"When did you become a Christian?" he asked. She paused, looking thoughtful.

"I have been brought up as a Christian but I didn't really begin believing in it for myself until I started going to my current church. They were so different, informal, but serious about Jesus."

Sherdan did his best to listen respectfully as she explained. His curiosity was piqued by her words, and he desperately wanted to understand.

"The church believes worship, the music and the band and everything about it, is important. It is modern and the words in the songs have real depth. It helps people connect to God and the Holy Spirit." She paused to think.

"Go on," he whispered.

"I hadn't realised the Holy Spirit was something I could tangibly feel. The first time I did, I felt so peaceful. I just knew I was home and had to keep coming back for more of that feeling, those moments when all that matters is God and being with Him."

He nodded. He didn't entirely understand, but he could see how important it was to her. It gave him a lot to think about. She didn't speak of prayers being answered, or logical reasons for God existing, but of feelings and experiences.

Her whole answer took him by surprise. It was the first time someone hadn't tried to argue him into believing but had simply explained their own feelings. Her face had also lit up in the most beautiful of ways. It evidently meant a lot to her.

"Thank you for being so honest. I think I understand more of it." She smiled and they kissed again. He had never spent time in such a sweet and innocent fashion.

Before long, Antonio meowed at Anya to make a fuss of him so they both played piggy in the middle with the cat for the next half an hour, rolling a small ball between them. Once the kitten was worn out she stood and picked the fluffy creature up.

"I should probably get some sleep." She stepped towards Sherdan and onto the tips of her toes to give him a kiss goodnight. He hugged her to him until Antonio began to wiggle between them.

It felt odd to be letting her go to sleep without joining her but he didn't protest. Her beliefs were important to her and every time he had acted against them, it had put a gulf between them.

He let her go and went through to his study. There was still a mountain of work to do and it was already almost midnight. He sat for a few minutes in his favourite chair, thinking of Anya, with no regard to his work schedule. He had not felt so happy in years.

Just before one, his radio squawked at him.

"Sherdan, are you awake, sir?" came Graham's voice. Sherdan grabbed his radio and pressed the button to reply.

"Yes. Why are you still up?"

"I was called into the command room. A small plane flew over about ten minutes ago."

"What did it do?"

"As far as we can tell, nothing; it just circled over and went back where it came from."

"Keep monitoring for now. Let me know if it happens again."

"Yes, sir." Sherdan put the radio down again, thoughtfully. They really needed to get some kind of air defence. He went back to his work, thinking no more of it.

"Sir, I think they may have dropped men."

"You 'think', commander?"

"Yes, sir. There have been civilian reports of two or possibly more men trying to sneak around."

"Have all the guard teams alerted. Let me know if anyone is spotted by officials."

"Are you going to come to the command room, sir?"

"No, not until we have confirmed sightings. I will stay here. I have things to do."

Sherdan went back to his work for a few minutes but Graham was soon calling for his attention again.

"No intruders found, sir, and the security teams have done a country-wide sweep."

"Do a second, just in case."

"Already doing so, sir."

Sherdan got up and went through to his own guards. Nathan had already turned to the door, expecting him after hearing the radio chatter.

"I assume you have been listening to the radio?" Sherdan asked.

"Of course, sir."

"Keep an eye out, just in case."

"Yes, sir."

Sherdan went back to his study. Normally he would have gone over to the command room but Anya was asleep and he didn't want to leave without her. He also had a lot of work to do.

Whatever it was that had caused the civilians to report something, it now had Sherdan so distracted that he found continuing the next items on his agenda impossible. He contemplated going to bed but decided on a small nightcap first.

Picking up the decanter, he poured the last of its liquid into a glass. He would need some more brandy in the morning.

"Sir, there's still no sign of anyone, but the soldiers think they may have seen movement, from a possible non-civilian source, near your house. I'm getting them to search the general area," the radio came to life.

"All right, Graham, keep me informed."

He contemplated going to wake Anya to take her to the compound with him but the thought just annoyed him. He left her where she was and paced his study, glass in one hand and radio in the other.

"Sir, we are getting some funky behaviour from a couple of our camera feeds," Nathan reported.

"What do you mean by 'funky', Nathan?"

"They have flashed on and off a couple of times. Just two of them at the back of the house."

"Ok... Graham can you send a squad of the guards over to the house?"

"Yes, sir."

Sherdan waited for a moment, now more concerned.

"They are on their way," Graham informed him.

"Thank you."

"Sir, I'm now getting the alarm on the kitchen door, someone's opened it."

"Come through and..."

"Wait, now it's fine," Nathan interrupted. "I think it was a false alarm. There is nothing on the camera feed in the kitchen."

"Is there or isn't there an intruder in the house?" Sherdan hissed.

"There isn't, sir."

"The extra guards are almost there, sir," Graham added. Sherdan sat down, noticing that the glass in his hand was very unsteady. His security team had unsettled him. He calmed himself as he decided whether it was best to get Anya and head to the compound.

Just as he was about to get up it occurred to him that to get to her, he had to go past the kitchen and he had left the door open. If it wasn't a false alarm he would be going towards danger.

He stood up when he decided he did not care. He couldn't let anything happen to her.

"Anya, are you awake?" he called into the radio. Before there was any chance of a reply the door handle began turning.

CHAPTER 36

Anya could hardly breathe as she walked up the flights of stairs to her room. She had finally gone to bed after the amazing evening with Sherdan.

He had been the perfect gentleman and not pushed her for anything further, but she had retreated anyway. Had she stayed any longer, she may have offered him something she would have regretted at a later date. The passion she felt for him had almost overwhelmed her as it was.

As she passed his room, she felt a tug from somewhere inside her suggesting getting into his bed rather than her own. After pausing a moment, she resisted it and walked into her own room instead.

She put Antonio down and stood, leaning against her closed door, still struggling to breathe with all the excitement and passion he had stirred in her.

Anya had decided she loved him and really believed he loved her too. Her thoughts that evening had not yet gone beyond that. What she would do if God told her to leave and not come back only then came to her mind. As Sherdan said, she was here now, but how much longer would she be?

She gnawed on her lip as she thought about how reckless she had actually been. Not only could she not guarantee she could stay, Sherdan wasn't a Christian. He may have taken an interest in her beliefs but that was a long way from a conversion.

On top of all these fears, she felt the first wave of doubt that she really loved him. Love was entirely new to her, and so far the relationship between them had been so mixed it could just be relief. She groaned.

Considering the circumstances, she did the best thing she could think of and fell to her knees to pray. She had possibly been very stupid and needed God to sort it out, but Anya could hardly concentrate on anything other than how she felt when Sherdan had been kissing her.

She still knelt, trying to pray for God's will, when the radio Sherdan had given her started squawking. She heard Graham call for Sherdan and the following reply. Feeling curious, she got up and took the radio to listen.

The messages confused her at first until she realised there were intruders. The dream she'd had flashed through her mind. She went invisible and the radio along with all her clothes dropped to the ground as she rushed straight for the stairs. She didn't even go through the doorway, but through the wall, in her haste.

Anya could hardly get down the two flights of stairs fast enough. As she reached the ground floor she slowed herself so she could move silently.

She walked into the study where she found Sherdan. He was pacing and walked through her a couple of times. It felt odd so she moved back towards the door to watch him and continue listening.

More information soon came in, although they were obviously confused by what was happening. She felt calm despite the air of panic around her.

When Sherdan was told the kitchen alarm had gone off, Anya almost gasped out loud. Thankfully he didn't hear the small stifled noise she made instead. She hadn't expected that her dream would come true. She froze to the spot in panic. After everything she had faced, and somehow managed to overcome, this made her feel frightened more than any of it ever had before.

Sherdan sat down, snapping her back to reality. She closed

her eyes and prayed, instantly feeling calmer. God wanted her to do it and she knew that. She had to be brave. The man she loved needed her help and she would do everything she could.

They both watched as the door handle turned. She moved swiftly to cover the opening and protect Sherdan. He seemed unable to move or respond.

As the door handle hit the bottom, the door was flung open. Anya was faced with two black-clad soldiers pointing guns straight at her. Without hesitating, she grabbed the front of the first gun and yanked it downwards.

The soldier pulled the trigger and peppered the floor with bullets. She gasped, giving her location away. She had to think fast and switch state as the second soldier shot in her direction.

Thankfully, Sherdan had moved out of the way and none of the bullets which passed through her found him. She stepped to her left and grabbed the gun again as she brought her knee up into the soldier's groin. He still held onto his weapon as she yanked on it for a third time.

She punched the soldier in the stomach and he let his grip go enough that a fourth tug dropped the weapon to the floor. The soldier moved forward and straight into her, sending her flying backwards. He was as stunned as she was.

Using the surprise of the assailants to her advantage, she scrambled to her feet and continued her attack in an invisible fury. Using the moves Nathan had taught her, she grabbed the soldier's arm, spun under it, and floored the man next to his own gun.

Improvising, she used the butt of the gun to hit his head. As more shots came her way she dropped the weapon again. All the shots passed through her, sending a chill up her spine. She really did not like things moving through her.

"What the?" the second soldier said as he followed into the room, only seeing his unconscious comrade and Sherdan. Anya turned and delivered an upper cut to the man's face. It wasn't strong enough to do any real damage, except make his nose bleed.

She took a step back and delivered a roundhouse to the soldier's side before grabbing the gun, yanking it up and bending his fingers back. A few more shots rang out and embedded themselves in the ceiling.

Her right hand met the nose of the soldier again as her other kept the gun pointed up. The poor soldier didn't know what had hit him as she battered him with blow after blow.

Anya was so exhilarated by landing so many moves, she didn't notice when the soldier took his second hand off the gun and punched forwards. He caught her right in the face, sending her onto her back again. Blood dripped from her mouth as the commando readied his gun to shoot at Sherdan.

"No!" she yelled as she scrambled to her feet. The soldier looked in her direction and swung the gun towards her, still unable to see where she was. As he did, one of the security guards snuck up behind and hit him on the head with the butt of his own P60.

"All clear, sir," the guard said, as another five of the security team filed in behind, followed very quickly by Nathan from the opposite side of the house.

"Anya, are you okay?" Sherdan asked, looking around as if he hoped to see her.

"Yes, I think so. I haven't been shot, at least." She went up to him and took his hand. "Are you okay?"

"Yes, thank you. That was... I'm not sure exactly, but thank you."

"You're welcome."

"Sir, what just happened?" Nathan asked.

"I used the karate you taught me to keep those soldiers at bay until you guys could arrive," Anya explained, from her invisible state beside Sherdan. Her words came out much faster, jumbling over each other so much she could only just make out what she had said.

The jaws of the other six guards hung open. None of them knew that it was the same girl who had been tortured by their team, and they definitely didn't know about her ability.

"Thank you, men, you may all return to your posts. Nathan, you too." Sherdan waved them all off and waited for them to leave. He kept a firm grip on her hand and she didn't try to pull away. He evidently wanted to know where she was and she had no intention of becoming visible and letting him see her naked.

On top of that, she knew her mouth had bled profusely and wasn't sure if it had stopped. She could taste the metallic salt of her own blood and knew she didn't want to see it yet.

As soon as everyone left, Sherdan tugged on Anya's hand.

"Come here, darling. Are you sure you are okay?" He reached out his arms to where he thought she was. She stepped into his embrace and hugged him tightly. She had begun to shake as the shock of the fight reared its ugly head.

While she sobbed, Sherdan held her and kissed every inch of her head and face that he could reach. The whole time he kept his hands firmly fixed to the same position on her back, preventing her from pulling away, even if she had wanted to. He didn't stop kissing her until she stopped crying and rested her head on his shoulders.

"I'm sorry," she whispered, completely ashamed of herself.

"Don't be. You just saved my life."

She tried to pull away but he still wouldn't let her go.

"I love you," he said in a more husky tone than normal. Her heart swelled as she kissed him, taking him by surprise.

His lips met hers again and again, while he wrapped his arms tighter around her until he had her crushed up against him.

"I should... I should go. I need to put some clothes on," she told him, with a great deal of effort. A part of her didn't really want to.

"Don't." He kissed her again, but she pulled away.

"I must." She ran from the room, and him, before she could change her mind. She could hardly believe what she had managed to do. It was a blur in her head already, replaced by the warmth of Sherdan's embrace.

As she pulled on her clothes she concentrated on her thoughts and feelings towards Sherdan so she wouldn't drift back into panic from what had happened.

It amused her that she had reacted so much more to something that was trivial in comparison to her ordeal six weeks earlier, especially when it had been over and done with in minutes. She smiled and she let herself go visible again. The image in the mirror made her stop. Blood covered her whole lower face and one of her hands.

Sherdan knocked on the door and came in before she could clean herself up.

"Oh, good God." He rushed over to her.

"It's okay. I'm not bleeding anymore." He didn't listen to her and quickly got a damp flannel. She waited, not really sure what to say.

Sherdan cleaned off all the blood from her skin, taking his time, while he sat beside her on her bed. She smiled at him, although it didn't reach her eyes.

"There, back to my beautiful Anya," Sherdan said when he had finished cleaning her up. She tried to get up and take the flannel away but she went dizzy as soon as she stood. He pushed her back and persuaded her to lie down.

"Let me. You need to rest." She allowed Sherdan to fuss over her as she lay there. She didn't think she wanted to be alone and he evidently didn't want to go. He tucked her into her covers and sat beside her.

"Please... don't leave me," she whispered as a few more tears welled up in her eyes.

"Of course. Why would I leave the side of my guardian?" He smiled at her. She wanted to smile back but another tear fell from her eyes. "I will stay here all night if you need me to."

"Thank you," she replied, taking his hand. He lifted it to his mouth and kissed. He then repeated the action again and again, working his way up to her wrist and then the rest of her arm. She had to pull herself away as he lay down beside her.

"Sherdan. Please."

"I'm not going to do anything. I'm just going to be here with you."

"I can't... I mean I shouldn't do any more than..."

"Sssshh. I do not intend to take advantage of your vulnerable state."

"Promise?"

"I promise, despite any temptations. I will just be here with you."

"It's been a very eventful day." She put her head back down and smiled again.

"It has, but it's over now. Sleep and know that I won't leave your side. You're completely safe now." She took his hand again and rolled over to snuggle up to him. When she was comfortable she closed her eyes. She breathed in the reassuring smell of him and allowed her exhausted body to drift to sleep.

CHAPTER 37

Lifting up his hand, Sherdan stroked the hair off Anya's face. She'd not been asleep long but he was relieved she was. He pondered over the day's events as he gazed at her peaceful face.

She'd saved his life, using her ability. He couldn't help but wonder if it did have something to do with God. It didn't completely match up with Hitchin's vision, but everything she had said now appeared true. She had been told to stay and, in staying, she had saved him.

He didn't know about the rest of her beliefs but he definitely believed in some kind of higher power. There was no way he could deny it any longer.

He fought to stay awake and enjoy the gentleness of being right beside the woman he loved. She filled his heart and made him feel alive in a way he had never felt before. Life was more complete with her by his side.

"Sir, are you awake?" a radio called from the floor. It still lay where Anya had dropped it earlier. She stirred as he got up off the bed and picked the interrupting item up.

"Yes, Nathan, what is wrong?" he replied as he tiptoed out of the room.

"Two more English commandos have been found."

"Where?"

"Near the compound. I don't think they had done anything."

"Thank you, Nathan. Get the guards to do another sweep."

"They already have."

"Do another," Sherdan growled.

"Yes, sir."

"And, Nathan, make sure nothing like this happens again."

Sherdan went back to Anya and resumed his position right next to her, feeling wide awake again. She had protected him and now he would make sure he was there to protect her.

He wished he had gone to her the second he had suspected any kind of trouble and whisked her off to safety. It had been his unwillingness to move that had stopped him going to her as soon as the first sign of danger had appeared, and it had put her in danger. He hadn't been frightened for himself. Hitchin's prophecy assured him of his own safety, but the thought of losing Anya now, when she had just given him such a reason to hope, terrified him.

He kissed her forehead and closed his eyes to sleep. Both of his arms were wrapped around her, keeping her close. Sleep passed over him, relieving his mind from all his thoughts and worries.

They stayed like that, entwined, the rest of the night, undisturbed and completely at peace. They didn't notice when Sherdan's alarm went off at its usual time across the hallway and neither woke when the radio called for Sherdan just after nine.

He opened his eyes naturally a little over an hour later. His attention fixed straight on Anya. She still slept right where she had been when he had drifted off. He smiled and kissed her on every part of her face, calling her name in between.

"We've overslept, darling. I need to go to work," he whispered. She kissed him full on his lips with more passion than he had expected.

"Thank you for not leaving me."

"I couldn't have left, even if you had wanted me to, but I have to now. You can come to the compound with me, if you want?"

"No. I will stay here. You'll be home for dinner?"

"I will try to be." He rubbed noses with her before kissing

her one last time and getting up.

He really didn't want to go but he knew he had to. He would be able to come back to her at least, and the following day she would be on his arm to introduce to all the citizens. The smile on his face grew as he thought of how he could present their future queen to them.

"What has made you grin so?" Anya asked.

"Just thinking of you... and having you as my wife."

"Steady on. We have only just started kissing."

"I know what you Christian women are like. Not much time between kissing and wedding," he teased her and laughed.

"We'll see." When she showed no signs of getting up while he remained, he leant over the bed

"I love you. I want to give you everything in my power to make you happy."

She reached up to stroke the side of his face but she didn't look happy to him.

"One day I shall be happy again. Until then, I shall take life one day at a time and I won't give up hope, but thank you for trying."

"I will do more than try; I shall succeed..."

She smiled at him but her words had been like an arrow through his heart. The pain of the things he had done to her flickered in her eyes, despite the attempt at a smile.

"I mean it. I love you."

"I love you too."

He kissed her again and left the room. She may have let him into her heart but there was further to go and there were many wounds along the way. Wounds he had inflicted. He hoped she would allow him the time to heal them.

Sherdan walked into the guard room to the instant silence of his two security guards.

"I'm going to walk to the compound this morning," Sherdan said and walked out, too involved in his thoughts of Anya to want to know why they had reacted to him appearing.

The day was crisp and fresh, and hinted at the possibility of more snow. He hardly noticed, distracted by the image of Anya's haunted face and the deep sorrow in his heart.

He longed to undo what he had done and the possibility that he might not be able to stabbed at his insides again. It baffled him that she could even say she loved him, but he felt grateful for at least that small flicker of hope.

As he walked, he resolved on finding her the best psychologist in the world to help her through everything. She would be happy again if he could manage it, and he would use every resource that he could draw on.

Sherdan marched into the compound thinking of the best way to get Anya well again and noticed nothing else until he almost bumped into Graham in Sherdan's own easy room. His commander had never come into the room uninvited before.

"Sir, there's bad news." Graham fidgeted and looked away.

"Bad news?"

"Yes, sir. It's those commandos last night. You weren't the only target."

"Who? Are they all right?" Sherdan replied much faster than normal.

"Hitchin's dead, sir." Sherdan sank into his chair.

"Hitchin?"

"Yes, sir. I'm sorry, sir."

"Leave me," he replied, barely above a whisper. Hitchin was the only person he had called friend. How had the British army even known to go after him?

For just a few minutes Sherdan had let his guard down and it had cost him Hitchin and almost Anya. He would need her at his side now, even more than he had thought before.

Tears fell from Sherdan's eyes as he sat and thought of his friend and co-worker. They had made so many memories and plans for the future together. Some of these memories popped into his head now.

He thought of the first day they had met when they were both eleven and at a new school. They had all the same classes and continued to study together all the way through to PHD level many years later.

Sherdan only allowed himself half an hour to stay in this emotional state. He had work to do and the four commandos needed questioning. He soon strode into the command room with the same facial expression he had worn on many occasions.

If they had not known Hitchin was dead, they would not have figured out Sherdan had just lost his best friend from both his demeanour and how he went about his work.

"Where are last night's infiltrators being held?" he demanded to know.

"They're here in the compound. All four of them," Graham replied as the rest of the room looked busy.

"Good. Have them interrogated. Find out who sent them and what information they know."

The commander nodded and passed on the orders to the relevant people.

"Does anyone outside of this room know of Hitchin's death?"

"Yes, the woman who found him and your two day guards."

"Fine. Make sure no one else finds out. Have the guards who know keep it secret and let me meet with the woman. I already have an idea of who she will be."

"As you wish, sir," Graham replied. "What should we tell the people? They'll wonder where he is."

"Tell them he is ill if they ask, for now at least." The commander nodded as Sherdan left the room again. He sat in his private quarters, thinking over what to say to this woman. He wanted the British government to think they had failed in their tasks.

He put his head in his hands as his thoughts turned to what almost happened. The country he had created was so delicate still. He would need to protect it from the shock waves of Hitchin's murder and was relieved that Anya had been there for him. His personal angel.

His thoughts settled on the warmth of her again. He could hardly help it after the events of the last twenty-four hours. Her affections, and the good memories of their time together, were a salve to the ache deep within him.

A knock on the door made him jump and look back up.

"Come in," he called as soon as he had composed both his face and manner again. A tall brunette walked into the room.

There were a few trace marks of mascara and puffiness around her eyes, but fresh makeup had been applied on top. She had her hands hidden in the pockets of a white lab coat which covered her standard clothes.

Sherdan had to stop the corners of his lips twitching up as he looked at her. She was every bit what he had expected, knowing Hitchin.

"Miss Miller, please sit down." Sherdan motioned to the seat opposite himself. "I would appreciate talking to you about my friend. I know that it's not easy for you to talk about this but I need to know."

She nodded in response as he reached for a nearby tissue box and put it much closer to her.

"Where did you find Hitchin?"

"Near one of the labs... He had been working late because of some extra tests he said he needed to do." She looked away, trying to stop the moisture dampening the edges of her eyes. She still didn't reach for a tissue. "They shot him, Dr Harper. They came for you, but shot him."

"I am sorry to add to your upset, Miss Miller, but unfortunately we have reason to suspect they were looking for Hitchin as well as me. That is one of the reasons I am talking to you now."

"They came for both of you?"

"Yes, they did. When I realised the enormity of what Hitchin and I were planning, I did everything I could to help Hitchin distance himself from me and the public eye, but right at the beginning there were several people who knew we worked together."

She finally reached for a tissue as the tears that had threatened to appear flowed over and tracked down her cheeks. Sherdan paused, less out of concern for her and more because of the lump in his own throat.

"Did the soldiers see you, Miss Miller?" She shook her head, "Good. We would hate for them to know there were any other scientists working with Hitchin. You were important to him. He was telling me that only yesterday."

"He was?"

"Yes, he stood in this room and spoke about you. You had put quite the spring in his step."

Sherdan smiled as her eyes brightened a little. He had lied, but it would do her no harm to think Hitchin cared for her more than he did.

"It is very important how we proceed from here, however. Our country is very fragile and this could both knock the confidence of our fellow citizens, as well as give the British government cause to increase their efforts against us. We don't want either of those things to happen."

She nodded and pursed her lips together. Sherdan hesitated before going on. He hoped Hitchin would forgive him for what he was doing.

"Could you keep it amongst us, how Hitchin died, at least for a month or so until our country is more stable?"

Her eyes went wide. She opened her mouth to respond but no words came out, leaving her with a fixed frown.

"I know it is a lot to ask. I wish to mourn him as well. He was my best friend, but we have to put this country first. It wouldn't honour him to let his death tear down everything he worked to build."

"What do you suggest instead?"

"I think, for the next few days, we should tell people that he is sick. It will give us time to plan the rest." She nodded and he had to stop himself sighing aloud with relief. "If you do need to talk about what really happened, just let my security guard, Julie, know. She will then inform me, or you could even talk to her if you would prefer."

"Thank you, Dr Harper."

"Please call me Sherdan. Now, is there anything you would like to add while you have me here?"

"No, thank you... Sherdan. I'll get back to my work. Someone needs to continue Hitchin's research, and I think I am the most qualified to do so, other than yourself, of course." She got up and shook hands with him, before leaving him alone with his thoughts again.

Sherdan sat back and breathed out. The conversation with Miss Miller had only added to the weight of his emotions. She had taken things well but he wished he didn't have to cover up his friend's death, nor trust anyone else with that burden.

The rest of the day was a blur for him as he rushed through all his tasks. He hardly looked forward to the ball the following evening anymore. Although, knowing Anya would be at his side brought him some comfort.

As a way of getting back at the British government, he phoned them again that afternoon. He was given another excuse for not getting to speak with anyone of any importance, but he didn't care. The main point was letting them know that he was still alive.

Sherdan also did a short radio interview to ensure the rest of the world had him fresh in their memories as well. Work helped him to forget the latest tragedy.

Not long before he was due to return to Anya, he received a return phone call from the Prime Minister.

"Dr Harper, I believe you called to speak to me?" the Minister said.

"Yes, I wanted to let you know I was still alive."

"I'm sorry. I didn't realise that was something I would be particularly interested in knowing."

"Really? Those four men you sent to try and kill me would say otherwise."

"I don't know what..."

"Cut the crap," Sherdan interjected. "You sent them to try and kill me. They have failed and I am more than happy to inform the public. The bodies of the four soldiers would be excellent proof."

"What do you want?"

"A ceasefire and an official statement from you saying we are entering negotiations."

"It doesn't mean we will reach an agreement," the Prime Minister pointed out.

"No, but I would like the opportunity." Sherdan did the best he could to sound sincere.

"Very well."

"If there is no announcement at some point before, I will let the six o'clock news know about last night's attempt on my life."

"Understood." The phone clicked in Sherdan's ear. He smiled, very pleased with how the conversation had gone. With the UK capitulating, and the resulting ceasefire, the country had achieved its first goal. They were finally established as a country.

Just to make sure, Sherdan stayed in the compound until the news came in that the British were backing down. Shortly before five, Graham pulled a feed from the twenty-four-hour news channel up onto the screens at the end of the room.

A lectern had been placed outside in Downing Street and many reporters were waiting for the announcement everyone expected. Thankfully, they didn't have to wait long before the front door of number ten opened and the PM came out. He put a sheet of paper on the lectern and looked out at the crowds before him.

"I am pleased to announce that, after a recent contact from Dr Harper, a ceasefire has been agreed upon. Negotiations with Utopia and its representatives will begin shortly. I plan to do everything I can to ensure, not only the safe return of our soldiers, but also the return of the homes and land stolen in that country's attempts at freedom. Thank you for all your patience in this matter."

Sherdan laughed as the Minister went back into his house. He had made it sound as if Sherdan had come running to him, but it didn't matter. He would look like the foolish one soon enough. Sherdan would let him save face where he could.

In response, he did a country-wide announcement, informing the Utopians that all the attacks were now over. He smiled as he thought of how happy the party would be. They had achieved their goal.

He could hardly wait to get back to Anya and tell her the good news, although he thought she was likely to have watched it on TV. Unfortunately, there were still several loose ends he had to tie up before he could leave.

Graham gave him a report from the interrogation team as Sherdan was about to exit the command room again. So far they had found out very little.

The soldiers had been ordered to avoid getting caught at all costs and had been definitely sent by the British government.

"Step up to the next level," he ordered and left the room. He was about to go through the mirror and get back to his girl when he heard a familiar tap on the door. Miss Miller came in without waiting. She had a bundle of papers, as well as the leather-bound journal he had seen Hitchin fetch to show him his visions of Anya.

"Dr Harper, I mean, Sherdan. I found these. They both seem to be Hitchin's diary. I'm not sure why he kept two, but there is a lot in them about you, our country and a woman called Anya," she said. Her gaze dropped down as she mentioned the last part. He smiled at the misunderstood rivalry.

"I have no idea why Hitchin would keep two separate diaries either but Anya is... Well, I am hoping she will be my wife shortly. She isn't a Utopian citizen yet. Hitchin was the only person I had told of her." Miss Miller sighed and smiled.

"That would explain a few things. I didn't read that much. As soon as I realised it was his diary I stopped. Here." She handed him everything she had brought with her.

"Thank you."

They shook hands again and she hurried off. He felt tempted to sit and read the documents before going home, but tucked them under his arm and opened his mirror entrance instead. The emotions of the day had worn him down and he wanted to be back in the company of his sweetheart.

He went through the underground tunnel as fast as he could manage. The recent events would be easier to process with a glass of brandy and a pretty face to look at.

Sherdan walked into his study expecting to see Anya, but she wasn't there. Antonio meowed at him indignantly from the sofa as he checked in the sitting room.

"Anya!" he yelled as he started running up the stairs. He heard no reply. Panic rose in him as he continued the ascent to the top floor. He hardly knocked on her door as he walked into her room, calling for her again. She wasn't there.

He checked every room of the house before seeing Anne.

"I've not seen her since lunch," Anne told him. She helped

him check every room again.

As he walked into his own room for a second time he noticed the envelope on his pillow. He snatched it up.

His name was written on the outside in Anya's handwriting. He didn't need to read the letter to know what it meant, and neither did Anne, who left the room, taking the cat and shutting the door behind her.

He sat down on the edge of the bed, unable to do anything but stare at the paper in his hands. Eventually his fingers managed to pull the flap of the envelope open and retrieve the letter from inside. His breath caught as he saw the back of the piece of paper and the last few words she had written on it.

Within moments he was sobbing so hard he couldn't even see, let alone read. He put the paper down. He'd not cried like this since he had been a small child, but no matter how hard he tried, he couldn't stop the tears flowing. He had lost everything.

CHAPTER 38

Anya lazed in bed for some time after Sherdan had left for work. His final few words echoed around her head. He still thought she was everything he needed and that he could provide everything required to heal her and make her happy.

She knew she could only find that in God. He would be her healing and hope, not Sherdan.

As she got out of bed her thoughts turned to the day before. Her task here was now done and for both her sake and Sherdan's she would need to leave. She had to decide when and how, if she was even strong enough to let go of her relationship with him.

The thoughts that went through her head brought tears to her eyes and an ache to her chest. She would need God to help her if she was to have the strength she needed. She thought she knew how to rely on God in this way, but the more time she spent in Utopia the more she realised she still had a lot to learn.

Anya had an early lunch while she pondered over the best way to leave. If she stayed another night she didn't think she would have the emotional strength, and she knew there would be no turning back at all if she went to the party with him.

Her dress caught her gaze. It had hung on the curtain rail since he had given it to her, so it would not get creased. She had to turn her back on it while she thought.

With feet like lead she got up and packed clothes into a small wheeled case she had found in Sherdan's room. As she folded the clothes and placed them inside, she picked up speed and confidence.

As soon as Anya was done, she sat down to write a goodbye letter to Sherdan. She didn't doubt that this would be the hardest part, so she had left it until last.

While stroking Antonio, she thought for a long time about what she wanted to say. She wanted him to know that her only reason for leaving was her belief in it being better in the long run. Doing so was going to hurt her as much as him. The right words wouldn't be easy to find.

Anya picked up the pen and paused again. Moisture spilled from her eyes and down her cheeks, but she ignored it and slowly made her message appear on the paper. She didn't want to still be there when Sherdan got back.

To Sherdan,

I am truly sorry for the hurt this letter is going to cause you, especially considering you will know that I have left when you find this. Please know that I do love you and I will leave a large part of me behind when I go. This place feels like home to me now as much as my flat in Bath ever did.

Not only is my task here now complete, but I know to find healing and wholeness I must return to my church, where God can minister to my needs and rejuvenate me for my next task. I will pray every day that it will somehow involve you and your country.

I will also pray for you. I know what I am doing will break your heart. I wish it wouldn't, but I will pray God heals you at the same time as me.

With all the love I am capable of, Anya

By the time she had finished writing her hands shook from holding back her emotion, and her heart ached in a physical way she had never felt before. It had never occurred to her that having a broken heart hurt in a very real sense.

Before she could change her mind she folded the paper, put it in an envelope and sealed it. She breathed out, not realising she had been holding her breath until that moment.

She thought she had done the hardest part, but she still had to put the letter somewhere he would find it. As she took it over to Sherdan's room she shivered and almost turned back. It took her over ten minutes to move from his bedroom doorway and place the message on his pillow. Even then, she looked back several times on the way out.

Once Anya was back in her own room her pace picked up. The adrenaline of sneaking out of his house and country helped her with the task. She grabbed her suitcase and walked downstairs as calmly as she could.

Her plan was to leave via the car tunnel in the garage. She had seen Nathan use it and thought she could remember what to do, although she would have to walk back rather than drive.

When she got to the garage door Julie stood waiting for her. "You can't leave, Anya. You can't." She blocked the door with her body and when Anya moved she went to grab hold of her.

"I have to. Please don't make this harder than it is. I have to go." She felt tears welling up in her eyes again.

"If it upsets you, then why?"

"It is very difficult to explain, but one day hopefully I will be able to come back. I do have to go now though." Julie frowned and still did not move. Anya waited, not knowing what else to say.

Julie bear-hugged her and then got out of her way. She gave Julie's hand a squeeze and the two women smiled at each other.

"Thank you for understanding."

She left before any more could happen to tempt her to stay. The button to get down into the secret tunnel was easy to find and Anya soon walked along the dimly lit passage. Her little suitcase made a gentle rumbling noise as she dragged it along behind her.

At first, the dark put her on edge and distracted her from her feelings as she trudged the long mile to the house at the other end, but it didn't last. A journey that normally only took a few minutes felt like a lifetime, with each step heaping more pain onto her.

When she reached the other end she paused. She hadn't thought about any more of her journey than getting back onto British soil. Anya was trapped in a locked garage. Normal garage doors opened from the inside, but for some reason this one didn't.

She rattled the main door, furious, before scanning the whole room for another way out. There was no other door.

Other than going back the way she had come, there was only one thing left she could do. She concentrated on the familiar feeling that turned on her ability.

Feeling free, she ran out into the late afternoon leaving all the clothes she had brought with her, and worn, behind.

With roughly an hour to get back before her ability faded, she jogged down the street, hoping there were clothes still in her flat. There did not seem to be any easy parts to leaving Sherdan.

As she ran down the street towards a bus stop she also realised she had no money on her. Even if she had got out of the garage she would have had to abandon her suitcase anyway. With no money she would have had to use her ability to get transport home.

Anya frowned as she stood alone at the bus shelter. There wouldn't be any way to get the bus to stop and pick her up without someone else with her. She had no choice but to start jogging along the bus route to try and get to the train station before she reappeared.

All the difficulties getting home almost made her turn around and walk back to Sherdan instead, but as the dark of evening began to fall she knew she could not. There was no going back now.

Her stomach churned as she spent the next ten minutes slowly running through the estate. She did not know where she was, and had to try and follow the bus stops on the route to know she was even going in the right direction. Several times she had to retrace her steps to find where the bus route went. There wasn't any way she would get home now without needing to spend some time, somewhere, visible.

Eventually she found someone waiting at a bus stop so she joined them, trying really hard not to breath too loudly and be heard – something not that easy after jogging for so long.

When the bus came along, she hesitated before getting on. She shivered at the thought of going visible in the middle of the packed bus. There was no better option, however, so she climbed on. She stood near the front, holding on to a nearby rail so she wasn't likely to get bumped into. Trying to use her power to its full extent so people could pass through her would make her even more likely to stretch herself to her limit and reappear.

Thankfully the journey was short. She had been much closer to the train station than she had realised. As soon as the bus stopped she ran off and into the building. Her ride had been so tense that her muscles cramped up in response but she carried on running anyway.

She sighed with relief once she was locked in a toilet cubicle at the station. This was the hardest journey of her life. She never thought anything could have been harder than the train journey to Bristol so many weeks earlier but she had been so wrong. So much had changed in such a small amount of time.

Being there had its downsides too. In the middle of the winter a train station was not the warmest of places and at least there had been a heater on the bus. She soon stood there shivering but she did not dare leave yet.

Tears fell from her eyes as everything she was doing hit her in a fresh wave. By now the letter would probably have been found. She hoped Sherdan would come to forgive her, but she didn't know if she would ever forgive herself.

She stifled her tears when she heard the scrape of the toilet door. There weren't many cubicles and she didn't want anyone to notice she had been in there for so long. She would have to move and hope she could get home now.

Thankfully, trains between Bristol and Bath were frequent and she soon hopped onto one and tried to stand out of the way. She managed to find a heater in one of the train toilets so she tucked herself away in there for the fifteen-minute journey back to her own city.

There were a few strange looks when she came out of the loo

and the passengers only saw an empty toilet cubicle that had said 'engaged' the entire time. She hoped they would assume it was some kind of malfunction, but it was too late to do anything about it if they did suspect anything.

Her flat was only a few minutes' walk from the train station and she prayed her key would be right where she had left it. Although she could just walk through the door, she didn't then want to be locked in the flat with no way out.

The flat itself would have been watched over by one of her friends. She had often wondered what they thought when most of her clothes had disappeared.

She walked up to the house and, behind the olive tree pot to the left of the door, she pulled a loose brick out of the wall. Behind it was her front door key, exactly where she had left it.

Anya didn't feel at peace until she had been into every room and checked everything else was still where it had always been. The majority of her clothes were gone, as she had expected, but she found some old worn clothes to wear for a little while until she could buy more.

She sank onto the edge of her bed, realising her journey had finished. She was home and safe. Her Bible was tucked under her pillow as the new one had been at Sherdan's house. She sighed as she stroked its leather cover.

When she had set out she had known the price of her task might be high. Had she known exactly what would happen she was not sure she would have had the strength to see it all through. As usual, God knew best.

Before she forgot, she flicked open her laptop and pulled up her email account. There were hundreds of unread messages but she ignored them all. They could all wait for another day. She sent a brief, but to-the-point, email to her church leadership team.

I'm back. There's lots to tell. Give me a day or so.
Anya.

She shut the lid on the laptop again and put it out of the way. There really was a lot to tell and, as she thought over it all, she sank into the corner of her bedroom. Unashamed tears poured from her eyes, and with them the vast, painful emotions she had been suppressing for the last six weeks. God had a lot of healing to do and that journey was still ahead of her.

CHAPTER 39

Sherdan couldn't say how long he had cried over Anya's letter. The whole evening passed in a blur of re-reading the same painful words and trying to get Anne to leave him alone and go home. Now and then, the tears gave way to angry outbursts, when he cursed Anya for coming to see him in the first place.

She had left her kitten behind and the sight of the abandoned gift only pained him more. Anne had the good sense to take the poor thing with her when she finally went back to her own family.

He had completely lost his desire for food and ignored everything he was offered. He considered getting a bottle of brandy but knew if he started drinking today he would go too far. There was also a small part of him that wanted to feel the pain he had in his heart, the deep ache of longing to see Anya's face again.

Sherdan wandered aimlessly about the house; first in her room, staring at its emptiness, then in his study, gazing at the screens he had first watched her on. All of it felt like daggers twisting in his core, and knowing Hitchin had been taken from the country made it all the worse.

In times like this his friend would have sat with him, reassuring him with words from his visions, stopping him from being alone in the dark.

The documents Miss Miller had given him had lain forgotten on his desk since he got back. He remembered them and picked them up. If Hitchin couldn't be there in person, perhaps reading his words would lessen some of the loss he felt.

He knew the second vision was in the leather-bound journal he had seen Hitchin fetch recently but Sherdan felt more curious about the typed documents. He flicked through the pages, checking the dates. There appeared to be an entry for each day and, as far as Sherdan could tell, it appeared a more thorough diary than the hand-written one.

Sherdan frowned, puzzled about why Hitchin would keep two, vastly different diaries. He stopped flicking through the pages when he reached mid-December in the previously unseen version and started skim-reading.

As he read, he grew more and more stunned. The day after Anya arrived, Hitchin had written at length about her, despite Sherdan having not yet said the intruder was a woman. Hitchin had met her. He had been in the lab she had run into when she had been breaking in.

Sherdan's jaw dropped open as he continued to read.

I knew then Sherdan would develop a crush on her and I am going to need to keep an eye on them both. I won't let Sherdan's fascination with the opposite sex put our plans in jeopardy.

He couldn't read on for a moment, overwhelmed by what he saw. After a pause, Sherdan skim-read through until Christmas when Anya was mentioned again.

I sat with Sherdan a lot today. His talk of Miss Price has me very concerned. She should be treated like any other security risk but he has her locked in one of his bedrooms. He is a fool for thinking she will be safe there. The only way to save him from ruin is to break her. The guards were close and Sherdan will have to finish the job. I have already told him I think another vision is on the way.

I know if I convince him it is meant to be, that he will force her to give him a child and have her completely submissive to his every will. He will just need pushing in the right direction, and the brilliant thing is, it was Sherdan himself who gave me the idea. The guards who interrogated her told me only yesterday that they thought he had stopped the interrogation to take over himself. He had said as much over the radio.

Once I have thought about all the details I will tell Sherdan he is meant to have her and he will do everything else for me. Maybe one day I will tell him the truth, but not until the next female has taken his fancy. For now this project is more important.

Sherdan couldn't read any further. He felt sick at the implications of what Hitchin had written. He had almost done exactly what Hitchin had expected him to, and only Anya herself had seen through it. No wonder she had left him.

The country they had been planning may well have achieved all its goals, but at what price? The damage they had done – he had done – to an innocent girl just because of the paranoid worries of one man. Even if the vision had been true, he realised he hadn't deserved her.

It had crossed his mind that evening on several occasions to demand Anya return to him but he could no longer do that. She was better off without him and far from his country.

He put his head in his hands and wept. Anya wasn't meant to be by his side, and now he'd found the person he'd always thought would be there had been against him. Sherdan really was alone in the dark.

THE END

ABOUT THE AUTHOR

Jess was born in the quaint village of Woodbridge in the UK, has spent some of her childhood in the States and now resides in the beautiful Roman city of Bath. She lives with her husband, Phil, and her very dapsy cat, Pleaides.
During her still relatively short life Jess has displayed an innate curiosity for learning new things and has, therefore, studied many subjects, from maths and the sciences, to history and drama. Jess now works full time as a writer, incorporating many of the subjects she has an interest in within her plots and characters.
You can find Jess on many social media platforms such as facebook and twitter as well as having her own website and blog at www.jessmountifield.co.uk. If you also wish to contact the author you can do so at books@jessmountifield.co.uk

LIST OF WORKS

Historical Adventure:
With Proud Humility (Hearts of the Seas: 1)
Victorious Ruin (Hearts of the Seas: 2) - Coming Autumn 2016
Chains of Freedom (Hearts of the Seas: 4)

Fantasy:
Tales of Ethanar: An Anthology (Containing the first 5 Tales of Ethanar - Wandering to Belong, Innocent Hearts, For Such a Time as This and A Fire's Sacrifice) - Coming Summer 2016
The Fire of Winter (Winter: 1) – Coming Summer 2016

Sci-Fi:
Sherdan's Prophecy (Sherdan: 1)
Sherdan's Legacy (Sherdan: 2)
Sherdan's Country (Sherdan: 3)

Printed in Great Britain
by Amazon

28558701R00155